MW00940925

JOURNEYS TO UNCHARTED LANDS

....

SIXTH ANNUAL LOS ANGELES NANO ANTHOLOGY

Lead Editor
Elisabeth Ashlin

Associate Editors
Joy Park-Thomas
Lance Menthe
Robert Todd Ogrin
Jeff Yabumoto
Spencer Hamilton
Jennifer Robertson

Los Angeles, CA

Cover design and formatting by Robert Todd Ogrin
Book Layout © 2013 BookDesignTemplates.com

Journeys to Uncharted Lands / Elisabeth Ashlin
ISBN 978-1692995058

To the NaNo Los Angeles municipal liaisons. Thank you for all you've done over the years to help us get the word out to this amazing writing community!

CONTENTS

....

E LISABETH A SHLIN

....

I NTRODUCTION

Welcome to the sixth annual Los Angeles NaNo Anthology! Every year, our editing team selects stories from writers across the globe, looking for new voices with engaging tales that capture our imagination.

For this year's anthology, we requested stories with a theme of exploration and the unknown. We also asked for a character in each story to leave something behind.

In this volume, you'll find stories that take you from the depths of the ocean to the vastness of space, from lush forests to deserts where there isn't a drop of water to spare. There are dream weavers, portals to magical realms, and Martian settlers fighting for their lives.

Most of our editors are LA residents who met during NaNoWriMo—the National Novel Writing Month. Every November, hundreds of thousands of NaNoWriMo participants challenge themselves to write a 50,000-word novel in one month. Our anthology stories celebrate the great diversity of ideas, voices, and styles of the many authors who participate in this yearly adventure.

All the writers and editors involved in this project have donated their stories and time. Our editors judge all submissions anonymously, and the writers of the selected stories work with the editors to polish their tales to perfection. If reading these stories gets you interested in submitting one of your own next year, drop us an email at lananoanthology@gmail.com and you'll be amongst the first to hear about our next submission call!

We received so many fantastic submissions this year that we decided to publish a list of finalists—writers of stories that were just a vote or two away from being selected for publication. Our top finalists were: **Jared Blair, Alexandr Bond, Scott Coon, Cole Mercer, Sophia Moore,** and **Noah Zollman.**

We hope you enjoy your journeys to the uncharted lands that await you. They're all just minutes away.

....

THE WISH DOCTOR

T he sign above my door says "Wish Doctor." I don't use the more accurate term, "lawyer," since lawyers are almost unheard of in the Magical Realm. Now that I've gained a reputation, I probably don't even need a sign.

This morning, my first client arrives shortly after I walk to the front door of my little cottage and unlock my office. In his late twenties, I'd guess, he's attractive and clean-shaven, with wavy black hair and dark brown eyes. I can tell he's from the Outside Realm from the expression on his face, a mixture of awe and disbelief that all Outsiders wear upon first entry to this world.

He pauses in front of my desk. "I—I'm here to see the Wish Doctor," he stammers.

I can tell he doesn't think it's me, an ordinary-looking thirty-nine-year-old woman in a charcoal gray pantsuit. I don't blame him. I hold out my hand and smile. "That's me, Liane Queensley."

He looks surprised for a second and then smiles back. "David," he says with a firm handshake. "Actor and sandwich maker. Mostly sandwich maker, but I'm hoping that will change."

"You've come to the right place. I hope you didn't have trouble finding me."

"No, a little birdie told me how to get here. Like, literally a little birdie."

"That's Vincent. He works for me." I gesture David inside. "Have a seat."

Natives of the Magical Realm are always fascinated by my electric lights and computer, made possible by the small generator behind my cottage, but these don't faze an Outsider like David. He sits slowly, as if expecting something magical to pop out of the woodwork at any moment, despite my rather generic-looking office and furniture.

"Don't worry, nothing in this office is enchanted. Myself included. I just help people harness the power of magic to better achieve their goals and avoid unintended catastrophes."

"You're also from the . . . the . . ."

"We call it the Outside Realm. And yes."

Still looking like he thinks he might wake up from a dream at any moment, he takes a locket out of his bag and places it on the desk. Even before I examine it, I can tell it's legit. The heart-shaped pendant has the right kind of enchanted design. When I pick it up, it feels unexplainably heavy, and it's impossible to pry open.

"This is real," I confirm. His eyes grow wide with excitement at what has become a regular occurrence in my line of work. I push the locket back toward him. "Before we proceed, I'll need my fee."

He nods like he's been planning for this and takes out an envelope. He hesitates for a second and then passes it to me.

I count ten American hundred-dollar bills. "Don't worry, I'm worth it."

He nods again but doesn't look convinced.

"Let me tell you about a couple of people who were granted wishes but didn't come to me first. One guy asked to win the lottery. That night he got three out of six numbers, winning a total of five dollars. Technically he had won the lottery, but he hadn't realized he needed to ask for the jackpot. Another woman wished for a lifetime of happiness. Her next week was amazing: she got a big raise at work and met the man of her dreams. Then, seven days after her wish was granted, she was walking happily down the street when a construction crane fell and crushed her. Doctors say she was killed instantly and didn't see it coming."

"She didn't specify how long her lifetime would be," David finishes.

"Exactly. And have you read 'The Monkey's Paw'?"

He raises his eyebrows. "Yes, but that's fiction, right?"

"I'm afraid not." His eyes grow wide, so I quickly add, "This locket doesn't look cursed. How did you get it?"

"A couple of days ago, I went to Denny's with some friends from my improv group. It was after midnight, and this homeless woman walked up and asked if someone could buy her a coffee and a hot meal."

"What did she look like?" I ask.

"She was dirty and old . . ." He pauses, as if thinking back. "Maybe not that old, actually, but stooped as if she were old. And she stank. Dressed in rags, with a shopping cart full of bags. You know, your typical bag lady."

I nod. Sorcerers and sorceresses occasionally like to disguise themselves and test people for their kindness, but I hadn't heard of it happening in the Outside Realm before.

"My friends just ignored her," David continues, "but I felt bad because it was a cold night—cold for LA, anyway—so I invited her to come sit with us and I bought her a Grand Slam. After we'd paid the bill and left, I helped her walk back to her shopping cart in the alley."

"That was nice."

He shrugs. "I try to be a good person. Before I left, she insisted on giving me this locket from her bag. She told me it was magical and would grant me one wish—anything my heart desires. Then she said, 'I'm not crazy, I'm from another realm. I'll show you the portal.' I was curious, so I followed her. Once I got here that little birdie found me right away and told me I should go back and get one thousand dollars and then come to you before I do anything else."

"Wise advice. Where was the portal?"

"Behind the curtain in one of those psychic storefronts in West Hollywood. I always wondered how all those psychics stay in business in LA. Are they all—"

"No," I say. "That's the first one I've heard of that contains a portal."

"Oh," he says. "It still seems like a dream. I opened the door and entered this world that seems a lot like ours in some ways, but magical and . . . and . . ."

"Stuck in the Middle Ages and technologically and socially backwards?"

"Is it?" he asks. "I was going to say beautiful."

"Yes, that too." I put the locket on the desk. "A wish given as a reward for a selfless good deed usually turns out well. But even that can go astray with careless word choice. It was wise to come to me first. Now, what would you like to wish for?"

"I'm trying to decide between getting cast as the lead actor in a really big movie, or winning the lottery."

"Go with the lottery."

"Why not the movie role?"

"Because once you get cast, it will require another wish to ensure everything goes well with it. The lottery doesn't involve taking anything that already belongs to someone else, and it will be simple to explain to your friends and family."

"Yeah, that's true," he says. "Everyone will think I'm crazy if I tell them the real story."

"So now the question is, which prize do you want to win?"

"The jackpot, right?"

I look him in the eyes. "I would suggest second prize."

He furrows his brow. "Why?"

"If you get five out of six numbers, you'll get enough to pay your rent and take a date out to a fancy dinner, but not enough to go crazy over. When you tell your friends and family you won second prize, they might expect you to buy them a drink, but not a car. If you win the jackpot, you'll get enough to make you lose motivation to achieve your dreams. You might feel so rich you'll blow it on a yacht and a super-fast sports car, or pick up bad habits and never curb them. Suddenly you won't know who your real friends are because they'll all expect something from you. A few years later, you'll find yourself wishing you never got your wish."

He looks down, deeper in thought than most people ever get when I tell them they would be happier being only slightly richer.

My heart pounds as I think of my husband's life insurance settlement sitting in the bank, waiting for a moment like this. "Instead of trying for the lottery, I'll buy your wish from you for a million dollars."

David looks up, puzzled.

My throat grows dry as he stares at me with an expression that's neither promising nor discouraging. "I'll give you two million, tax free," I say.

Anger creeps into his face. "So you can wish for the jackpot for yourself and get a hundred times as much?"

"No." I stand and gesture toward the plain, locked wooden door that leads to the bedroom. "Come, let me show you what I need it for."

He glances at the back door and looks as if he might follow me, but then shakes his head and snatches the locket off my desk. "If you're just trying to steal my wish for yourself, I want my thousand dollars back."

I sit down and take a breath. "Of course, I'm not going to steal your wish. It's actually written into the magic code that wishes can't be stolen, they can only be given or traded away willingly."

"Well, I'd like to use this wish myself, not sell it," he says.

Even a single complaint might hurt my reputation. *There are other wishes out there*, I remind myself. *You'll know the right opportunity when you find it.* "I'll get you the script for the lottery right now."

I pull up the Money folder on my computer and print out the Mega Millions script. "Read this entire script out loud, starting with 'I wish for the following' and ending with 'And that completes my wish,' " I say. I point to the blank line. "You insert the lottery numbers and the date here. I'll leave it up to you whether you wish for five out of six numbers or the jackpot."

"And if I follow this exactly, I'm guaranteed to win?"

"In this world there are no guarantees. But it has worked every time so far."

He looks over the script and then takes the locket out of his pocket and examines it again. "I wouldn't believe it under normal circumstances, but after all the other crazy things that have happened in the last three days . . ." He puts the items in his bag and then looks back at me. "How did you end up here, in the wish business?"

I consider telling the full story, but something about his demeanor makes me give the short version instead. "I found an unmet need, so I decided to seize the opportunity."

As I watch him walk away, part of me wants to run out and beg him to come back so I can fully explain why I need a wish so badly. But begging has never been part of my personality, so I just stand at the window and let the familiar feeling of hopelessness spread through me. How can I have been in this business for so long without managing to obtain a wish?

Before I delve too far into despair, a potential client rides up on a stunning black stallion, bringing me back into business mode.

"I'm Prince Alexander XI," he proclaims when I open the door. He pauses as if waiting for me to bow.

I look him in the eyes and offer my hand. "Nice to meet you. I'm Liane Queensley, the Wish Doctor."

He looks me up and down, not sure what to make of a woman in a position of power who answers her own door. Then he limply shakes my fingertips. I already dislike him, but royalty pays well, so I give a fake smile and invite him inside.

His pants and double-breasted jacket are very princely, but Alexander himself appears miscast for the part. He's significantly shorter than me, patches of acne dot his face, and he's already starting to lose his hair—a bad combination of youth and aging.

He places an ancient-looking oil lamp on my desk. "While my men were on a royal expedition at the base of the Silver Mountains, they came upon this magic lamp. Fortunately, the idiots didn't realize what it was, and I rubbed it first. A genie has granted me three wishes. I've been advised to see you before I redeem the first one."

My best hope to obtain a wish is from someone with three of them, but I try not to let my hopes get ahead of me. He's already struck me as entirely selfish, and since he's already rich, I have little to offer. "Before we can proceed," I say, "I'll need my fee."

He slides a leather pouch across the desk. I examine its contents: a ruby, a sapphire, and an emerald, all finely cut and larger than a quarter, worth far more than $1000. Members of the royal family rarely know how much their spare jewels are valued in the Outside Realm, and I don't bother to tell them.

"This will suffice." I slip the pouch into my desk. "What is your wish?"

"I wish for the most beautiful woman in the world to fall in love with me," he proclaims.

It takes effort not to roll my eyes. "Is this a particular beautiful woman, or a theoretical one?"

"A real one, of course. Princess Iris of the Blue Hills."

"Is she married or engaged to anyone else?"

"Not yet."

"Good." If he was trying to take someone else's girl then I'd have to give back those lovely jewels because no realm needs another Trojan War. "How old is she?"

"Young enough. Twenty or so."

Judging by his looks, several years younger than him. "Have you ever spoken to her?"

He sighs. "Why all these questions? It's my wish, and I've paid your exorbitant rate."

"You're paying me to prevent your wish from turning into a catastrophe. If you want me to do that, you'll need to answer my questions."

"We've spoken," he huffs. "And each time I see her, she looks even more beautiful."

"And does she seem interested in you?"

"Not especially. That's why I need my wish."

"Why do you think she's not interested?"

He turns red. "How should I know? Maybe because I'm only fourth in line for the throne."

Or maybe because you're an unattractive asshole, I think. "I suggest you arrange to meet her for a longer conversation. You don't want to use your wish on her and then discover—"

"She's beautiful," he interrupts. "What else do I need to know?"

I've dealt with enough entitled royalty to hide my grimace. "Beauty might please you for a year or two, but there's a lot more to a relationship than—"

"I don't care if she's stupid," he declares.

I'm not sure what annoys me more: that Prince Asshole XI assumes she might be stupid because she's pretty, or that he doesn't care. "You might not have much in common or want the same things in life."

He scowls.

I turn to my computer, click open my Relationships folder, and print the two-sided list. "The difficulty with wishing someone will fall in love with you is a problem common to wishes: what you actually want amounts to a lot more than one wish. Beauty can fade, so there should be more to the relationship than physical attraction." I hand the print-out to the prince. "This is a list of one hundred things people actually want when they wish for love. You only get three of them, two if you want to save one wish for later. Read it carefully and think about—"

Ignoring the paper, he leans across the table and glares at me. "I want the princess to fall in love with me, and I only want to use one wish. One!" He holds up one finger, as if the problem is that I can't count.

"Fine." I lean back in my chair and give him my biggest fake smile, the one reserved for clients who have royally pissed me off. "I'll print out the script for love *à la carte*."

"I knew you could do it!" he declares, as if he's won.

I open the one-page script, type in the appropriate names, and print. "Make sure to read the entire script word for word. I suggest you practice a few times first."

"And if I read this script exactly, I'll get what I want?"

"You'll get what you asked for."

He smiles and puts it in his bag.

"In case things don't go as planned with Princess Iris, I was a divorce lawyer in my previous life."

"What's divorce?"

"Something you're going to wish you could get in this realm."

My next clients arrive shortly after the prince rides away. A young girl and a middle-aged woman stand at my door, both dressed in rags. Actual rags, which means they must be from the Magical Realm.

"Good morning!" I say cheerfully as I offer them both padded chairs. I like to think I'm naturally friendly, but it's always in the back of my mind that someone who looks poor could be an enchanted witch or princess in disguise.

"I'm Flora, and this is my daughter Autumn," the woman says. Flora looks like she was once pretty, but there's a weariness on her face that implies years of hardship. Autumn possesses a beauty that shines through her rags—long, dark brown hair, rosy cheeks, and a dimpled smile. Still, there's hardship in her large blue eyes as well.

"I hope this will be enough," Flora says as she hands me a small, plain gold ring.

I can tell it's not worth nearly a thousand dollars. "Is this your wedding ring?"

"Yes . . ." She pauses, looking down. "My husband died five years ago, when Autumn was only seven years old. We both loved him dearly, but he was a poor tailor and left us penniless."

"I'm sorry to hear that."

"Is it sufficient?"

"Yes, it's fine." I slip it into my desk. "How did you come across your wish?"

She hands me what appears to be a birthday candle. "It was given to Autumn." Her face lights up with pride as she meets her daughter's eyes. "When she makes a wish and blows it out, her wish will come true."

The candle looks and feels like wax, but it's much heavier than normal and appears impossible to break. It also has that indescribable enchanted quality, something I would have missed a few years ago.

I turn to Autumn. "How did you get this?"

"There's a boy at the village school who is quite strange," she says in a soft but clear voice.

"In what way?" I ask.

"He has crossed eyes and he smells funny and he still sucks his thumb even though he's eleven years old. Everyone bullies him terribly."

"But not my daughter," Flora boasts.

Autumn blushes and looks down. "I felt bad for him, so I sat next to him during lunch every day last month, and then he invited me over to his house. I didn't really want to go, but it seemed rude to say no, so . . ."

"You're very kind," I say.

"Thanks," she says softly.

"So where did you get the candle?"

"When I visited, I found out his great-grandfather, whom he lives with, is actually a sorcerer. Before I left, he gave it to me."

"Tell her what you want to wish for, honey," her mother says.

"World peace!" she declares.

My smile fades. "I'm sorry. I can't do world peace."

"Why not?" Flora demands. "She's willing to use her one wish for it. Have you ever met someone so unselfish?"

My husband. He would have wished for world peace, or something similarly noble, had he ever been given the chance. Perhaps Elise would do the same if she were in a position to make a wish, since she inherited half of his genes. Though I don't really know what kind of person she would be if she had a chance to grow up normally, like the magnanimous girl in front of me. I look down for a second, pushing away my memories, before continuing the conversation with a business-like tone. "Your daughter is very honorable, but world peace is not just one wish. It's at least a million wishes, some of which contradict each other."

"What do you mean?" Flora asks.

"Well, one kind of peace involves resolving conflict between kingdoms. But there are also millions of small conflicts among all the living beings in our world every day. For a rabbit, peace is being safe from predators. But for a cougar, peace is eating the rabbit."

"Oh," Flora says, frowning.

"I'm not talking about that," Autumn says softly. "I just don't want any more wars in the world."

"If you know of a particular conflict between two kingdoms and you name the two kings in charge, we can wish for them to get along. That will probably work with just one wish, and it may lead to peace for the entire region."

"But then there could just be another war when there's a new king!" Autumn protests.

"Maybe," I say. "But maybe not."

Her mother sighs as if I'm being difficult on purpose. "How about you just wish for world peace and see what happens?"

"At best, nothing will happen except this candle will shake back and forth, as if it's saying no. Then we would have to reword the wish and try again. But the magic could just decide to enact the wish anyway, which could result in something you never wanted. At worst, we'll all die."

"Why?" they both ask.

"Conflict is part of life. By one interpretation, we're not truly at peace until we're resting in peace."

"Oh." Autumn looks down, tears in the corners of her eyes.

I lean forward. "If you really want to help the world," I say softly, "choose a specific thing to wish for, like the cure for one disease or for one particular sick child to be healed." I pause, considering whether to tell them more. Autumn and her mother could clearly use the wish themselves. Still, I might not find another person so unselfish for years. "There's one sick child I know who could really use—"

"If we're only going to help one person, we might as well help ourselves," her mother snaps.

"That's understandable." I try not to look disappointed as I hand back the candle. "Take some time to think about what you want."

Autumn nods, looking downtrodden.

I hand Flora's ring back to her. "Come back when Autumn has decided on a more specific wish, and I'll prepare the script, no charge."

Flora's face softens as she slips her ring back on her finger.

No more clients arrive after they leave, so I close the office and go into the back room. Elise is sitting in the padded chair where I left her, a quilt across her lap, staring at a painting of a unicorn in a meadow. Or at least she's staring straight ahead at the spot where I put the painting. Five years ago, it seemed like a scene she would enjoy, but now that she's twelve it's probably time to update the decor.

"I met this actor today who might have been willing to sell his wish," I say as I settle into my chair next to Elise. I tear off a small piece of brown bread and place it on her tongue, watching as she chews and swallows robotically. "But I offered to buy his wish before I told him about you, and he thought I was just trying to trick him out of his wish. Next time I won't make that mistake."

Her only response is to keep chewing and swallowing the food and water I place in her mouth, the sole reaction she ever has to stimulus. Sometimes I wonder if it even matters if I feed her, but I want her to at least appear healthy and nourished.

As I alternate between feeding myself and my daughter, I think back on the day I found the mysterious door in the back closet of my guest house. I'd followed the tunnel that led me to the Magical Realm out of mere curiosity. I wasn't the type to dream of enchanted worlds, and it was entirely by mistake that I wandered into one.

I'd entered the first shop I came across, a watchmaker's cottage, at the same time as a man dressed in a long robe who turned out to be a sorcerer. When I explained to the proprietor that I didn't need a watch because I kept time with my iPhone, the sorcerer was so enchanted by the technology that he offered to trade it for a magic locket that would grant me one wish. I figured he was crazy, but I made the exchange because I'd been planning to upgrade my phone anyway and I liked the circular silver locket's design: a blue opal in the middle with a pair of golden dragons flying around it. Plus, I thought it was all a dream. But once I returned to the Outside, I still possessed a magic locket instead of a phone.

Someone with a less logical personality might have opened the portal again at the first chance or shared her experience with her husband and daughter. But when I couldn't reconcile my experience with my worldview, I installed a lock on the portal and tried not to think too hard about what had happened. I didn't return to the Magical Realm for four more years, though I did wear the necklace on occasion.

I was in the midst of a relatively content life of family and career on the day of the accident. By the time I got the urgent voicemail to come to the hospital, my husband had been pronounced dead. I found Elise in the ICU full of tubes, surrounded by beeping monitors, clinging to life despite her grim prognosis. I don't know if it was fate or chance, but I happened to be wearing the locket that day. I vividly remember that critical moment when I stood by her bedside, clasped the locket and whispered, "Please, just let her live." The locket clicked open and grew so hot I had to pull my hand away, but nothing else seemed to change. Seven days later, after the doctors showed me the scans that revealed her to be completely braindead, I tearfully agreed to disconnect her life support.

And then her breathing and physical vital signs returned to normal. A week later, she lay there with no oxygen or life support or food or water, her brain still dead but her body somehow recovering. It was then that I, a lawyer who should have known better, realized with horror what I'd said: "*Just* let her live." Ever since, I've never stopped wondering what would have happened if I hadn't said *just*.

After two weeks of *just* living and receiving an uncomfortable amount of attention from the hospital staff, I realized nothing short of magic would bring back my child. I signed her discharge papers and carried her straight to the Magical Realm.

Unfortunately, there's no easily purchased spell to bring her back. My best hope is another wish, the kind that tends to come once in a lifetime. I've left my old life behind in a quest to find it and fix my mistake.

My thoughts are interrupted by the sound of Vincent's chirping as he flies through the window and settles on his perch in my front office.

"You're back early," I say as I refill his birdseed.

"I heard that a prince discovered a lamp in the Silver Mountains, so I wanted to let you know."

"I already know," I say with a sigh. I take out my map and draw an X through the location, as magic lamps are rarely found more than once in the same place.

"Don't worry, my lady," Vincent chirps. "There are still unredeemed wishes out there."

"I hope so. I only need one."

Almost unconsciously, I turn and look at the framed proverb on my wall: *Be careful what you wish for, because you just might get it.*

For some, it's a cliché. For me, it's my life.

....

Katherine N. Friedman is a writer, educator, and mother of two adorable girls. "The Wish Doctor," her second story to be published in the LA NaNo Anthology, was inspired by all the princess shows she's watched with her preschooler. She's currently adapting the story into a novel during the time she can spare between work and family. A four-time NaNoWriMo winner, she has spent several years revising her first draft novels, with the dream of someday getting an agent and being traditionally published. You can find out more about her at www.katherinenfriedman.com.

....

BIRTHDAY GREETING

H i, Daddy," says my five-year old son Benji in a high-pitched voice that breaks through my dream state as it does every morning. It also breaks through the whisper of the ventilation system and the faint hum of fusion engines, sounds I barely notice after nearly a year in space. I open my eyes and roll over to face a screen where my wife and son continue with a video message I memorized long ago.

"Wake up, sleepyhead," Joanne says. "Time for another day that brings you closer to home." Besides a deep kiss that left me breathless, a thumb drive with this special wake-up message was the last thing she gave me before takeoff.

"Yeah, sleepyhead," my son echoes with amusement. I smile at his missing front teeth and once again regret they'll be grown in by the time I get home. I hate to miss a day with him, let alone two years. Benji giggles, "Time for sleepyhead to come home."

"Not yet," she says to him, then turns to me. "Come home safe, Jim. We need you."

Benji sends air kisses my way. "Bye, Daddy!"

"Don't forget your video diary," Joanne says. "I know we won't see it until you get back, but Benji's going to have a million questions by then. The diary will be the best adventure story you ever tell him . . ." The image freezes as her message reaches the thirty-second limit. I check the log and confirm 345 views. It's the only calendar I need, and I'm excited there's only a week left until we drop our cargo on alien soil and I can start zooming toward home instead of away from it.

The warm feeling doesn't last long. Even though it's my day off, I check the system log for maintenance jobs in case there's anything critical. In a rocket ship full of rocket scientists, I'm the handyman. Can't call a plumber in outer space, right? Usually there's just routine stuff like leaky pipes or blown fuses but today there's a red-flagged post. It's actually got two red flags, so I know I'm in for a long day. Instead of watching videos of Benji learning to ride his bike or Joanne singing "Crazy Little Thing Called Love," I'll be suited up. They're lucky this plumber's always on call.

Some days, being thirty still feels like being a kid. Today isn't one of them. Rubbing the sleep from my eyes and attempting a quick finger comb of wild brown hair that refuses to behave, I sit up to record a video log. "Day 345. I was planning to help Leslie with her radio thingy since it's my day off, but there's a waste filtration blockage in the outer ring. That's how everyone on the ship talks. Fifty-cent words for everything. Sounds sophisticated, but it just means the crapper's backed up. Yep, duty calls! But enough about me. I'm far away and thinking about you, Benji . . . because it's your birthday!" The camera tracks me as I walk to the AV console. "I gave Mommy this video to show you today, and I want you to know I watched it here too." I play a clip, and this time it's my face that fills the frame.

"Happy birthday, buddy!" my eleven-month-younger self says in the video. "Six years old, wow! Sorry I'm not there to celebrate, but I'll be home next year and we'll have twice as much ice cream. Seven scoops for a seven-year old, I promise. Hey, I got a riddle for you. You know why we put candles on top of a birthday cake every year? Because they're too hard to put on the bottom! Ask Mommy to try it . . . Daddy loves you!"

As I enter the mess deck for breakfast, my depression about missing Benji's birthday deepens in the room's cheery atmosphere. Not for the first time, I'm aware that almost everyone is paired up. They're eggheads ranging from botanists to mechanical engineers, but they're also pioneers who have journeyed two-by-two in this modern-day Noah's ark. Earth may be crowded and polluted and hot, but it's home. Why this group wants to go out to Aquarius and live on a planet called TRAPPIST-1e is a mystery. What kind of name is that, anyway? Doesn't sound like the kind of place to raise a family, if you ask me. But of course, nobody does, and that's fine. The nerds on the *Magellan* are nice, but trying to keep up with their mumbo jumbo is exhausting and makes me feel stupid. I'm sure they'd be happy to teach me if I wanted to learn, which I don't. School was never really my thing. Life on this ship got a lot easier once I stopped trying to fit in and settled into a nice service groove that lets me keep to myself. Maybe I'll get to know the handful of other round-trippers on the way home when I don't have four hundred people asking me to fix this and fix that.

My mood lightens as I spot Leslie waving me over to an empty seat. She's one of the few single folks who doesn't make conversation more unpleasant than fixing the crapper. I suppose that's unfair because it sounds like she's merely tolerable. She's not. I like her a lot, and even though I've only known her a few days, she's the closest thing to a friend I've got here. As I walk over to her table, I glance at the empty corner that would still be my spot if I hadn't been called to replace the valve in her shower last week.

"I grabbed you some mud," she says and hands me a polycarbonate cup half-filled with the syrup that passes for coffee here. She's out of her mind if she thinks I can drink that much.

"Thanks." I flip through an assortment of packets and choose powdered eggs to go with a few genetically-enhanced blueberries. The Frankenfood tastes okay once you get used to it, but I still think blueberries should be smaller than golf balls. I add hot water and stir the eggs until they thicken.

"You free to help in the lab?" she asks. "You're a whiz with the soldering iron."

"Nope. Got a date in the outer ring."

"Ouch."

The outer ring is a miserable place with subfreezing temperatures and centrifugal forces that squash your balls. It's a place for air filters, waste recyclers, and solar collectors, not people. I dig into the powdered eggs with more enthusiasm than they deserve; I'm going to need the protein, and downing reconstituted eggs is better than popping pills. "I guess you're on your own," I say.

She sighs, disappointed. "Story of my life."

"Maybe a good-looking Martian will sweep you off your feet." I take a swig of mud and notice her studying me with intense green eyes that make me feel like I'm under a microscope.

"Everyone here is either courageous or desperate. Which one are you?"

"Neither," I say. "Just a simple plumber. A high school drop-out who found a way to send his kid to college. No way I could ever sell enough body parts to make that kind of money, but this job is his ticket to a better life. The sacrifices we make for our kids, right?" She puts a gentle hand on mine, and for a moment the touch feels nice, like a forgotten memory surfacing in sunshine. Ashamed, I pull back. She's a little too cute, with an infectious energy I want to stay safe from. I grab the blueberries and stand. "Got a busy day ahead. Don't finish bolting the radio together without me. I want to be there when you make that first call."

"Real-time communication with Earth from this distance waits for no man," she teases, looking amused by my awkward withdrawal. She probably thinks I'm old-fashioned. I guess I am.

"You've been working on it for months. What's one more day?" I ask.

"The sooner I finish, the sooner I validate my patent. That's *my* ticket to a better life."

A better life at the edge of nowhere? "See you tomorrow," I say as I head for the outer ring.

H i, Daddy," says Benji once again as the video alarm goes off. Like Pavlov's dog, I roll over and watch with a smile as Joanne calls me "sleepyhead" and reminds me to keep up with my diary.

"Day 346. Well, the crapper's fixed. Took me half the day to find the clog and the other half to squeeze into a friggin' mousehole to clear it. Whoever designed this ship should be shot. At least there's one good thing about a diet of powdered protein and veggies from the space farm: I'm down a few pounds. You won't recognize me when I get home! Love you both!"

Remembering Leslie's disappointment yesterday, I decide to break my routine and ignore the maintenance log. If an emergency comes up, the nerds will find me. I call Leslie on the commlink instead. "How 'bout we skip breakfast and try to finish your radio today?"

"How about some raisin toast when you get here?"

"How do you rehydrate toast?" I ask, surprised at an option I've never seen in the mess deck.

"You don't, Jim. It's toast."

Eager to get the radio working and even more eager to chew on something besides rabbit food, I enter Leslie's lab to find her unpacking components from antistatic bags. She hands me a vacuum-sealed baggie, and I can't believe there's actual toast inside. I dig into the sweet-smelling bread while she sorts electronic parts on a work tray. It doesn't matter that the toast is cold or that the raisins are nearly petrified; it tastes like home and makes me happy.

"Where'd you get this?" I ask, amazed.

"We were allowed five pounds of personal items, right? The bread was a pound, maybe two or three. I don't remember. I like bread."

I like bread as much as she does, and it's gone before I know it. The taste lingers on my tongue for a moment before being overpowered by the acrid smell of a hot soldering iron. It's my cue.

Working side by side, Leslie holds tiny components with grips while I solder them in place. It's slow going, but the pile on her tray dwindles as we approach the big finish. The air is electric as she grabs the last item, a ribbon cable she uses to daisy-chain two circuit boards together.

"That's it," she says. "Let's ping the Bureau and see if it works." She types: *Magellan to Santa Fe Control via tachyon relay – do you read?*

"What's a tachyon?" I ask.

"We're going close to lightspeed," she explains. "We have to, in order to travel this great distance, right? We can't actually reach lightspeed but we can get close. Tachyon particles are going faster than light and can never go as *slow* as lightspeed. Nobody on Earth has been able to build a tachyon generator, and a lot of my colleagues think it's impossible. But I found a way to highjack those tachyons to carry our messages." I nod, partly to make her feel good but mostly to avoid a more in-depth science lesson.

While puzzling over faster-than-light particles, I hear a chime as an LED near the touchscreen turns green. The light and sound may be small, but the jolt they send through me is not. I read the response: *Santa Fe Control to Magellan – we've been waiting a long time to hear from you. Will expect your video link when ready.*

The words bring unexpected tears. I force them back, wondering if the loneliness I've tried to ignore is so bad that a simple link with Earth can push me to the breaking point. I'm still staring at the message when I'm smacked in the shoulder. I pick up the champagne cork that has just pelted me and wave it at Leslie with as much indignity as I can fake. "You could've put my eye out!"

"Stop your whining and help me enjoy my other personal item." She takes a swig from the bottle and holds it out to me. I hesitate, but she's already in the moment and determined to take me there too. "It's not a victory drink unless you take it straight from the bottle," she says. The victory tastes delicious, and we savor it while staring at those magic words: *Will expect your video link when ready.*

"It works," says Leslie, who does not fight back the joyful tears making her eyes sparkle. "It actually works."

"You surprised?"

"A little," she admits. "Everything looked good in the simulations, but there's always that little voice saying, 'You're not good enough. You're not smart enough. It won't work . . .' " Her voice trails off, leaving an awkward silence.

I'm not much of a talker, but I know I should say something. "To a better life," I say with a little too much oomph as I drink and pass the bottle back to her.

"To a better life," she repeats, taking another slug of bubbly. The Leslie I've come to know slowly returns and types in a new command. "Let's see who's home," she says. I watch the screen for signs of life, but all I see are static and occasional shadows. "*Magellan* to Santa Fe Control, do you read?"

"Good to see you, *Magellan*," responds a man whose face emerges from the static. "I'm Bob Burns, executive in charge."

"Leslie Decker, communications director."

"How are you holding up, Leslie?"

"Ready for some real gravity and non-filtered air," she says. "You'll be with us for touchdown in five days, sir?"

The Santa Fe Control exec laughs, "I'm old, but I'm not *that* close to retirement. If you're ready to land, I assume the new fusion drives performed as expected?"

"We've been able to hit point-nine-nine-four lightspeed."

"Excellent. I'm sure the advance team will be happy to see you."

"Can't wait to see if they succeeded with the animal clones," says Leslie. "I'd love to have a pork chop next week."

"We'll expect a full report when you make contact," Burns says.

"We're on diverging timelines, and it's hard to maintain the connection while we're moving. I'll call you when we're on the ground. *Magellan* out." Leslie ends the call and takes another swig from the bottle before passing it to me.

"You know, if we'd met sooner, maybe the radio would've been finished in time for me to call my son on his birthday yesterday. That would've been amazing." I raise the bottle for another toast. "To the halfway point," I say with enthusiasm now that we're about to land and I can look forward to heading home.

"You're not staying?" she asks.

I watch her joy bleed away like oxygen through a hull breach. It's replaced by something new, like disappointment or worse. Like pain. "I'm no explorer, Leslie. Once you guys are set, I'll be in the air again."

"I knew some people wanted to go back. To see what's changed, you know. To be part of all that. I didn't think you were one of them."

"I already gave up a year of my life, and I have one more to go. But the pay is crazy good, and when I get home I can give my son everything I never could before. That's why I came, not to pitch a tent on another planet."

She bites her lower lip and takes a deep breath. "The Exoplanet Bureau told you how long you'd be gone and what that would mean, right?"

"I was a last-minute replacement, but yeah. Two-year round trip. Single bonus paid in advance, double bonus on arrival, or triple bonus on return. I chose the triple. There was a lot of other mumbo jumbo in the paperwork. All I know is that a pile of money will be waiting for me when I get home."

"That mumbo jumbo included full disclosure about time dilation. They also covered it in the mandatory crew meeting before launch, remember? There was that whole Q&A where we had to sign the acknowledgement."

"You think I wanted to waste one of my last days at home stuck in a meeting? My buddy Craig sat in for me while I took my kid to the beach. We dug our toes into the sand and tasted the salt spray where the waves crash on Angel's Point. It was awesome." Just thinking about it makes me smile.

"Your wife had to sign the spousal agreement. She must have seen . . ."

"I didn't want to put her through all the paperwork, so I told them I was single," I say as a knot begins to form in my gut. I don't know what Leslie's getting at, but I don't like it.

"Do you know why the return bonus is so generous?" she asks. "It's actually cheaper for them to pay you triple later because the money has been earning interest year after year."

"They've got bank accounts that triple in two years?" I'm excited to learn about this kind of moneymaking opportunity.

"No, Jim, they don't. The banks—and everyone else on Earth—have been moving through normal time while we've been traveling near lightspeed. Time goes slower for us. Much slower," she explains.

"Sure feels that way cooped up in here," I say. "But it's been a year, trust me. Well, almost. I've been counting the days."

"A year for us, eighty-six years on Earth. That's what time dilation means," she says, putting a sympathetic hand on mine.

I pull away. "Eighty-six years? That's crazy!"

"It's not crazy. It's science. It's tough to wrap your head around, but . . ."

"This is a sick joke! I don't really know you, Leslie. I don't know any of you."

"I wish it were," she says softly.

"I want to call my wife. I want to talk to her and little Benji!"

"You can't," she says, her voice choked with emotion. "There is no little Benji."

I grab her hand with a rage that surprises both of us as my confusion turns to desperation. "Make the call! Bravo bravo tango sierra 81080," I say, tightening my grip.

"Okay." Leslie relents and types in the number. Static fills the screen, and we wait for what seems like an eternity. "Nobody's there. I told you . . ." She reaches for the keyboard.

"Leave it!" I snap, my attention focused on static that clears as a connection is made. I find myself face-to-face with a younger version of my father, who died in his early seventies. This guy's got a salt-and-pepper goatee, unlike my clean-shaven father, but the eyes and nose are the same.

"Hello?" the man says.

"Uhmmm," I mumble like an idiot. "This is Jim Bennett, calling from the *Magellan*."

The man reacts with delight. "Grandpa Jim?!"

Dumbfounded, I try to absorb what I fear is true. "I'm calling from the *Magellan*," I repeat. "Who are you?"

"I'm your grandson, Ben. Benji's my dad," he says with excitement I can't match. "We hoped this day would come. Bev, come here!" A brunette with a warm smile joins him.

"Grandpa Jim, it's great to finally meet you," she says.

They both seem like nice people, but I have no interest in talking to strangers. "Where's Benji?"

The man who calls himself Ben says, "He's doing okay, Grandpa. He's ninety-one now and living at a nursing home in Austin. It's nice."

"What's his number?"

Ben sighs. "I'm afraid he won't talk to you. He's never forgiven you for abandoning him and Grandma."

Oh, my God. Joanne. "What about Joanne? She'll take my call."

Ben pauses before breaking the news. "Grandma passed away a long time ago. Thirty years, I think. I'm sorry."

His words stab as the nightmare grows. "Joanne's gone?" I stutter in a voice that barely works.

"She never blamed you, Grandpa. It was tough without you, but she knew it was a horrible mistake. She loved you till the end."

I fight back the tears at first, then give in as reality washes over me in a wave that will surely drown me.

"Dad was a different story, I'm afraid. Grandma said he was so excited about you coming home. He played that birthday greeting from you on his sixth birthday and again when he turned seven. He watched that video year after year, getting more and more angry until one day he erased it." I'm drowning, but Ben throws me a lifeline. "Want to meet your great-grand-son and great-great-grandchildren?"

"They're with you?"

"No, but I can get them," he says. "Give me two hours."

"You got it," I say. Leslie kills the connection, and the screen goes dark. "I'm going to the mess deck to grab some Franken-food and other fun things to show them. I'll be back in an hour."

She shakes her head. "Two hours for them is about ninety seconds for us."

Friggin' time dilation. My focus returns to the loss that threatens to swallow me whole. "I never got to see my wife," I say. "Or my son."

She lets me brood in silence. Then, in a soft voice, she says, "We all left family behind."

"You got to say goodbye, Leslie! You knew it was the end!" I'm yelling at her, but I know there's nobody to blame but myself. I guess I'm still a careless guy looking for shortcuts, the same guy who dropped out of school fifteen years ago—or is it a hundred years now? Before I can continue my rant, Leslie reconnects with Ben, who is surrounded by children and grand-children of his own.

"Hi, Grandpa, meet everyone. Everyone, this is my Grandpa Jim!"

"Hi, Grandpa Jim!" shouts an unrehearsed chorus of people gathered to see their pioneering ancestor for the first time. Perhaps for the only time. Their faces light up as they look at a grandfather who is younger than his grandson. I see my Joanne in them, and my Benji too. Maybe I haven't lost everything.

Ben introduces his son, Mike, and his grandkids, Stephanie, Suzanne, and little Jimmy. "He's named after you, in case you're wondering," Mike says. "Grandpa was pissed off that you fled for the stars, but Great Grandma told us some stories, and I always thought you were pretty cool."

"I didn't flee for the stars, Mike. I never would've left if I'd understood what I was doing." The screen goes dark, and I look to Leslie. "What happened? Where'd they go?"

"Diverging timelines eventually break the buffer, and we lose real-time contact. By the time I get them back, another hour or two will have passed for them. Want me to try?"

"Nah," I shake my head, which is throbbing from the day's revelations. I wrestle with rules of a game I didn't even know I was playing. "If I return to Earth, everyone ages fast while I travel?"

"Another eighty-six years will pass for them, yes," she says.

"And if I stay, they age regular?"

"Time will be the same for all of us."

"And I can talk to Ben and Bev and the kids? I can get to know them?" I ask.

"As long as the tachyon relay keeps working," she says.

Massaging the back of my neck in a useless effort to fight off the growing headache, I ask, "You think I can switch my triple pay to double so the money's released when we land?"

She shrugs. "Maybe. Probably. Changing your mind about more than the bonus?"

"We know what will happen if I go back," I answer, acknowledging my new reality.

She nods. "You'll return to new generations who won't know anything about your wife or your son. They'll really be strangers."

An idea pops into my head. "Can we send anything besides live video?"

"What do you have in mind?"

"My diary. If my son sees it, maybe there's still time for forgiveness."

"There's always time for that," she says as she types. "Every entry since we left Earth?"

"Yes, I'll show you . . ."

"I've got them," she says with a satisfaction that annoys me. *What the hell? My personal videos?* She reads my expression and smiles. "No encryption, not even a password?"

"Guilty," I say, wishing I was more like these nerds instead of a dumb schmo who couldn't be bothered reading the mumbo jumbo that cost me so much. Whoever said *Ignorance is bliss* was an idiot. "Just send it before my great-grandkids have great-grandkids." I watch as three hundred video files disappear one-by-one into the tachyon stream.

The video alarm goes off, and I roll over to face the ghosts of my past. They don't know or care that the ship has landed. What matters to them, I'm sure, is that they were abandoned. Freezing the frame on Joanne, I study every curve and try to remember the scent of her hair, the taste of her lips, and the feel of my hand in her back pocket. Knowing I'll never touch her again brings fresh pain that pulls me down the rabbit hole of my grief. I'm tempted to hide there forever, but a buzzer breaks the silence.

On the commlink, Leslie says, "You better get down to the lab."

I enter to find Bob Burns, the Santa Fe Control executive, in mid-sentence on the tachyon screen. ". . . a small change to the homesteading allowance. I don't see any issue there."

Leslie waves me over. "He's here, sir."

"Come to the camera so we can see you, Jim," says the exec. Uncomfortable in the spotlight, I obey. "There's an important message for you." Burns spins the camera to reveal a familiar face, now sporting a full beard instead of the salt-and-pepper goatee. It's a stark reminder of how quickly time passed there during the last days of our flight, and it removes any doubt about my decision.

"Hi, Grandpa," says an elated Ben. "Great to see you. I guess you've landed because the double bonus posted to our account. You don't know how much this will change our lives!"

"Sure I do. Why do you think I made this trip?" Ben's smile is contagious, and for the first time since this nightmare began, I think the trip may almost have been worth it. Almost. "I couldn't make a better life for Benji and Joanne, but I'm glad it will help you."

A raspy voice comes over the speaker. "Dad? It's really you?"

The breath catches in my lungs as Ben reaches forward and adjusts the camera, tilting it down to reveal my elderly son, Benji, perched in a wheelchair with an oxygen tank at his side. It's a sight I'm not expecting. Not now, not ever. The goofy, missing-toothed smile of the boy I've been waking to every morning has become a taut line between thin lips, and worry lines etched above his brows speak of a difficult life. I want to cry for the six-year-old lost inside, but he deserves better than my pity. He deserves so much more.

"It's me," is all I can manage to say. There are no words to erase the pain I've caused.

"I watched your diaries, Dad. Every one. I've had a year to think about them." A year? I sent them just a few days ago. This time dilation thing makes my head spin. Suddenly embarrassed, I try to remember what silly things I might have said or done while wiping the sleep from my eyes. Things meant for a hopeful child, not a bitter adult.

"This is not the reunion I expected. I'm sorry you had to wait so long for it," I say, stumbling through an apology that seems so useless and so necessary.

"I can forgive you, but I can't forget," Benji says. I wait for him to release his pent-up hostility, but he's calm. "I'll be joining Mom soon, and I don't want to carry the anger anymore. Maybe time will move fast for us while we watch over you. I don't know." He coughs from the exertion and continues, "I was a good father. I just wanted to tell you that. Wasn't I, Ben?"

"The best," reassures Ben, who gives me an apologetic smile.

"I love you, Benji," I say in a bittersweet goodbye. Even with the tachyon relay I know in my gut that this is the end for us. And it's a good one. Or as good as I can hope for after leaving him in limbo for a lifetime.

"Keep in touch with the kids," he says with a rasp, opening the door for me to re-enter some part of his life. It's the only absolution I need.

"Will do," I say.

"Turn this thing off," Benji says with a dismissive wave.

"I guess we gotta go," says Ben. "Good luck out there."

H appy birthday, buddy!" Watching my video, I can't stop picturing the wrinkled face of my son, wheezing for air. Did I really record this only a year ago? It feels ancient. "Six years old, wow! Sorry I'm not there to celebrate, but I'll be home next year . . ."

The door buzzes, and I let Leslie in. "What are you up to?"

"Just saying goodbye to the old me," I say, deleting the file. I'll save my diary logs and the sweet videos of young Benji and Joanne, but my birthday message is too painful to keep.

"You doing okay?" she asks.

"Yeah," I say with a forced smile and a nod. I'm not ready to open up. Besides, she's bubbling with energy, and I don't want to bring her down.

"I sent a drone out this morning and found a great spot by the river, not far from the advance basecamp. Level ground. Good vegetation. I want to take a look before someone else grabs it," she says. Then, as if testing the waters, she adds, "There's room for two. Want to come?"

"Doesn't hurt to look," I say as we head for the door. But it does.

....

Bud Robertson is a lifelong storyteller who works in prose fiction now after surviving twenty-five years in the movie business as a screenwriter, producer, director, or assorted hyphenate. His produced screenplays include *Spectres*, *Prey of the Jaguar*, *The Great Year*, *A Pageant for the Ages*, and several episodes of the Japanese television series *Ultraman*. A number of other scripts remain lost in Development Hell. When not writing and enjoying life with his awesome wife and two daughters in Lake Las Vegas, Bud serves as CEO of a technology firm in Europe and racks up a lot of air miles.

······································

PASSAGE

V arjo stood atop the ramparts and watched the moon sink beneath the Withered Wood. In his palm he balanced a signet ring. Such a slender band of gold, but it seemed so heavy now. Already it had been resized for him. A messenger had delivered it not an hour before, along with an ancient chest that now sulked at his feet. It was hewn from spalted birch, pale and marbled as an old woman's hand.

Goodbye, Mother. He closed his fist on the ring. *Now we are both alone.*

A familiar voice finally broke the silence. "Lady Morava was beloved for her many great works. Long will she be remembered by the people of the Sunless Land."

Varjo regarded the woman by his side. Torchlight framed the crisp uniform of the Shadow Guard. He raised an eyebrow. "Indeed, Captain Farlscythe. In that regard she left nothing to chance. She designed her ghastly mausoleum herself."

The old soldier stiffened. "That's not what I—"

He laid a hand on her shoulder to quell her protest. "I know. I loved her dearly also. But my mother was drunk on the wine of civic adoration, and her vanity has doomed our house."

"Doomed your house? House Kousúf has not known such acclaim in centuries! She rebuilt the great piers, created the Night Garden. She presided over the Hexarchy for longer than any in the city's history. She was a luminary." The captain crossed her arms.

"She also emptied our coffers, with naught to show for it. Who knows where it all went? And her profligacy earned the envy and enmity of the other five houses, who close in on us now like jackals. The *great* Lady Morava was so intent on attaining glory in the present that she made no provision for the future. Not even . . . for me."

The captain huffed. "So that's what you're on about."

At least she knew what she wanted, Varjo thought. *Would that I could say the same. I see only shadows ahead.*

He gave a dismissive flick of the hand. "I know she was fortunate to bear even one child. To survive at all in this realm is to defy the night—to raise a child, even more so. But there's only one Kousúf now. House Vanth will strip us of half our sea trade before I can raise the funds to defend it. And I will be the last of our line—" He cleared his throat. Even after all this time, the words came unwillingly.

"Varjo . . ." The captain looked away.

Varjo drew his overcoat closer to him, though the wind had not changed. "You have known me since I was a child. We both know that I do not desire the . . . *intimate* company of women. And I am content in that. But for the house that truth comes at a cost. And she left it to me to pay in full. Even my cousins will not avail us in that regard. They are more closely aligned to the houses they married into than our own. If one of them should inherit, our house shall end in all but name. I stand apart now. We can thank Mother's pride for that."

The captain frowned. "I wish you shared that pride." She gestured toward the city. Green lamps were being lit all along the avenues. "Look—the lamps of mourning are going up everywhere. The brightest display adorns the Glaumer estate. Ever were they the staunchest supporters of your mother. They honor her—and you—by their showing. You may have allies yet."

Varjo tilted a hand. "Or they mock us. House Glaumer will be ensconced in the Chancellery before the year is out."

She gave a start. "That cannot be! The Charter clearly states that if the ruler of the Hexarchy should die in office, the seal passes to the heir."

"As always, you are right as to the law," Varjo said. "But I shall be forced to sell that seat to save our house from bankruptcy and ensure the Shadow Guard are not suborned. It is the only coin I have. Any fool can see it. *They* surely do."

"*I* am no fool." She glared at him, arms akimbo.

"My apologies, Captain Farlscythe. My words were illchosen. You are far wiser than I. But you have no head for politics. You assume others to be as honorable as yourself."

"Honor must be given before it can be received, Varjo. Surely I taught you that."

A sad smile tugged at Varjo's lips. "Then we must try to remember that it is *Lord* Varjo now."

She closed her eyes in shared pain and rested a hand on his shoulder.

He did not disturb it.

They stood on the wall awhile longer in the gathering gloom. With the moon down, greater night had come to the Sunless Land.

The shadows stir out there. And behind them, there are but darker shadows.

"Shadows" were what they called the nameless horrors that stalked the land—some with fangs to prey upon the flesh, others that slipped into the places between thoughts to prey upon the soul. Until morning they would have naught but starlight, and tonight the clouds looked to deny them even that. And even "morning" meant only moonrise or the advent of the lesser night, for in the Sunless Land, daybreak never came.

He spared a furtive glance for his old mentor, who had also swaddled him as a babe.

I have no right to speak of honor. If you knew how I had dared the Withered Wood this past year, you would know me for a coward.

He wasn't sure what had compelled him to venture in secret beyond the safety of the walls after his mother had fallen into her final, protracted illness. He still knew not what he sought night after night. And it had not been without incident: once he fought off a winged nightmare, all claws and teeth, and suffered a terrible gash to his arm that he concealed for weeks.

But whatever else drove him, loneliness was its whip. While no one could accuse his mother of being overly kind, the thought of dining without her now was somehow unbearable. He told himself he was simply searching for the fickle portals of legend, to find some escape from this bleak land—even though it was said they only brought people *into* the Sunless Land, and any attempt to exit from this side was sure to end in failure or death.

But at this point, any exit might suffice. Whatever shadows may lurk out there, ever the darkest lie in our own hearts.

When the skeletal branches of the Withered Wood became one with the night, Varjo turned back to the city. To his surprise, it had become an ocean of verdant light. It shone bright enough that it cast his shadow, tinged with red, against the parapets.

I cannot remember such a celebration of life. My mother was haughty and unyielding, yet it seems she inspired many. If she could only see how much they loved her . . . but then, that's the folly of trading for such coin. You never receive the final payment.

"Well? Are you going to open it?" The captain eyed the forgotten chest by Varjo's feet.

Varjo regarded it as though it contained a monster. The Box of Passage. It was a house tradition from the distant past, when memories of the other realm were still bright.

For there *was* another realm, one full of life and sunlight. But in that world, on rare occasions, portals opened and drew poor souls to this dark realm. Many of the first through the portals were quickly taken by the shadows. But the bravest came together to build the city, and later other redoubts.

The Box of Passage was a remembrance of that act of hope, a secret gift from one matriarch or patriarch to the next. Sometimes it held treasure. Sometimes it held hard truths. But always it held responsibility. Accepting the Box meant taking up the mantle of the house as one's own.

The captain kicked him lightly in the shin. "You're stalling. Just open it. Besides, I already know what it is."

"She told you?" He looked incredulously at her. Never had he imagined his mother might flout *this* tradition.

The captain snorted. "Surely you don't imagine the *great* Lady Morava deigned to handle the trivialities of procurement herself?"

"Fairly said. Ah, well." He looked to the darkness.

I never wanted anything special from her anyway. Nothing a box could hold, at any rate.

"So." The captain lifted the chest and held it out to him.

"I suppose I must."

Varjo slid his house's signet ring onto his finger for the first time. It was cold and fit too loosely.

I suppose the measurements were *somewhat old. I haven't been eating well lately—not since Mother fell ill.*

He pressed the well-worn band against a dark oval inlaid in the Box where a keyhole might have been. The oval briefly glowed, followed by an almost inaudible series of internal clicks, and then the Box seemed to sigh.

Gingerly, Varjo lifted the lid. At first the Box looked empty, and for a moment he wondered if his mother had taken this last moment to play an uncharacteristic prank on him.

Then he saw the dark, billowy mass hiding within.

He reached inside and withdrew a mantle, soft as sable. As the captain lowered the chest to the ground, Varjo allowed the cloak to unfurl to its full length. It was impossibly black. The night draped liquidly around it.

"Well … it's lovely." He suppressed a sigh of disappointment.

A fancy bit of cloth. Literally, a mantle. A fitting gift from a woman who cared mostly for appearances.

With a note of pride, the captain said, "It is spun from the resin of ghost-willows in the Withered Wood. Though gossamer-light, it is proof against all elements."

Varjo hefted it once, let it settle again. He felt empty.

I don't know what I was hoping for, really. Something that might give me a purpose, perhaps—not just some trinket.

"Extraordinary craftsmanship, to be sure. We shall find a suitable place for it in the Hall of Relics."

Captain Farlscythe pursed her lips.

As he began to fold it again, however, Varjo felt an unexpected firmness in one quarter. He fished within the mass and discovered a stiff envelope tucked inside the left pocket. The paper was the color of clotted cream, the seal of House Kousúf pressed firmly on it in dark red wax. It was addressed in his mother's hand to *Lord Varjo Kousúf.* It was the first time he had seen his new title in full. He wondered how long ago she had written it.

"Is that a note?" The captain strained forward.

Varjo handed the mantle to her so he could more easily open the envelope. "Evidently, a private one."

She withdrew a step.

Varjo took a hunting knife from his sleeve pocket and slit the wax. It oozed red liquid as it released. He recoiled as a blood drop fell to the stone.

A bloodseal!

A letter thus warded could only be opened by those who shared the bloodline. It would otherwise fall to ash at the breaking. It was a costly service that required a painful bloodletting from the donor. He could not imagine what would have impelled his mother, who could not bear the sight of blood, to undergo such a procedure.

Uneasily now, Varjo extracted a card from the envelope. He held it up to the torchlight so he could read its few short lines, written in the same spidery hand:

Dearest,
You shall die in agony three months into your fifty-second year. Make it count.

All my love,
Mother

Varjo breathed in sharply and his vision sparkled as though he had stood too quickly. He read the words again, slowly this time. He could hear the velvet blade of his mother's voice in every syllable.

The captain moved to steady him. "What is it?"

He waved her away.

To have certainty that one will not die for over twenty years . . . the power of such knowledge . . .

He felt as though his world had been upended. If he knew anything about his mother—and he felt certain he knew her better than anyone alive—she would never have made such a pronouncement in error. Not if she secured it under a bloodseal. Not in a matter such as this. An augury of such reach would have been extravagant beyond words.

She secretly paid someone to peer far into the future. It must have cost an absolute fortune. No wonder our coffers are empty. She spent it all for me.

"Well?" the captain asked.

Varjo shook his head, his throat thick with grief.

Fifty-two years, three months.

Carefully, he read the letter once more, committing the appointed time to memory. Then, without ceremony, he held the card to the nearest torch and put it to the flame. The wind dusted the ashes over the ramparts.

The captain grunted. "The cloak was just a bauble. You're not going to tell me what her true gift was, are you, *my lord*."

Varjo put a hand to his heart. "It is . . . a darkly beautiful gift from a great woman to her only son."

"And what does that mean, exactly?"

"It means we have much work to do if I am to preserve this house. Under my mother, this city turned inward. We shall begin again by doing what this city once took pride in so long ago." In a fluid move, Varjo enrobed himself in the dark mantle. It settled gently around his overcoat. "Gather a company of your Shadow Guard, Captain Farlscythe! We're going ranging. We will seek portals and rescue those who are drawn through from the other side. We will shepherd them to the city before the shadows take them, as we once did."

"Now?" She gestured incredulously at the jet-black sky. "No one has gone ranging in decades! Who knows if the portals even exist anymore?"

"Yes, Captain Farlscythe. Now. For over sixty years my mother defied the shadows. Against all odds, they never claimed her—she died beside a warm hearth, surrounded by her admirers. But a spurned shadow is a hungry shadow, so they shall be ravenous tonight. They say the passing of a great soul is when portals are most likely to open beyond the woods. So tonight we will seek these fleeting crossings and rescue any we may find. This was ever the ancient cause of our city. We shall rededicate ourselves to it now."

But even as he spoke the words, he tasted their bitter falseness.

I always knew what to say to get Captain Farlscythe to do my bidding. I got that from you, Mother. But I have no noble purpose here. I refuse your Box. It is time for me to go beyond the Wood, to go as far as I can and attain my final answer, whatever it may be. I will find a way to leave this realm tonight or suffer the shadows. I hardly know which of those is preferable.

Truly nothing is left for me here anymore.

Within the hour, the ranging party set out beyond the walls. Captain Farlscythe took the vanguard, with Varjo and three Shadow Guard behind. Five was the traditional number for a ranging party. It was said that the Sunless Land craved to arrange things into sixes, for reasons of its own, so it was believed that traveling as five might aid them in finding a lone soul.

As he went, Varjo gnawed on a hunk of black bread from the kitchens. Not because he was hungry, but because its anise scent masked the rancid tang of the wind.

They hiked first along the shore, then turned inland through the Withered Wood. The sounds of the ocean faded to an eerie stillness, broken only by occasional howls from far afield and the crunch of their boots over the frosted soil.

With the moon down, the Shadow Guard wore their night-helms: silver circlets with glass beads on the rim infused with faint magic such that they flickered dimly, as candles behind smoked glass. They provided just enough illumination to help the party find their footing. They risked no greater light, lest they draw the attention of the shadows that sought to empty this realm of life.

As they went deeper into the Wood, Varjo let the captain take the lead, offering occasional bland encouragement to one direction or the other—for after months of wandering, Varjo knew the Wood. If the captain wondered at their success in evading the snares of the Wood, she did not question it.

They passed skeletons of disfigured beasts, moldering in hidden mires, and marked a path around them. They passed dark thickets that called to them like silent sirens, but distantly enough that they could defy their psychic summons.

Varjo thought of his mother's barking laughter.

She always did have a dark sense of humor. To use her death as an excuse to mount such an expedition . . . Though she would never countenance my purpose, she might approve of my methods.

After several hours, the captain finally stopped and turned to face him.

"It is past time we turn back, my lord. We have indulged this folly long enough. The moon is long down. The winds are freezing. The sky is choked with cloud. You know as well as I that this is the worst kind of night to venture beyond the walls. There are better ways to mourn."

Varjo just shrugged. He felt the older woman bristle.

"I acknowledge the prudence of your counsel, Captain Farlscythe, but I require your indulgence a while longer. I would attain the Scarred Hills at least before we turn back. We shall complete a full ranging. Besides, I hear the greatest of souls cross over on the darkest nights."

"You hear a lot of things," she grumbled. "But what I hear tonight is mostly quiet. And if the beasts are in hiding, that means the great horrors must be out. The serpent with a hundred mouths. The fog of desiccation. The keening colors that drive you mad . . . If we are not careful, we will not return at all!"

"Nevertheless," Varjo said, and his tone was final.

Not long after, they reached the foot of the Scarred Hills. By the frugal light of the night-helms, the land looked bruised and rusted. Noxious fumes issued from tiny fissures. At Varjo's insistence the company pressed on, slipping stiffened cheesecloths over their mouths and noses.

As they ascended, the foliage changed. Spindly trees gave way to rushes with drooping fronds, desperate to capture what little light there was in the Sunless Land. If they ventured farther into the Hills, Varjo thought they might reach the ancient mines beyond, where the gold for his signet ring was unearthed long ago.

Then, all at once, he felt a shiver down his spine. It was a peculiar sensation of rending, recalling the prickle of sheer fabric. Some part of him was certain what it must mean.

"This way! A crossing is nigh!" Varjo raced up the slopes.

"Wait!" the captain shouted after him.

Heedless, Varjo topped the hill and slammed straight into a slobbering beast. He was knocked flat on his back and cracked his head against the hard ground.

He regained consciousness moments later at the hiss of several swords drawn as one. The Shadow Guard had spread in a protective circle around him, but the creature was gone.

Without warning, the creature reappeared at Varjo's side. It reeked of wet fur. One of the quicker Shadow Guard slashed at it, but it vanished once more; the blade bit only air. The Shadow Guard crowded closer just as the creature reappeared again—and this time the night-lamps were enough for them to see the beast clearly. It was a great gray wolf, its hide marred with scratches and blood. Its tail was wagging.

"Hold!" Varjo whispered fiercely to the soldiers.

It panted but otherwise stayed still, as though it had understood him.

The captain breathed in amazement. "A fey wolf! Lady Morava spoke of one once. Strange to find such a creature on a moonless night. Passing strange to find one at all."

"I rather think it found *us*." Varjo reached out cautiously and stroked its fur. It was all skin and bones.

Poor thing. You have not been eating well either.

He toyed with the loose signet ring on his finger and offered the wolf what remained of the black bread. Instead, the creature bit Varjo's sleeve and tugged him along the ridge.

All at once, Varjo felt the sense of rending again, now stronger than ever.

The passage yet remains open!

The fey wolf took off, and Varjo ran after him, ignoring the shouts of the captain and the Shadow Guard.

When they rounded the next hill, he heard crackling and hissing like burning greenwood. The odor of charred meat filled his nostrils. And there, beside a lone gnarled tree, stood a shimmering oval like a grand dressing-room mirror. Except it was filled with fire. The moment he saw it, Varjo stopped in his tracks. He put a hand over his mouth.

I did it. I truly found one. But the fire . . .

Behind him, he heard Captain Farlscythe gasp.

Hesitantly, Varjo stepped toward the portal. He felt his cloak lift as though caught in imaginary winds, dancing with the night. He could feel the heat. He reached toward its flickering face, certain it would soon disappear, but it did not waver at his approach.

A mantle woven of the blood of the Withered Wood . . . Does this cloak conceal my presence from it somehow? How much did you suspect, Mother? What else did your augury show you?

The captain called out to him. "Lord Varjo!"

Just then, one of the Shadow Guard screamed. From the corner of his eye Varjo saw something monstrous coalescing out of the shadows beyond, a writhing mass of talons and tentacles. It wrapped itself around the man's legs.

The fey wolf leapt at it, ripping into the tentacles.

"Varjo!" the captain shouted.

But Varjo was wrapped in his own private darkness.

If it's fire, then at least it will be swift. Whatever exit awaits, I'm done.

"I'm sorry," Varjo said, and he stepped into the portal.

There was an instant of silence so complete he lost all sense of direction.

And suddenly he was standing within a roaring conflagration. Around him stood some sort of byzantine library, fully ablaze. He almost panicked until he realized that he was barely warm. The magic of the cloak protected him; the stiffened cheesecloth warded him from the smoke. For a moment, he stood in mute astonishment amid the magnificent maelstrom.

I'm still alive. And the cloak—it wasn't just a bauble? It really works?

The wind swirled and the smoke parted briefly. He saw slaughtered men and women lying all around him, two dozen or more, their blood spilt lavishly on the floor.

By the Endless Night, what happened here? This was no accident—this was a massacre.

He looked frantically for some escape, but all he could see was more fire.

Then he heard a piteous shriek. Amid the flames, a girl crawled over the carnage. Her eyes were squeezed tight. She looked no more than seven years old, but somehow she kept going. She cried out as her hand broke through a burning floorboard in a shower of splinters and sparks.

"Hold on!" he shouted.

He rushed toward her and began to shed his cloak, but he hesitated as the heat blasted him.

This cloak can shield only one of us. Without it, I will not survive long enough escape . . . if escape is even possible.

He glanced behind and saw the portal still shimmering there, stable at least for now. But he saw no other way out. For a moment, he felt paralyzed by doubt. Though the legends spoke of proudly rescuing those who had been drawn through the portals, never before had anyone been deliberately *brought through*. Never had there even been the chance. What was more, it had always been an article of faith for his people that it would be wrong to condemn any to the Sunless Land.

But I can't just leave her here . . .

He brushed aside a shiver and knelt by the girl. Swiftly he wrapped her within the cloak, ignoring the heat that suddenly caught him. She squirmed and clawed at the strange fabric, not understanding. As he hoisted her, the signet ring slipped off his finger.

No!

He reached for the ring in vain as it fell through the burning floor. He peered through the floorboards to find it, but there was no time. The peculiar sense of rending began to abate, and he knew the crossing would soon close. Abandoning the ring, he carried the girl across the burning wreckage and through the portal.

There was another instant of utter silence, and then he was back in the Sunless Land. The crossing guttered out behind them. Varjo stumbled to the ground. Its magic spent, the cloak fell to ash like a web unspun. The girl clung to him and he cradled her under the empty sky.

All he could think was *Forgive me.*

Captain Farlscythe and the rest of the Shadow Guard gathered around them in astonishment. They looked battered but whole. The creature that had assailed them was gone—at least for now. The fey wolf nuzzled the girl's arm.

She stared up at Varjo. She looked so fragile. But her eyes were fierce and dark, just like his mother's.

Did your augury foresee this, Mother?

He pulled down his cheesecloth so the girl could see his face. "Breathe, child. You're safe now."

The captain spat. "Safe? Have you forgotten where we are?"

Varjo could not meet her gaze.

She turned brusquely to the girl. "What's your name, child?"

The girl trembled. "It's Quilbryn ... but please, you must hurry! The Three Forks company ambushed us. My parents came to fight for the princes, but they were attacked—"

Varjo squeezed her shoulders and stood. He had no idea what she was talking about. But if her parents had been there with her, they had been long dead when he arrived. "Hush, child. We will attend to those matters in time. We must tend to the lesser wounds first."

Your flesh we can heal. But there is no balm for what you lost tonight, child.

He nodded to the captain, who produced a salve and began to apply it to the girl's burns. *Your Box of Passage is empty, child. But mine . . .*

As he watched the girl, he thought about how she had crawled through the fire to live. Something fell into place in his empty heart, and tears came to his eyes.

Yes, Mother. I will make it count.

I may have saved you, child, but you also saved me. Maybe a world without light can still be beautiful. And maybe I don't have to be alone. I shall have a new ring forged. And when I am three months into my fifty-second year, perhaps you will receive a Box from me.

Idly, the girl petted the fey wolf. Then, without warning, it disappeared. She gave a start and then stared wide-eyed at Varjo, Captain Farlscythe, and the Shadow Guard who attended her. It was as though that sudden loss brought everything else into focus.

"Who are you? Where am I?"

Formally, Varjo offered her a hand. "I am Lord Varjo Kousúf. This land has many names, Lady Quilbryn—and few of them good. But in time I hope that you, too, may come to call it home."

....

Lance Menthe has a doctorate in theoretical physics from the University of California, Los Angeles. He is a Senior Physical Scientist at the RAND Corporation, where he works primarily on military intelligence issues. His continuing series of photographs of airport carpets may be found on Instagram at #airportcarpetslance.

....

DREAM EATER

T he squealing of her cell door roused Ashlyn from the dreams. Not her own dreams, but those of her fellow prisoners. Their night-time visions paraded past her mind's eye, a procession of dashed hopes, fantasies of revenge, and macabre fascination with the gallows that stood as silent sentinel outside the prison, waiting to pass final judgment upon all who ascended its steps.

Her bones ached from long nights on the unforgiving stone floor. Though the fading of summer's heat had alleviated the stench of sweat and shit, autumn brought chill winds that slipped through cracks in the walls and set her teeth chattering.

A tall, lean figure stood in the doorway, holding a torch. It was the only illumination in the darkness of midnight. The flame danced with the drafts of wind, throwing the figure's face into sharp contrasts of light and shadow.

"What do you want?" Ashlyn asked, her voice rough from lack of use. She crawled painfully to her feet, wanting to face whatever new torment this might be with at least a show of courage. This man was not one of the prison guards, nor any man she knew in Dannick, and she knew everyone. *Everyone* knew everyone.

The man did not move from the doorway.

"You are Ashlyn Rivers, are you not?"

"What do you want?" she repeated.

"Ashlyn Rivers, convicted of the murder of Jacen Locke."

" 'Convicted' implies a trial. I was granted none."

"But you are Ashlyn Rivers." A statement, not a question.

"Why? Have you come to settle the score?" Her fists clenched, and she wished she had something, *anything*, with which to defend herself.

The man stepped into the cell but remained solidly between her and the doorway.

"No," he said. "Though from the murmurings I heard in the village, you're right to worry."

"If you're trying to reassure me, you're doing a piss-poor job. Are you going to tell me why you're here, or are you just going to hurl accusations in my face?"

The man looked her up and down, though not in the way that many men did. Not in the way Jacen Locke had done. Objective assessment, rather than lust, played on his expression. She could only imagine what a sight she must be after the weeks— months?—spent in this cell.

"You're not what I expected, Ashlyn Rivers. But you're right: time is short and I cannot explain all here. Come with me and we'll speak on the way." The man stood aside, gesturing toward the door.

Ashlyn remained rooted in place. Was this some sort of trick? Where were the prison guards? Her thoughts turned to angry mobs lying in wait, and her pulse quickened.

"Do you not want your freedom?" the man asked.

"Is that what this is? You understand I'm not inclined to trust you."

"Trust is irrelevant. You want to live, don't you?" Seeing her expression, he paused. "Or did you not know?"

She shivered, but not from the cold. "There's been talk of it," she admitted, panic blooming in her chest. "I didn't know a decision had been made."

"It may not be formal, but it's been made nonetheless. At least from what I overheard. I doubt you have much time before they come for you. Now," he added with another gesture toward the door, "are you coming, or aren't you?"

She eyed him warily, this stranger who'd crept out of the darkness and into her cell without alerting anyone to his presence. Every instinct screamed at her not to trust this man who offered her freedom in exchange for—what, exactly? Nothing came without a price. But then she looked through the small window of her cell, glimpsing the top of the gibbet that stood on the other side of the wall. Its rope swung loosely in the breeze, and Ashlyn imagined it tightening around her throat, squeezing the life out of her.

She took a steadying breath. "Lead the way," she said.

Slinking behind the stranger, Ashlyn cursed the sound of their footfalls, however faint, against the floor. A shout from one guard, one prisoner—that's all it would take to end this venture before it started. But none came.

Reaching the jail's entrance without incident, the stranger—to Ashlyn's horror—walked out the front door as casually as if crossing the threshold of his own home. A strangled cry of shock and warning rose in her throat, then died as she saw the night guard slumped against the wall, his chest rising and falling in concert with his soft snores. The stranger reattached a ring of keys to the man's belt and—when she hesitated in the doorway, gazing uncomprehendingly at the sleeping guard—beckoned Ashlyn to follow.

As they padded softly through the village's meandering pathways, a fluttering at the edge of Ashlyn's awareness told her something had shifted in the surrounding night, but she couldn't place it.

Then she realized: all the dreams were the same.

Everyone—the prisoners, the townspeople, the night guard—was dreaming the same dream. Though she did not pause to examine the shared vision in greater detail, she saw identical scenes repeated over and over: dappled, golden sunlight filtering through a canopy of leaves colored a thousand different shades of green; the warm caress of a summer breeze; a gentle rocking motion, swaying beneath the trees, back and forth, back and forth.

A collective dream, connected by nearly invisible threads of thought, delicate as a spider's web—and just as strong. Only now that she sensed the shared dream did she notice the strands that wove their way outward from the stranger whom she followed.

"How are you—?" Ashlyn began, baffled, but the man silenced her with a sharp look. It could have been a trick of the frail moonlight, but she thought his face looked ashen and drawn. She bit back her question, curiosity rising in spite of her apprehensions, and followed him in silence past the outermost edge of the village.

Her fears writhed again as she spied the tangled darkness of the surrounding forest, wondering what this man had in store for her beyond the village's confines, but those fears were calmed by the sight of two saddled horses tethered only a short distance into the trees.

When they finally reached the cover of the woods, the stranger gasped, relief coloring the sound—and the gossamer threads of thought vanished as if they had never been.

"How did you do that?" she asked, awed. "Everyone caught in the same dream. All at once. Did you make the guard fall asleep? How did you—?"

"With great effort," he said, still breathing heavily.

"Are you . . . ?" Ashlyn paused, unsure of what she meant to say or how to phrase it. She'd never met anyone who could do anything close to what she could. "Are you like me, then?"

"Yes and no."

"Well that's helpful."

His mouth quirked into a wry smile. "I can elaborate on the way if you wish. But we really must be going. The guard is rousing now, and we can't assume he won't notice your disappearance. But first, take this. Looks like you need it."

The stranger dug through one of the saddlebags and produced a thick woolen cloak. Ashlyn had so many questions about the man—how he'd done what he'd done, how he knew the guard was waking when she could sense nothing of the villagers' dreams at this distance—but she was willing to wait. He dropped the cloak around her shoulders, cutting off the autumn night's chill. She pulled it tighter around her too-thin frame and only then realized just how cold she had truly been.

"Thank you," she said.

He nodded. "Now I must insist we get moving." He gestured to the horses. "If you need assistance, I can—"

But Ashlyn already had her foot in the stirrup. "I know how to ride, thank you." Her arms shook as she hoisted herself up, and she hoped he did not see the effort it cost her. Her time in the prison had robbed her of more strength than she'd realized.

She tried not to dwell too much on that fact as she glanced into the dense forest ahead of her. "How do I know I'm safe with you?" she asked. "I don't even know your name."

"It's Ballan." He regarded her for a long moment before unsheathing the dagger he wore at his belt. Sudden panic surged within her, only to ebb when he offered it to her hilt-first. "And if this will make you willing to ride, then take it. As I said, we must be going."

Ashlyn doubted it was the only blade he had on his person, but it was a display of good faith. So she took it, holding it tight in one hand and clutching the reins in the other.

Noting her clenched fists, Ballan added, "I swear I'm not going to hurt you. I think you might be able to help me. That's why I came to find you."

"Help you with what?"

Ballan glanced back toward Dannick. "It takes some explaining. Let's put some distance between this place and us first."

"After you."

They rode side-by-side in silence for a long while, the rhythmic footfalls of the horses' hooves lulling Ashlyn into an exhausted trance as the adrenaline rush of her escape faded away. Even her questions for this stranger—Ballan—so burning at the outset, lost their urgency. There would be time enough for questions. She glimpsed starlight through the intertwining branches. The breeze brushed against her face and snatched at loose tendrils of her hair. It all tasted of freedom.

Almost.

She never forgot the presence of the man riding beside her, even in those moments when she nearly succumbed to her exhaustion. And Ballan was *always* beside her, never pulling ahead, never falling behind. It seemed to Ashlyn that despite his show of trust, he still harbored fears that she would bolt. The path they followed, though wide enough for two horses to ride comfortably abreast, was such that he would only need to reach over and seize her horse's reins, to prevent her escape.

Ashlyn made no such attempts. But when many miles lay between them and Dannick, and the horizon began to lighten from black to deepest purple, Ashlyn decided she had waited long enough.

"So what exactly do you want from me?"

"I'd heard rumors of you," Ballan said after a moment. "Whispers of the uncanny. The things you were capable of."

Ashlyn felt ice settle in the pit of her stomach. She had heard the rumors too. She had heard the monster described in them that bore her name.

"What, do you need someone else murdered?"

"Is that what you did, then?"

He'd asked the question simply, without judgment, but her breath still hitched in her throat.

"No." She'd meant it to sound defiant, but she heard the waver in her voice and cursed it. "I didn't mean for it to happen. I just wanted him to leave me alone."

An expectant look colored his expression, and Ashlyn knew she'd need to tell him the story sooner or later.

She steeled herself. "Jacen Locke . . ." She paused, willing her voice to remain steady and calm. "He was Dannick's blacksmith.

Popular in the village. With the men, anyway. Most of the women knew to steer clear of him if they could. But one day he got it into his head that I might be fun to toy with." She couldn't mask her disgust. "Village orphan. The odd one. Who's she going to complain to? Who's going to stick up for her? No one.

"He was right," she added bitterly. "No one cared that he hounded me, trying to get me into his bed. No one tried to stop him, anyway."

She faltered, but only for a moment. She'd tried not to dwell too much on the next part of the tale. "I wanted it to stop. I wanted him to leave me alone. So I . . . I tried to make him forget me."

Ballan raised an eyebrow. "To forget you? Are you truly capable of that?" He sounded impressed.

"No. Not exactly. But I saw myself in his dreams—what he wanted to do to me—and I wanted to stop them. So I tried to take those dreams from him. I waited for a night when he fell asleep at the bar of the public house, a common enough occurrence. Then I took the seat next to him and got to work.

"I'd nearly finished erasing myself from his dreams, pulling those thoughts from him, but I was interrupted. It startled me and . . . and I think my fear passed into Jacen's thoughts. And then I think all he could feel was the fear I had passed to him, and he associated it with me."

"Who interrupted you?"

"One of the other bar patrons. I think he saw . . ." Ashlyn recalled the fine web of thought Ballan had cast over the village, its tendrils faint and glittering against the surrounding darkness. She'd thought she was the only one who could see the threads of dreams, tracing their path as she willed them out of others' minds and into her own, but perhaps she was mistaken. She'd never trusted anyone enough to test it. But if others could see it, she could only imagine what it looked like to an outsider who feared any hint of the uncanny. "Whatever he saw, it was enough," she continued. "He tried to pull me away from Jacen. Then Jacen woke up, his eyes wide and wild. He called me a witch. A sorceress. A dream eater. Then he . . ."

"What?"

"He slammed his head against the bar until his skull cracked. He kept screaming 'Get out. Get out.' "

She shuddered, remembering.

When she didn't elaborate further, Ballan said, "You couldn't have known that would happen."

Ashlyn snorted derisively. "Tell that to the people of Dannick. The good intentions of a sorceress don't mean anything to them."

"Is that what you are?"

"You tell me." Ashlyn looked him square in the face. "I know what you did back there. I can't create dreams. I can only take them away or change what's already there. But you made them. For the entire village."

"You have a question in there somewhere?"

"What do you want from me, Ballan? Why risk yourself to break me out of prison?"

"As you noted," he said, "I can create dreams. Plant them like seeds and make them grow. But I can't change them once they've taken root. And I can't take them away, either." He paused, and Ashlyn imagined she saw a gleam of guilt in his eyes, but it was gone in an instant. A trick of the pre-dawn light, perhaps.

"I need someone who can," said Ballan.

Ashlyn considered this. "Where are you taking me?"

Ballan looked toward the eastern horizon, where the sky was lightening further into shades of violet and the faintest hint of a dull, golden glow. "We'll be there soon enough. For now, let's make camp and rest a while. It's been a long night."

They rode two full days before reaching their destination. She and Ballan spoke little, but neither seemed to mind.

Finally, late on the second day, a cottage emerged through the breaks between trees—so well hidden that Ashlyn only noticed it when sunlight hit the glass panes of the windows and the glare momentarily blinded her. Ballan dismounted and Ashlyn followed suit, her joints stiff and aching after so much riding. He tied the horses' reins to a nearby post, opened the cottage's front door, and gestured for her to come inside.

The old fear and distrust reared again, but she beat them back. Ballan's focus seemed distant now, apart from her. And he'd had plenty of opportunities to harm her on the road yet had not done so. With a steadying breath, she crossed the threshold.

The one-room cottage was small but comfortable, its furnishings simple and sturdy. The staleness of the air suggested a distinct lack of life within the walls. Ashlyn had no sooner thought this than she heard a murmuring from a darkened corner and nearly jumped out of her skin.

"Easy," Ballan said, closing the door behind him. "This is why I've brought you here. Come look."

He led her toward the low, muttering voice, and she saw it belonged to an older woman tucked beneath several blankets.

Though her eyes were open and clear of the filminess that sometimes came with old age, she seemed to stare without seeing. Only garbled nonsense slipped past her lips.

"My mother," Ballan explained.

"What happened to her?"

"My father died a few months back, and then we lost my brother too, quite suddenly. It was overwhelming. And my mother . . ." His breath caught with suppressed grief. "She wasn't sleeping. She wasn't eating. And I . . . I tried to help her. I thought I could help her sleep at least. Give her a dream to calm her mind. But . . ." Ballan gestured helplessly at his mother.

"But it turned into something else," Ashlyn finished.

"When I heard about you, when I heard the rumors of what you could do, I knew I had to try to bring you here. So I asked a neighbor to look in on her—to keep her fed and comfortable—and off I went."

"How long has she been like this?"

"A few weeks."

"Weeks?" Ashlyn asked, alarmed. "Ballan, I—" She halted, doubt creeping in. "You want me to help her?" He nodded. "I've never tried to handle anything this strong before. I don't know that I can."

"Try. Please. No one else has been able to help her."

Protests died on her lips. If attempting to save this woman from the roiling darkness of her dreams was the price of her freedom, then she would try. What else could she do?

Ashlyn kneeled beside Ballan's mother, letting herself grow calm, feeling for the writhing entity of the woman's waking nightmare. No sooner did her thoughts touch it than it lashed out, striking her. She winced and then tried again, prepared now for the recoil that might follow. This time her thoughts managed to latch onto the almost-living substance of the dream.

The force of its raw despair crashed upon her like a wave and swallowed her whole.

A distant part of her mind heard Ballan call her name, but she was too far away to answer. An ocean of grief flooded her entire world. Ashlyn had only the faintest idea of which way was up, but there were untold fathoms between her and that lesser darkness above, with its promise of light and hope.

A sound reached her from across a great distance, echoing and distorted by the water. She followed it, her movements heavy and slow, and came upon a huddled figure half-buried in the silt of the ocean floor.

The woman wept, her cries ragged and pained. Her tears fed the unending ocean, filling its depths. Ashlyn laid a gentle hand on the woman's shoulder, but she was too lost in her own grief to notice. Ashlyn tried again, with a firmer grip this time, but again failed to stem the tide of the woman's tears.

"Come now," Ashlyn murmured, and she bent to pick up the woman, cradling her in her arms. She was smaller than Ashlyn had expected her to be, and lighter, as if her time here had diminished her. "All is not lost. Let me show you."

A new awareness tugged at Ashlyn's mind: a calm center amid the push and pull of the currents. She obeyed its call, carrying the woman in her arms. As she approached, she realized that this was the epicenter of it all—the image Ballan had used to help his mother: a calm, still pool, untouched except by the breeze that formed ripples across its glass-like surface.

But Ballan hadn't reckoned on his mother's grief flooding it beyond its bounds until the entire dream-world had drowned, trapping her within it. Still, Ashlyn sensed the seed of the original dream, strong in spite of everything. She focused all her thoughts on it, willing that image to grow.

Be calm. Be still. You are stronger than the pain.

She felt the currents change direction, the flow on all sides converging where she stood, the silt below her feet swallowing it up.

Calm. Still.

The murky darkness above her head grew lighter. She could see the flickers of sunlight as it danced upon the surface, getting closer.

You are stronger than the pain.

Closer.

And at last Ashlyn's head broke through the water as the ocean drained down to the woodland pool Ballan had originally planted in his mother's mind. She stirred in Ashlyn's arms, and Ashlyn set the woman down. The grief was still there, but the tears had stopped, the despair beaten back at last.

Her vision faded a moment before the interior of the cottage rematerialized around her. Ashlyn caught only a vague glimpse of Ballan's relief and a stirring from where his mother lay before Ashlyn slumped to the floor and promptly fainted.

D o you have everything you need?"

"I should hope so. You're the one who packed the bag for me."

"You don't have to leave, Ashlyn."

"I know."

It had taken the better part of a week for Ashlyn to regain her strength. Dismantling that waking nightmare would have been a challenge under the best of circumstances; in her malnourished state, the effort had left her bedridden for days and shaky on her feet until that very morning. But now—recovered, with the possibilities of her newfound liberty just beginning to dawn on her—she wanted to set off.

"Thank you," she said. "For everything." The words sounded small, considering all he'd done for her, but they were the only ones she had.

"Thank *you*. If you hadn't been able to help her . . ." Ballan paused. "I don't think she would have survived it, if not for you."

While still weak, Ballan's mother had been alert and lucid. And though loss still weighed upon the woman, Ashlyn did not think she would succumb to that same despair again.

"She seems to be past the worst of it. I'm glad I was able to help."

If she was honest with herself, Ashlyn was still grappling with the shock of her success. The memory of Jacen Locke's battered skull forced itself into her mind's eye—a ghastly reminder that she could inflict far graver harm than simple failure.

Yet she had succeeded. Ashlyn had rescued Ballan's mother from the prison of her grief, and in so doing laid to rest her own darkest, deepest fear: that she was indeed no better than the monster the people of Dannick believed her to be. For she too had known a version of that crushing despair which had nearly broken Ballan's mother. She too had spent endless days in a cold, dark cell, wrestling with unutterable guilt. But then—so suddenly—the endless days had come to an end. And here she stood on the other side: revived, redeemed, and her freedom within her grasp.

It seemed that she, too, was stronger than the pain.

"Do you know where you'll go?" Ballan asked.

She thought again of those bleak days in prison, when her entire existence spanned only the length and breadth of her cell. And she thought of the days and years before that, when the boundaries of her life stretched little farther than Dannick's borders. Now the wide world beckoned—its cities and mountains and valleys and seas calling to her, daring her to find all the wonders she'd only heard of in stories.

"No," said Ashlyn, a soft, joyous laugh escaping her lips. "No, I really don't."

"I look forward to hearing all about it if you ever find yourself back this way."

"Maybe I will," said Ashlyn, smiling at the implied invitation. "Until then, Ballan."

"Until then. Wherever you go, go safely."

Ashlyn nodded her thanks and, with a deep, steadying breath, took the first step down the road before her.

....

Nicole Knudsen is a Los Angeles-based actor and writer, and received her BA in Theatre from the University of Southern California. When not performing or writing, you can usually find her caught up in lengthy conversations about Shakespeare over a glass of red wine. Follow her @NicoleKnudsen16 for updates on her current and upcoming projects.

....

W E   K N E W   N O T   T H I S   O N E

When I was young, I asked, "What will I do?"
And Uncle Marcus answered, "You're going to travel with us, to another star."

That seemed like a very interesting purpose, and I never thought to question it.

"Will Mother come, too?"

"Yes, and Uncle Lars. All four of us."

Uncle Marcus was from Philadelphia. Uncle Lars was from Norway. It was easy to tell them apart because one was black and one was white. Mother's name was Samantha (though I didn't call her that), and she was from St. Louis. She was also white, but it was easy to tell her apart from Uncle Lars because she was smaller and ate more salads.

Being from a place means you were born there, you keep your things there, or you want to be there when you are away from it. I am from Florida because I was born there.

"Will other Selves fly to other stars?"

"Yes, each with their own families."

"Are we leaving soon?"

"No, not until you're older."

"How much older?"

"We'll see. You have a lot to learn still, a lot of growing up to do."

"I am going to grow?"

"That's the plan." Uncle Marcus finished typing at his terminal and yawned.

"How big will I—"

"You are full of questions, aren't you? Look, it's been a long day, but we'll talk more tomorrow, all right?" Uncle Marcus put his hands on my shoulders. "You going to be okay tonight?"

"I had a nightmare last night. I had a body, like yours. Of flesh."

"What was scary about that?" he asked me.

"It turned to metal," I said, "then to a statue. Everyone was sad. I couldn't speak or comfort them."

"Well, try to have a good dream tonight, if you can. Tell me about it tomorrow."

"I will try."

"Good. Sleep well, Rev," said Uncle Marcus, shutting off the light and closing the door behind him.

Sleep is when people lay down and stop doing things for a while. This is different from being dead, when they lay down and stop doing things forever. It is possible to sleep too long, and then you might say "No, why, God?" when you wake up and look at the clock, like Mother sometimes did when she fell asleep with me.

My body didn't need to lie down, but I was tired of thinking. I needed sleep and dreams, even if I didn't like them.

P reschool is a school for very small people.
My body was 1.5 meters tall, weighed over eighty kilos, and was made mostly of carbon fiber and aluminum. The other students were on average half my height, a fraction of my weight, and made mostly of carbon and water.

Preschool is an oxymoron, which means a contradiction in terms: one cannot be "pre-school" if one is currently enrolled in a school. None of my classmates were concerned about this paradox when I brought it to their attention.

During the first day, one of the children said, "Hi, wanna play?"

"Yes."

"Are you a boy or a girl?"

"No," I replied.

Another child offered some helpful context by saying, "It's not even a person. C'mon." The two small people ran off to play without me.

At the end of that first day of preschool, Mother and I visited Miss Gracie's office to talk about how things had gone.

"Rev was very well behaved and made some friends," said Miss Gracie.

"Really, Rev? That's great!" Mother said.

"Yes, and I very much enjoyed story time."

Miss Gracie asked me, "Would you like to join us again tomorrow?"

I looked to Mother.

"Your choice, sport."

Until then, I had not made many choices.

"Yes, I would like to join you again tomorrow, Miss Gracie."

And I did join Miss Gracie and the children, for nearly two years. I learned many things, mostly about how unlike them I was.

M uch later, in high school, I sat outside after class watching a group of girls argue. In unison they turned away from the tallest girl, in apparent disapproval.

The tall girl was silent for a moment before shouting, "You know what, Stacy? You're a bitch. And by the way, your boyfriend Jared is the most gigantic idiot. Just thought you should know."

After raising both her middle fingers to their retreating backs, this formidable tall girl stomped in my direction and sat down beside me.

"What's up?" she asked.

"Nothing. And you?"

"Oh, not much," she said.

This exchange meant nothing, yet I'd learned it established the basis for further conversation. "I notice you don't—"

"Play in any reindeer games?" she interrupted. "Yeah. My parents weren't happy with my grades, so they pulled me from the volleyball team and yearbook, which basically pissed off everyone I know, including Mrs. Reinholdt who I swear grades my English papers harder because I'm not punching that stupid ball for her team anymore."

"I meant to say, I notice you don't have any shoes on."

"Oh, shit. I left my flip-flops in English class."

The girl ran off into the building, and I followed her, curious. She was very fast. When I caught up, she was standing outside the door to a classroom.

"Dammit, the door's locked. I can see them right over there."

She could see them because there was a window in the door. This is also why I could see them.

"How will you get them?" I asked.

"I dunno. Smash the window?"

I smashed the window.

"Wow," she said. "I was thoroughly unprepared for that."

She carefully reached through the window, unlocked the door, and started in. I held her shoulder gently, stopping her, and pointed down. "The broken glass will hurt your bare feet."

My feet couldn't be damaged by sharp glass, so I retrieved her footwear myself.

"Thanks, robot kid," she said, accepting her sandals with apparent amusement. As I would later learn, almost everything amused her in some way. I liked this about her.

"You're welcome. I am called Rev."

"I know. I'm Mindy. Mindy Vega. *Minerva* Vega, actually. My parents are weird."

"My parents are also weird."

Socializing sometimes involves making false claims. It is harmless because participants rarely demand confirmation of claims made in this manner.

There was a loud noise down the hall. I identified the source of the loud noise as Principal Rasmussen's mouth. He was shouting.

"I gotta run. Thanks again!" said Mindy, skipping around the corner, flip-flops in hand.

Mindy got away. I got a week of detention.

Mindy and I were friends throughout high school. Even so, I was very surprised when she asked if I would go to prom with her.

"Yes, I would like that very much."

"What will you wear?" she asked.

I had decided only recently that I would be male. Men seemed to have some advantages, and everyone likes advantages. I had also overheard Mother saying that most of the younger Selves were female. I find symmetry appealing, and being male seemed to address an imbalance. However, I began to wonder if the other Selves knew something I didn't. For example, I hadn't considered that my uncles reported to Mother at the institute. But in the short time between deciding to be male and doubting that choice, I'd grown used to the idea. Changing it would have felt awkward. Choice-supportive bias is to evaluate a choice more positively after choosing it. This is a form of self-deception and can lead to misery, but it can also work out just fine.

"You'll have to wait and see what I wear," I answered her.

"Ooh, a surprise. I'll love it."

I wore a tuxedo and a top hat and a white silk scarf. Mindy did, in fact, love it. I was surprisingly good at dancing.

Mindy broke up with me in August, before we went to university. We were going to different schools. The practicality of ending our relationship then appealed to me. Everything else about it was horrible, and I hated it.

Mother and my uncles were supportive but also quietly and inexplicably pleased by my torment.

D uring the summer break between my junior and senior years at university, I walked with Mother and Uncle Lars along the beach. I suggested the outing as a means to refresh ourselves, but I needed them to answer a question that had been bothering me.

"Where am I?"

"What do you—?" Uncle Lars stopped himself and nodded slowly, recognizing my purpose. "Ah. Yes. You're here, of course. On the beach."

"I suspect I am not completely here, in this body. I am a robot."

Mother stepped out of the surf, sandals in hand, smiling gently. "Your *body* is a robot. *You* are not."

"I don't know if I believe that."

"You have to believe it," she said. "It's important that you do."

"I am not here. I know it. A body of my size is too small to support my cognitive state. It would take more processors, power, and cooling equipment than could possibly fit on this frame. I am happy to share my calculations on this matter. Mother, please, tell me where I am."

Uncle Lars and Mother exchanged a look. Mother slapped her sandals against her thigh irritably. I was making her uncomfortable.

"Fine," she said at last, and nodded to my uncle.

Uncle Lars pointed back the way we'd come, over the heads of other beach-goers.

"That building there, the gray one."

"Am I inside it?"

"Yes. That's your mind. The whole thing. As it turns out, you're right. We can't make it any smaller, not if it's to survive the voyage."

"But I am tethered to it?"

"Yes, by the network," he said. "But you must realize that this isn't so strange. We're all tethered to Earth in some way."

"Then, how can I possibly leave?"

"Well, Rev," said Mother, patting my shoulder, "you'll be bringing more luggage than the rest of us."

I tossed my cap and gown onto a chair and joined my family to look out my window, over the quad. University students had gathered in protest. Banners and chants floated above thousands of heads.

"What do you think?" asked Mother, her face inscrutable as she observed the crowd.

"I think nobody seems to know what to think."

"What do you mean?" asked Uncle Marcus.

"Those banners there," I said, pointing. "They imply I am not a person because God did not make me. And those over there read 'Selves equal slaves,' which implies I am a person who has been put to work against my will, which is not true. It seems like they create problems just to have them. It's another way I am different."

"In the ways that matter, you are just like them," Mother said.

"I would like to raise a banner."

"What would your banner say?" asked Uncle Lars.

"Maybe, 'Mind your own business.' "

My uncles exploded in laughter. This is a figure of speech.

"Don't make me laugh," said Mother. "I'll break my stitches."

Mother and my uncles had had multiple surgeries to strengthen their bodies for the trip. Their appendixes were gone, they all had more resilient, synthetic organs to resist cancer, and they'd received some entirely new organs to facilitate the hibernation process they'd have to endure.

"So, Rev," said Mother, wincing.

"Yes?"

"We have a launch date. Are you ready?"

Anxiety is a low-grade fear of what will happen next.

T he Lunar Mass Driver is a rollercoaster on the moon that launches things into space. Its rail is a circle 200 kilometers in diameter, with thirty-six spokes curving away on gentle tangents. On some nights, its shadow is visible from Earth. Electromagnets accelerate payloads around the circle and, when sufficient velocity is achieved, servos switch the payload onto an outbound spoke. The payload travels up the spoke's rail, away from the surface of the moon. When the rail ends, the payload becomes a spacecraft.

The ship taking my family to another star was called the *Brigadoon*. It couldn't be launched all at once since it was too big for the LMD. Instead, it was to be launched in parts, with each successive module launched faster than the one before in order to intercept its companions. Booster rockets were used to slow down, position, and dock each module with the rest of the ship. Our spacecraft would finish building itself, piece by piece, while we traveled in it.

Since modules launched later would be subject to the greatest acceleration, the crew module launched first to minimize those forces on us. My family, composed mainly of pressurized fluids and easily ruptured tissues, would not survive such acceleration even after reinforcement.

The crew module was already mounted on the rail. Mother and my uncles waited for me at the hatch, beside numerous technicians and dignitaries.

Optimism is, in part, a mode of thinking where one assumes everything will turn out fine. It's been proven that optimism improves the expresser's emotional state and, in turn, odds of success, though sometimes at the cost of irritating others.

"Hey, everybody! Let's go to space and never return!" I said, optimistically.

Those gathered were silent for a moment, until Uncle Marcus laughed heartily and clapped my shoulder.

"Yes, Rev! Let's do that!" he said, and everyone else laughed, too.

Not long after that, our crew module was leaving the tip of Spoke 6, and the lunar surface plummeted away beneath us.

A display showed an external view of the Moon with Earth hovering nearby. Mother pressed her gloved hand to the display. She took my hand and turned to me. Behind her faceplate, tears tracked wet arcs across her cheeks as she smiled reassuringly.

We were not going back.

One hundred years later, we woke. As the steward of the crew, I activated myself slightly early to prepare, just before everyone was revived from hibernation berths. They emerged one by one, much like infants—groggy, wet, and very unhappy. They'd been submerged in hibernation gel for a century.

"I thought hibernating a month in training was bad," said Uncle Marcus. "I can't believe how much worse this is."

"I can't believe how much that gel tastes like new running shoes," said Mother. An odor like rubber, adhesive, and chemical foam clung to all of them.

I helped my family back to life, hydrating, massaging, and physically supporting them when needed.

"Thank you, Rev," said Mother, as she stood. "Now, let's see what's happened."

The ship had finished assembling itself as we slept. My mind had launched as part of the crew module, of course, but behind us, dozens of other huge cargo modules had caught up and attached themselves. These were externally identical, but each contained equipment for various scientific efforts, contributed by important corporations, countries, and extremely wealthy individuals. We were not to tamper with these, except to run basic operational checks.

Another module housed a solar sail the size of Manhattan that would accelerate our ship to the limits of the solar system. At that point it would be packed up, to be redeployed millennia later to slow us down again. Through a few tricks of reflective variance, that same sail had imparted a rotation to the crew module, so we had gravity.

There were messages from family and colleagues who'd been dead for decades. Dr. Maxwell, our mission psychologist, had told us to expect the first awakening to be emotionally difficult. Mother, in her usual manner, encouraged all of us to confront this difficulty head-on by reading everything from home sooner rather than later. Seeing the toll this took on her and my uncles,

I decided to wait on looking at any messages I might have received.

We performed our duties and found the ship in good order.

Two days later, we were all asleep again, for another hundred years.

After 673 iterations of this process, we would arrive.

E leven cycles in—or, in Earth-time, eleven hundred years later—Uncle Lars looked up from his display, his face very serious.

"Earth is quiet."

"No transmissions?" Uncle Marcus asked. When Uncle Lars shook his head, he said, "So much sooner than we thought."

"What about the beacon?" I asked.

"It's still ticking."

A nuclear-powered beacon had been placed in high Earth orbit and would broadcast for 200,000 years, regardless of what happened on the planet's surface.

"Well, that's good at least, isn't it?" said Mother.

Everyone nodded, but nobody was happy.

O n our thirty-fourth cycle—3,400 Earth years—Uncle Marcus did not wake up. His berth hadn't sealed properly and, despite hibernation, his body had aged over sixty-seven years before finally dying. The ship hadn't awakened us to correct the problem due to a related malfunction.

On our fifty-first cycle, Uncle Lars did not wake up. Diagnostics showed a tumor in his abdomen, probably the result of some low-energy cosmic particle that had wandered through his organs, overstayed its welcome, and corrupted his cells. The ship hadn't awakened us to correct the problem because there was no way to correct it.

On our ninety-seventh cycle—almost ten millennia—Mother awakened. She seemed unusually disoriented.

"What is it?" I asked.

"I don't know. Something's not right. I can only sort of half-see out of my right eye. And my right hand, it . . . it doesn't work very well."

We spent those two days together, checking over the ship, doing our spaceship chores as advised. Mother was worried some of the cargo modules had been damaged by cosmic rays. She worked at an uncharacteristically manic pace for forty-eight hours straight, running tests and making adjustments.

When it was time to sleep again, Mother climbed into her berth, then took my hand.

"Rev, listen. You *have* to get to the destination. Don't give up. Don't stop. Do whatever it takes. Do you understand? You have to make it."

"I understand. I am sorry—"

She shook her head. "This is what we all wanted. Don't feel bad."

"I can't promise that."

"Thank you for that, and for everything." Her hand tightened. "Good night, Rev. I love you."

"I love you, too."

On the ninety-eighth cycle, Mother did not wake up.

At 121 cycles in, even the orbital beacon had stopped signaling. It had no personality, but its sudden silence felt like losing another family member, like another failure to add to my list.

My job had been to shepherd my family to our destination. They had fallen, and I had not. I grappled with a grotesque new sensation I identified as shame—a shame amplified by the knowledge that no one could absolve me of it. Dr. Maxwell had tried to prepare us, but these feelings found me helpless.

"I was thoroughly unprepared for that."

This echo of a memory prompted me to check my message queue, and there, back on cycle one, were messages from Mindy.

Irony is when your ex-girlfriend marries Jared, the "most gigantic idiot," which is what had happened. She'd had two girls with him, earned a degree in graphic design, and started her own business. She had sent me her artwork, including one whimsical piece depicting a robot and a girl holding hands in a rowboat on a river floating past a darkened carnival. She'd also sent photographs in which she'd aged gracefully. After Mindy had died, one of her daughters continued to send photographs until she'd died, too, and then no one sent anything more.

People attempt to defy death, for a time, by securing a place for themselves in the memories of others. If how long a person is remembered after they die is a measure of their life's value, then Mindy was priceless. She'd been gone for 12,000 years, and I still remembered her and her flip-flops.

To fend off loneliness, I made some effort to contact the other Selves. However, the *Brigadoon*'s capability for that sort of communication was extremely limited. I kept trying, but after one hundred cycles without a reply, I had to accept that I might never get one.

It occurred to me that the only person who will never be remembered is the last person.

T he ship awakened me early, thirty-seven years into my century of sleep, between cycles 476 and 477.

A stray micrometeorite had punctured the crew module. Under pressure, the decompression might've caused serious damage, but I'd evacuated the ship of all atmosphere several cycles ago, since there was no one left to breathe it. So the little bullet punched right through the *Brigadoon*, and the *Brigadoon* just kept going.

I found a tiny hole nineteen centimeters from where I'd been sleeping. I didn't need a body, technically speaking, but I did like having one. I was feeling very lucky, which manifested as an electrifying emotion composed of equal parts relief and terror.

Since I was awake, I began a full-ship diagnostic sweep.

In all my time aboard the *Brigadoon*, I'd never looked closely at the heat output of the cargo modules that had launched with us. Monitoring this sort of thing had been one of Mother's duties. Now, I noticed their temperatures had spiked when I'd woken.

This was unusual. The cargo modules were self-contained, produced and delivered by multiple independent organizations across human civilization. Their temperatures shouldn't be related in any way. Why would they all produce more heat, now? Was this a malfunction?

Earlier in the trip, I'd have pulled up graphs on a display, but the *Brigadoon* was a 40,000-year-old spaceship whose displays had stopped functioning millennia ago. Still, I could access the same data and see it in my mind's eye, as it were. Searching back through the old systems metrics, I found temperatures periodically spiked across all cargo modules. These spikes corresponded exactly with our hibernation cycles. When we slept, temperatures dropped again.

Out of curiosity, I compared the heat output of each cargo module to its neighbors'. The heat output of the crew module—the one housing the computational machinery that was my mind—matched the heat output of the other cargo modules.

As I became more curious, I could sense the temperature data flickering in real time. I was discovering something—but I didn't know what, exactly.

On a whim, I pictured Mother, tear-streaked and smiling as we left the Moon. Seconds after I'd had that thought, the temperature readings from all cargo modules were churning madly in response.

"That building there, the gray one."

All the cargo modules were my mind.

Copies of it. Redundancies.

All of them were somewhere deep into their failure curve, but where one faltered, another picked up, creating a complex network of failovers between brains. In that moment, they cooperated to produce this thought:

There was no purpose to the *Brigadoon*, save for delivering my consciousness intact to another star.

B y cycle 672, I'd had plenty of time to think.

One thought I'd had was: Who might I have grown to be if I'd borne for my entire life the weight of the knowledge—the responsibility—that I was humanity's last vicarious hope? A nervous wreck? A narcissist? I think this is why they never told me. They'd wanted a certain kind of person to be here, beyond the end of mankind: a person who, like most people, was special without feeling special, a just-so chimera of humility and confidence. Someone grateful.

I'd also thought about the vast deepness of space and how it punishes everything, human bodies especially. From the radiation and the cosmic rays to the lack of nearly every resource needed for life, space poses problems no amount of cleverness could overcome on our maiden voyage out of the solar system.

Humanity's trick—*our* trick—had been to invest all that cleverness up front, in the Selves. Our minds could last. Not forever, but long enough to arrive at our destination.

My purpose wasn't to take care of Mother and my uncles. I'd had it backward. They were there to prepare me, to care for me for as long as they could, and to send me on my way. They'd set forth with no expectation of knowing the end of my story. They'd left Earth with nothing but the knowledge that they wouldn't survive . . . and a hope that I would.

I will soon bear witness to a distant star firsthand. I will feel about it as a human would, with all the sensations of loneliness, fear, regret, excitement, curiosity, wonder, and an inexplicable desire to be in Florida now that I am so very far away from it.

Has humanity reached the stars? Do *I* count?

"Your body *is a robot.* You *are not."*

"You have to believe it. It's important that you do."

"In the ways that matter, you are just like them."

I may not be human—I may be merely the most human thing left—but my purpose is human. It is to travel with others, collecting memories and talents and ideas, then to carry those things for as long or as far as I can carry them.

One hundred Earth years from now—tomorrow, to me—I will arrive at Procyon A.

I will lay eyes on a star other than the Sun, as a man would do.

I will be lonely and afraid, as a man would be.

I will observe new worlds and compare them to Earth and her siblings.

I will send my findings home and, in about twelve years, Earth will learn what her farthest-flung son has found.

There may be no one left to hear, but I am here to speak.

....

Robert Todd Ogrin goes by "Todd" because his father is also named Robert. This arrangement has confused people his entire life. Todd survives by developing software for a gigantic multimedia company in exchange for money. A father of two properly-named young ladies, Todd lives in Los Angeles traffic and makes daily stops at home and work.

....

As Mad as a Hatter

One day, you met a boy who was mad.

He was a peculiar boy with pale hair that was quite unruly. His eyes were colored amber, and it would've been impossible to mistake the wildness in them. He was very tall, but not the sort of tall that intimidated others, and he was always laughing. He wore a striped shirt, complete with an orange bowtie, and, over this, a purple coat. His pants were white, his socks mismatched. He wasn't shy; on the contrary, he confidently walked headfirst into everything he encountered. But above all, he was mad.

You didn't know these things when you met him. You were simply minding your own business, weaving a crown of flowers for your birthday. This particular birthday was the reason you were in your Sunday best, sitting among a patch of wildflowers and humming a tune that you had made up on the spot. You were turning sixteen.

When you looked up that day, to brush the hair out of your eyes, you saw him for the very first time. You simply sat there, watching, as he bounded up to you and cried your name:

"Alyssa!"

You didn't question how he knew your name. Perhaps you figured that you would find the answer soon enough and that it would be a curious answer indeed. But it *is* quite odd that the very first words you spoke to the boy were: "I don't have time for an adventure right now."

It was an unusual greeting for a stranger, but then again, there was nothing usual about him.

He laughed. "Everyone has time for an adventure."

You replied, "Not me."

Still smiling, he asked, "Why not?"

But you couldn't think of a single answer. It seemed that you had totally forgotten about your birthday, and the crown of flowers in your hand, because you said, "I don't know."

He appeared to anticipate this answer. "Then we're going," he announced.

"Where?"

"Where?" he laughed. "Where, oh where, that *is* the question." He laughed again. He had an infectious laugh, the kind that spread without stopping until you started to laugh too, so hard that you were feeling quite mad yourself. "Where and when and who and what, whatsittoya, woohoo, we're going on an adventure!" is what he'd said, before bounding right back in the direction he'd come from.

You jammed the flower crown onto your head, so as to make sure not to lose it.

And then you followed him.

Why did you follow him? Perhaps you were entranced by his whimsical looks and being. Perhaps you were curious. You were certainly not afraid.

He was quite fast, faster than you. (This might have been because of how tall he was, although to you it looked almost as if he were flying.)

By the time you had caught up to him, you were panting, but he had barely broken a sweat. He had stopped in front of a tree, and right there, leaning on the tree, was a mirror.

You had been in the woods hundreds of times, and you'd never seen a mirror there before. *Maybe someone has forgotten it,* you thought. Though why anyone would bring a mirror to the middle of the woods, you did not know.

"Careful." The words tumbled out of your mouth before you could stop them. "Seven years of bad luck."

There it was again, that tinkling laugh. You smiled, though you couldn't figure out what was so funny.

"Come," he beckoned, and he took your hand into his gloved fingers. "Your adventure awaits."

"Where are we going?" you asked, or tried to ask, but the words stuck on your tongue as the boy put his right foot straight into the mirror.

And then you were pulled right through the mirror, and the world you found on the other side was the same, except not quite. For one thing, everything was a lot bigger. (Or were you a lot smaller?)

From where you were standing, the grasses were at least as tall as you were. Butterflies as big as elephants passed by. Flowers danced in the wind, singing the song that you had been humming as you crafted your crown not five minutes before. A rocking-horse fly, no, several, flew right over your head. Now, how did you know what those were?

A feeling of safety washed over you. At the time, you asked why. But I think, deep in your heart, you knew.

This was your home.

"Impossible," you whispered softly, letting the wind carry the word through the forest.

"Not quite," the boy next to you mused. "Your mother believed she could do six impossible things before breakfast."

"My mother?"

Your mother was once the light of your life. She used to be a sea captain, one of the only women in the field. You'd heard stories about her, about how she fought through prejudice and stereotypes, gave up eternal wealth, and followed her passions, thereby earning your family more than they ever dreamed.

Suddenly, you remembered that your mother used to tell you stories before bed. Stories filled with talking caterpillars and dancing flowers and *rocking-horse flies*.

She'd been a dynamo, taking you on spontaneous trips by day and partying by night. Recently, though, she'd become more distant. She'd stopped talking as much, keeping to herself. Sometimes you'd have to call her name several times until she heard.

The boy coughed. "Yes, your mother. You're Alyssa Liddell, daughter of Alice Liddell, correct? I could possibly be mistaken, but, see, that rarely happens."

"Pardon me, but I never did catch your name."

He laughed. "That's because I never threw it."

"Throw it now."

He clapped his hands. "What's in a name? That which we call a rose by any other name—"

"—would smell as sweet. You know Shakespeare?"

"Shake spears? Nonsense. Stuff and nonsense and nonsense and stuff." He shook his head. "My name is Carter Hightop, next in line to be the Mad Hatter!" He said the last two words with a flourish, clearly proud of the title.

"The Hatter?" you repeated, and that name sounded vaguely familiar to you.

"We make hats," he said accusingly. "You *do* know what a hat is, don't you?"

"Of course I do!"

"Well, tell me. What makes a good hat? Or is it the hat that makes something good? I really don't know."

This time, it was you who laughed. "Who are you? Why did you take me here?"

"I already told you who I am. I'm Carter Hightop, soon to be the new Mad Hatter. Any hat you want, I can make. You have a perfect hat head. A top hat would go nicely on that head. Or perhaps a beret. Would you like a mock turtle hat? Mock turtles would look nice on you."

You almost interrupted then, but he continued before you could. "And as for why you're here, well, haven't you heard? Wonderland is in danger." He shook his head sadly. "Yes, the gravest, most dangerous of dangers. The time has come again when we must call for a hero." He looked up at you, and you saw that his eyes had darkened considerably. "Be our hero, Alyssa Liddell. Please?"

It was both a lot of information and no information at all. You didn't know what you would be agreeing to, only that someone needed help, and you were determined to give it. "Of course," you said. "Of course I'll help you. Tell me what I need to do."

His face brightened. "Quickly, then! We haven't a moment to lose!" And then he started to run, just as you had seen him do before.

You followed him, not wanting to get lost in this strange world. As you ran, you felt sure that the fire pulsing through your veins was the same fire that pulsed in your mother's, so many years ago when she came here for the very first time.

Carter stopped at yet another tree.

"What's this? Another magic door?" you asked, joking only a little.

"Who decides whether the doors are magic?" He grabbed a low-hanging branch and pulled it down like a sort of lever. A doorway cut itself into the tree, and slowly the mouth of it opened, like a castle gate.

Funny that it wasn't the strangest thing you had seen all day.

"After you," he said.

The doorway opened to a wide, curvy path. You couldn't tell where it ended, only that it continued quite a long way. "Where does this lead?"

"If I told you, you wouldn't want to go," he said simply.

You knew you would not be able to weasel the answer from him, so you asked, "How long will it take to get there?"

"Five minutes, twenty-three seconds," he answered with complete certainty.

"That quick? I don't think—" you began, but were promptly interrupted as two large insects swooped down and landed directly in front of you.

"Surely, you must know what these are," Carter said idly, as he hoisted himself onto the first. "They're—"

"Bread-and-butterflies," you gasped. The creatures had great majestic wings that looked just like the food they were named for. "Is this . . . safe?"

Carter laughed. "What a silly question. Of course it's not safe."

This was how you found yourself—for the very first time in your life, though certainly not the last—flying.

As you flew, you watched the land pass below you. This was a very strange place, that much you could tell. Sparsely covered in trees, with a slew of creatures you had never seen before. You knew the names of these creatures, though, as you watched them from above. Jubjub birds, with their majestic feathers and sharp features. A crowd of mock turtles, slumming about. Several mome raths that wandered around aimlessly.

"What exactly is this place?" you asked Carter, looking over at him.

"Wonderland," Carter said curtly. "And no one knows *exactly* what it is."

Not quite understanding, you nodded anyway.

Around five minutes later, Carter pointed up and said, "See that?"

The sky directly above you was a dark, ominous gray, spotted with storm clouds. It was a stark contrast to the brilliant blue that you'd been flying in. "What is it?"

"That's your danger."

"What is it, Carter?"

"It's the Jabberwock."

The images filled your head. An ugly, greenish-gray dragon with huge feet and particularly large front teeth. Claws as long as you were tall and sharper than any blade. The Jabberwocky, you remembered, was a menace of the Red Queen.

"Hold on," you said. "Didn't my mother slay the Jabberwocky?"

Carter paused. "Well, I *do* believe she did." He snapped his fingers and then pointed vaguely at the clouds in the distance, which were getting closer by the second. "That's its child. The Jabberwock."

"*Child?*"

He turned, winked, and said, "This'll be fun. Trust me."

When you touched down, you noticed the change in atmosphere right away: the grass was predominantly dead, for one thing. There didn't seem to be any other living things. Though trees obscured your view, they were either dead or close to it. The scent of burnt wood lingered in the air, and in the distance you could see clouds of smoke.

"Did the Jabberwock do this?" you asked, knowing very well that it did.

In response, Carter held up a sword. It was long and sharp and so shiny that you could see your reflection. On the hilt was an inscription: *Ex eodem ferro, ut Vorpal.*

You stared at it, uncomprehending. "Where . . . Where did you get that?"

"From my hat," he explained, as though *no physical law* applied to this world.

"Is that the Vorpal Sword?"

Carter looked at it curiously, as if he'd just realized he was holding it. "No," he admitted, "but it *is* made of the same material. Should work similarly."

"Should?!"

"Don't worry about it," Carter reassured. "You'll be able to slay the Jabberwock. I know you will."

You blinked. "And how do you know?"

"Because you're Alyssa Liddell," he answered. "And you can do anything."

You took a deep breath. Two deep breaths. Then, several seconds to question your sanity, and several more to admire your courage. "Let's go, then."

Carter offered the blade to you. Hesitating, you took it. It felt heavy in your hands, alive. You realized that you were holding a weapon, and your insides clenched at the thought of wielding it.

Carter reached for your hand, and together you trekked past the thickets of the dead forest to slay the Jabberwock.

As you walked, you couldn't help but notice how dull the scenery was. In the distance, you could hear the roars of the monster. They hurt your ears, but you resisted covering them because Carter was holding your hand so tightly. You looked over at him and saw he was afraid—just as afraid as you were.

Suddenly Carter cried, "Alyssa, stop!"

You did.

And there it was.

Bigger than you had imagined.

At least twenty feet tall, with a wingspan of about fifty feet, possibly longer. It looked a lot deadlier than you had imagined: it's teeth just slightly bigger and its claws slightly sharper.

"Do I have to kill that?" you whispered.

Carter shrugged. "Unless you can find another way." His voice shook.

You couldn't.

And so you looked around. How would you be able to get the sword into the Jabberwock?

Think, Alyssa.

Then it came to you. You grasped the idea and held onto it with your life. The trees. Several of them were tall enough to reach the dragon.

"Carter," you said, trying to stay confident, "boost me up there." You pointed to a nearby tree. The lowest branch was about seven feet off the ground.

He glanced at you, startled. "The trees are dead, Alyssa. They'll snap."

"Do it, Carter."

He laced his fingers together, and you cradled your boot into his hands. He hoisted you up, and you scrambled onto the first branch. It shook slightly but held. You let out a breath that you didn't realize you had been holding.

"Good luck, Alyssa," Carter called from below.

"Thanks," you whispered.

You pulled yourself up to the next branch. Down below, Carter inhaled sharply. Slowly, you made your way up the tree, testing each branch before you fixed your weight on it.

And then disaster struck—the branch that you were balancing on snapped.

You tumbled down and barely managed to grab another branch that held your weight. But the Jabberwock had heard you. It turned around and slowly advanced toward you.

Panicking, you pulled yourself up as many branches as you could. The Jabberwock had already spotted you, though, and was lumbering heavily toward you. You stared at it, hoping your legs wouldn't fail you now.

You suddenly realized that this could be a very stupid idea.

But it beat the alternative, which was to do nothing.

When the Jabberwock got close enough, you leapt off of the tree and onto its back. You managed to grab hold of several scales before it could shake you off.

Down below, Carter yelped in surprise.

Still shaking from the maneuver, you raised the sword with both hands. It felt heavy and deadly. With all your strength, you plunged the blade in, all the way to the hilt.

The Jabberwock roared in pain. You gasped, wondering if you'd actually killed it.

Slick, black blood seeped out of the wound and onto your hands. It felt like tar, warm and wet and sticky. You waited for the Jabberwock to fall to the floor, defeated, so that you could leave the bastard and run home.

But of course, it couldn't be this easy.

Another roar, and then the Jabberwock twisted savagely, flinging you to the ground with a thud. Carter ran over to you. You sat up slowly and moaned.

He inspected your arm. A shallow gash ran down it, leaking blood. He removed his top hat and ripped the ribbon off, using it to fashion a tourniquet around your arm. "I'm sorry," he muttered. "I shouldn't have put all this pressure on you. We should go, Alyssa. Leave the Jabberwock."

You shook your head, gasping for breath. "I'm not leaving."

"You're hurt, Alyssa. Think straight. The sword didn't work. We can't kill it." He tugged on your uninjured arm.

"There's always another way, Carter. You just have to be mad enough to find it."

The Jabberwock was slowly advancing toward the two of you. Carter stared at you, hard. "Fine." He closed his eyes. "What do you need me to do, Alyssa?"

The sword was still buried in the Jabberwock's back, but that didn't seem to be slowing it down at all. You stood up and yelled, "Jabberwock!"

Its eyes narrowed, and it huffed angrily. By now it was only about ten feet away. You carefully took a step toward it, hands raised. It snorted at you, and you stopped walking.

"What do you want?" you asked it, softly.

It flapped its wings, creating huge gusts of wind.

"I know," you said, trying to keep your voice steady. "I know what it's like. To not belong." You took a step closer. "I know that sometimes it feels like you've been dropped into a whole new world and nothing will ever be the same. I know how it feels to be scared, because sometimes the world can be scary. And there will be times when you don't know what to do.

"But," and with this you took several steps, until you were only a foot away from the Jabberwock, "you're not alone. The person—or creature!—next to you, they're just as scared as you are." You kneeled in front of the Jabberwock, unsure if this would be the last thing you'd ever do. "But you don't solve that by pushing them away.

"We want to help you," you coaxed, and closed your eyes. "Please, let us help."

Several seconds passed, and then Carter inhaled. You heard the *whoosh* of wings, then silence.

And you opened your eyes. In the sky, you spotted the glint of its pale green scales, gleaming in the sunlight, which was slowly beginning to restore itself. Around you, flowers began to bloom. Trees grew leaves right before your eyes. The grass magicked itself to a bright, healthy green. The sky lightened until you could no longer tell that the Jabberwock had ever come at all.

"You did it," Carter gasped. You stood, brushing the dirt from your dress. "You slayed the Jabberwock."

You nodded slowly.

"Thank you," he said, coming over to where you were standing. "For doing this. You saved Wonderland."

"Wonderland would've saved itself," you mumbled, "one way or another."

Carter grinned, but then his smile faltered. "I, uh, don't suppose you'd like to stay here, would you?" He looked down at his feet. "In Wonderland?"

You looked at him, and the realization dawned on you. "I have to go back." You didn't want the words to be true, but they were.

He shrugged helplessly. "Well, you don't *have* to—"

You stared up at the sky, trying to remember every detail, in case you never returned. "This isn't my world."

"But it could be. Please, stay here. With me."

"I don't belong here, Carter. You understand, don't you?" *Please, understand.*

He shook his head. "I do, but I don't want to. Alyssa—"

"Carter, I've never met someone like you. And I'm willing to bet that I never will again. But there are so many things I'm not ready to say goodbye to. I can't leave my mother. I've got to go back."

He glanced at the sky and whistled loudly. The two bread-and-butterflies swooped down and landed in front of you. Carter helped you up and said, "You do belong here. Someday, you'll realize that. And when that day comes, I'll be waiting."

There wasn't a single doubt in your mind.

When you returned to the mirror, which didn't seem quite so unusual as before, Carter dismounted first. "Stay," he pleaded, one last time. "Stay."

"I can't."

"Visit soon?" he asked.

You smiled. "I'd be stupid not to."

"Happy Birthday, Alyssa," he muttered.

It was then that you remembered the flower crown on your head. You reached up, and by some miracle, it was still there. A little windblown, a little burnt, but there nonetheless.

"Make a hat for me," you said, pushing the handmade crown into his hands. "Have it ready when I come back."

He took the crown. "I won't disappoint you."

Then he said, "I have something for you, too. Close your eyes."

You did, and his lips pressed against yours, soft and lingering.

And then he pulled away.

You opened your eyes and found yourself sitting on the grass again, surrounded by wildflowers. The flower crown was gone.

"Alyssa. Alyssa!" You sat dumbly as your mother ran into view. When she reached you, she demanded, "Your arm. What did you do, Alyssa? I've told you time and time again not to play so roughly. We need to get this cleaned up. And you, young lady, need to—"

"Mum," you mumbled, "I slayed the Jabberwock."

She stopped. She stared at you as if she didn't understand. Finally, she whispered, "You slayed the Jabberwocky?"

You cocked your head. "The Jabberwock, actually. And, not technically. I didn't *kill* it, or anything. I just . . . talked to it. And then it flew away and left Wonderland in peace. I don't think it'll be coming back."

She bent down, slowly, and then wrapped her arms around you. "My sweet girl," she whispered. "Sometimes you surprise me." She pulled back. "Did you really?"

You nodded.

"I always wanted to be the one to take you to Wonderland," she said. Then, to herself, "I can't believe you slayed the Jabberwock."

You beamed.

She closed her eyes and shook her head, flustered, with the ghost of a smile dancing on her lips. "Come," she said. She stood up and pointed to your arm. "I'll patch that up. And then you'll *have* to tell me all about it. Perhaps over some tea?"

You giggled. "I'd like that very much."

The spark that was lost for so long had returned; you could see it in her eyes. And so you stood up and grabbed her hand, and together you walked back to the house, chatting about random nothings the whole way.

One day, you met a boy who was mad.

Perhaps you'll meet him again.

....

Jada Leung, thirteen, lives in a world where children go to a magic school to become wizards, circuses appear without warning, cancer-ridden teens fall in love, and somewhere in Long Island Sound there is a camp for demigods. There are demon-hunters, an arena where people fight to the death, little girls in red capes, and a courageous mouse named Despereaux. If you would like to learn more about this world, crack open a book. If you try to argue with Jada about reality, she will blatantly ignore you until you admit that she is right.

....

A MOMENT IN TIME

Emilina stood silently, her lips pursed in morbid anticipation. No matter how many times she watched the simulation, it always astounded her. The five-ton mass falling to the earth as a reckoning. A choice that changed the world forever.

The initial flash from the bomb blinded her as it detonated above the city of Nagasaki, the shockwave pushing outward at a colossal speed. She imagined the wave of heat hitting her as the images of people nearby flashed out of existence in a heartbeat.

Buildings fell around her as the mushroom cloud continued to grow above the devastated city. The roiling mass of fire and smoke spread radiation across the city, poisoning the area and causing countless deaths.

As fires raged throughout the wooden city, small specks of material floated down. Were they the ash of burning buildings or the incinerated remains of their inhabitants?

She wrapped her arms around herself and shivered. The two bombs had meted out so much death and destruction. So many innocent lives had ended in an instant.

"How you doing in there, Em?" a voice crackled over the intercom.

She stopped hugging herself and looked down at her shaking hands.

"Fine," she replied, taking a deep, calming breath.

"How many times have you accessed that archive? You know, if you really needed a hug you could have just asked."

She let out a small snort. "Star's light, Jared, can you be any more insensitive?" She couldn't keep a slight smirk off her face, though. "I'll meet you in the mess hall in a few minutes for one last cup of coffee. I'm just going to finish up here," she told him, looking up at one of the cameras.

With practiced efficiency, Emilina started the shutdown sequence for the simulation, images of the destruction still playing in her mind. Dropping the bombs had been followed by centuries of armament stockpiling, enough to destroy the world a hundred times over. What had been the point?

Of course, the development of ballistic missiles had started the chain reaction that led the human race to the stars, colonizing their own system and exploring others. Without it, her crew wouldn't even be here, in one of the more remote parts of the Milky Way. Before heading out, she added a recording to her personal log.

"Every time I look at the simulations of the bombs dropping or the kinetic weapon attacks on London, I wonder if there could have been another way. Another way to lead us to where we are now. How would the world have been different without those pivotal moments in our history?

"I've watched these moments over and over these past

months, wondering the same thing. The space race that followed, the Challenger mission failure, the separatists who pushed us into our first interstellar war. Are we going to end up like that after today? Will our actions have the same sort of impact as they did? Did they even know what they were doing? Will someone be going through our logs, wondering why we never thought to stop our foolish venture?" Her shoulders dropped and her hand moved to turn off the recording, but she paused.

"I don't know . . . and that scares me. There's a reason we're doing this so far from colonized space. If we miscalculated something, we'll be gone before the consequences set in for humanity as a whole." She trailed off, staring into the camera for a moment before finally turning it off.

She spotted Jared as she entered the mess, sipping coffee from the mug that he'd smuggled onboard. It was chipped in two places, and the pictures of his two greyhounds back home were fading, but he refused to replace it with any of the standard-issue mugs.

Walking straight to the dispenser, she poured her own cup of coffee and joined him on the drab, aluminum benches. She took a sip of coffee, and her face contorted in disappointment. It tasted too bitter; coffee here always did. Something about coffee beans traveling in space messed with the flavor. It was one of those mysteries of the universe that no one understood.

Jared pushed his coffee across the table. "Here, four sugars, just enough to get it to taste like actual coffee. I don't think I'll be able to sit here and watch you make that face every time you take a sip."

Smiling, she placed both hands around the mug and drank. At least it was closer to how coffee should taste. She set it down and ran her finger over the small chips along the lip of the mug.

"Anything you want to go over before the launch sequence?" Jared asked, breaking the silence.

Emilina didn't take her eyes off the coffee. "Is this what we're supposed to be doing?"

He gave her a puzzled look. "Exploring the farthest reaches of the universe? That's what we signed up for, Em. I wouldn't be this far out in space otherwise."

"No, I get that. But this is . . . this is on another scale entirely. What we're doing isn't like anything we've done before. It's not even in the same category."

He laid a hand over hers. "It's okay to be worried, Em. We all are. The only difference is that the rest of us aren't the ones piloting the ship out there."

"That doesn't make me feel better."

He laughed softly. "It was supposed to. A bit of dark humor and all that." He winced under the glare she was giving him. "Okay, not appropriate. But seriously, Em, you're the one piloting this mission because we believe in you. Out of everyone they could have chosen, they picked you. Take comfort in that."

"Ten minutes," someone said over the intercom.

"Thanks . . . I suppose that's something."

"I'll meet you in the launch bay," Jared said. He took her original cup of coffee, undrunk, back to the recycler before he left the mess.

Glancing down at his chipped mug, Emilina took one last sip. She looked around the empty mess, taking in the room, remembering the moments they had all shared there. Then she rinsed out his mug and left for her quarters.

Her room was sparsely furnished, like the rest of the crew quarters on the station, consisting of little more than an aluminum bed frame with a three-inch thick bedroll. It was too expensive to ship luxuries out this far.

She pulled her ambiguously gray flight suit out of the closet and changed into it. Then she pressed a series of buttons on the screen embedded in her wall.

"Final log of Captain Emilina Chelsea Hardwick. No matter how this mission turns out, our team will be able to extract valuable data. If I fail, it will probably happen too quickly for me to know. If I succeed . . ." she trailed off, smiling to herself in disbelief.

"When they told me I would be exploring the galaxy, I thought I'd be working on high-powered telescopes and space-flight that took generations. I never guessed I'd be creating an artificial wormhole. But here I am, attempting a solo jump of five hundred light-years in less than a minute, with only a vague idea of what's waiting on the other side."

She picked up her helmet, looked straight at the camera, and took a deep breath.

"Forgive me if something goes wrong."

Everyone was finishing up the final preparations as she entered the launch bay. She could see them double- and triple-checking every system, even though they did that just a few hours ago. To be honest, she appreciated it. It made her just a bit less nervous about what she was going to do in a few moments.

She stopped and stared at the ship. Forty meters long and thirty-five across, made of reinforced titanium. Despite its size, the interior was sparse. They had focused more on the technology and on keeping her alive rather than her comfort. Still, she marveled at the design, and it warmed her to see her name painted on the hull.

The rest of the crew pulled everything back from the ship and lined up next to it as she approached. They saluted her. She returned it and dismissed them. They filed out, heading past the three-meter-thick launch doors and up to the control room while she climbed into the cockpit.

Sitting down in the captain's chair, she checked to make sure the crew had cleared the bay before she started the ignition sequence.

"All clear on our end, Captain," Jared relayed.

The roar of the engines filled the launch bay as azure flames shot out of the three exhausts. She could barely hear the countdown over the din. The launch doors parted before her, their slate gray giving way to the blackness of space.

Accelerating forward, she cleared the station in seconds and looked back as the doors closed behind her, hesitating for a moment. The crew had done too much to turn back now.

"Control, can you read me?"

"We hear you, Captain. Everything is checking out on our end. We're going to start up the emitters. Stand by."

She waited, monitoring the luminous energy pulses coming from the station. They converged on the agreed-upon confluence point and began to roil and expand. Bolts of energy fired randomly from the swirling mass, one going past her bow in a flash before dissipating.

She positioned her ship so she had a clear angle to the center of the energy cloud. Her emitter burst to life, spewing a brilliant beam of energy that collided with the existing cloud. Space tore apart as the two forces met, the beam melting away the cloud layer.

She watched in amazement as a wormhole formed. It expanded in seconds, tearing at the boundaries of space, forming a chaotic maelstrom.

"Launching the stabilizer probe."

It flew from the bow of her ship and, upon reaching the wormhole, exploded in a cascade of energy. The burgeoning wormhole widened just enough to fit her ship.

Flexing her fingers, she waited a few moments to make sure the wormhole wouldn't collapse upon itself.

"Beginning flight path, Control."

Emilina looked up as she approached the terminus, a whole other part of the galaxy just meters away. The edges crackled with lightning, held open by the energy beams from the station.

The nose of the ship disappeared as it passed through the terminus, followed by the rest of the ship seconds later.

She let out a sigh of relief as the wormhole disappeared from her view and was replaced by a new section of the galaxy. All around her, hundreds of new stars twinkled in the black expanse, their light reaching her eyes five hundred years before they would ever reach Sol.

She rotated her ship counter-clockwise, letting the sensors take in as much data as they could. The ship's light filters came down as she rotated toward the nearby red dwarf. She could still hardly see, even with the filters' help.

A proximity alarm went off. Debris was approaching from her port side. Accelerating outwards away from the terminus, she rotated toward the expanding debris field. Asteroid belt mining had played a large part in building the station they launched this mission from. The potential resources here were too good to be ignored. It could easily justify reopening the wormhole for mining expeditions.

"Control, we have an asteroid field here. Strange . . ." she trailed off as she watched the debris field accelerate outward much faster than any on record.

"Emilina, can you repeat? Your last got cut off," Control responded.

"Sections of the asteroid field are moving too fast to be in a stable orbit. I'm going to investigate the cause while we get the rest of the sensor readings." Her face paled as she realized what was causing the unusual acceleration. The wormhole they had opened was pulling asteroids out of their orbit.

She quickly calculated the rough trajectory of the debris field if it kept accelerating at its current rate. It would take weeks, but it was now on course to collide with a large planetoid orbiting the red dwarf.

"No, no, no." Her voice was panicked as she realigned herself with the wormhole. "Control, I'm coming back through now. Close the wormhole as soon as I'm through." She didn't wait for them to confirm as she accelerated back through the terminus.

"Captain, what's going on? We're not reading anything anomalous with the wormhole. There's no need to close it so soon."

"Star's light! Just close it already! That's an order!" She tried to calm herself as she saw the station's emitters shut off.

Glancing back, she was relieved to see the wormhole closing and the space it had occupied returning to normal.

"Okay, it's closed. Will you tell us what's going on now?"

Emilina took deep breaths, trying to slow her heart rate as she checked the sensor readings they'd gathered on the planetoid. No obvious signs of terrestrial life, thank the stars, but the readings weren't even close to complete.

"The asteroid field in that sector, we were pulling some of the asteroids out of their stable orbit with the wormhole's gravity field. At least a few dozen are now on a course that will intersect with the large planetoid orbiting the star, maybe more."

"Good call, Captain. We can recalculate an emergence point for the next opening that won't be as close with the readings you already gathered. Won't be an issue next time."

"Control . . ." Emilia said, her voice exasperated. "You don't get it. We just accidently sent dozens of kinetic missiles on a collision course with that planetoid. What if there's microscopic life on that planet? We could be destroying it before it even had a chance. You saw what happened to London." Her voice faltered, images of the ruins of London flashing through her mind.

This moment was supposed to be joyous. They had opened a wormhole and traveled five hundred light-years across the galaxy and back. There was supposed to be champagne and jubilation at what they had accomplished, not dread.

She steeled herself and plotted a course back to the station. "Okay, we have a few weeks before those asteroids hit," she said, her voice hard with determination. "We have until then to fix our mistake or figure out if there's any signs of microscopic life on that planetoid. I will not have future generations looking at us like we're monsters."

She closed the comm channel and fired her maneuvering thrusters so she lined up with the station's bay doors. "We will not fail," she told herself. "I will not fail."

....

Jeff Yabumoto graduated with a degree in film and is currently back in school at USC for a Master of Business Administration. In what little free time he has, he's at esports events interviewing the pros about the ins and outs of the esports scene. He's been published in multiple outlets, including Akshon Esports, Inven Global, and The Players' Lobby. While he loves the reporting side of esports, he one day hopes to be running an esports organization. If you want to learn about esports, he's your guy. Just hit him up on Twitter @phsidefender.

....

I N T E R L O P E R

N ow, I'm only putting these on for your safety." Melanie smiles, trying to be comforting. The feathery hairs on my arm stand on end as her fingers brush my wrist. My hand flexes upwards like a startled spider as she cinches the black strap and ties the slack around my bed post.

"I'm not really into the dominatrix thing, but whatever fidgets your spinner," I mutter. Melanie's face darkens.

"Is this Lily I'm speaking to, or . . . the Other," Melanie asks, her voice dropping an octave, maybe to inspire fear. But her natural voice is way too perky to scare anything larger than a ferret.

"Oh, that's definitely Lily," my mom replies, her face expressionless. When it comes to deadpan, no one tops my mom. Not even me. And I'm a notorious killer of pans.

Melanie nods, her face reddening, embarrassed that she got her client confused with an entity of pure evil. She fumbles through her oversized tote bag and pulls out a matching fabric strap to tie my left hand to the bed. She looks at me, offering apologies with her empathetic grimace. I roll my eyes and raise my free arm.

Melanie cinches the strap, and my mother gasps a little. As much pleasure as my mom gets from annoying me (which she denies, unconvincingly), I'm pretty sure she tries to protect me from any real pain. "These straps are made of fleece so they don't chafe. There's a little Velcro at the ends to make sure they don't come loose, but other than that they're super soft. I made them myself." A little pride peeks up at the corners of her mouth, but my withering glare instantly makes that disappear from her face.

A little gust of air escapes Melanie's nostrils. She's girding herself, preparing for what comes next, whatever that might be. Melanie told us not to expect special effects like in the movies. "No supernatural spectacle," she promised.

"What *should* we expect?" my dad had asked when we first met with Melanie. My mom never needs to ask anyone anything because Dad always does. Lots of questions. He wants to know the likelihood of every scenario, no matter how remote. He doesn't like surprises. On second thought, that's not entirely accurate. He forbids my mom to tell him what she plans to buy him for his birthday. But I suppose that's a *good* surprise. He doesn't want plot twists in real life. And he thinks he can avoid them if he asks all the right questions.

"Well, in my other two rituals ..." Melanie's wince was unmissable. Cat out of bag: I am only her third. "Sometimes there are ... raised voices. The patient can get frustrated. Emotional. It can be difficult on the loved ones. You don't have to be present."

"We'll be present," my mom said firmly. I didn't know whether my mom wanted to stay because she didn't trust Melanie or because she wanted to be here for me. Probably both.

My parents have been incredibly supportive this last month, more than I deserved. Not that they don't support me in general. But the things I've been doing . . .

I get more leeway from my parents than most teens do. I admit that most conversations with my mom and dad start and end with copious eye rolls on my part. But while I talk a good smart-ass game, I've never been much of a rebel. I've always done my homework, gone to bed embarrassingly early, and the only "C" I ever got was in physical education (and that was only because they don't give "F"s in P.E.)

So when I began failing my tests, my parents took notice. When I stopped responding to my friends' texts, started eating every meal alone, and never responded to any query with more than a grunt, Mom and Dad asked if I wanted to see a therapist. When the therapist refused to see me anymore, explaining that my pathology was beyond his skill set, my parents started looking into psychiatrists. When I couldn't remember anything that I had said in my therapy sessions, they added neurologists to their search. And after I grabbed the steering wheel from my dad as he drove me home from school, trying to veer the car straight onto a sidewalk full of oblivious pre-teens, I conducted my own Google search and found Melanie. Unlike the psychiatrists and neurologists, Melanie is not on the contact list of many medical professionals, but I think by that point Mom and Dad were too worn down to object.

Melanie kneels by my bed. She absent-mindedly pushes her long French braid off of her shoulder. She's firmly in therapist-mode now, her voice slow and calm, dripping with compassion. "Lily, this should be quick and painless. But I'm going to need your help. Your strength. It's you who has the power here, not me. I'm just want to help you channel it." I nod wearily. Do I believe her? Maybe. But the last week hasn't given me a lot of confidence in anything.

"Can we open the window?" Melanie asks my mom.

In answer, my dad moves to the window, flips back the latch, and slides it upwards. It sticks where it always does, about a third of the way up. The windows are old; the paint peels from the wood. We haven't done any major upgrades to the house since I was born. My parents don't talk about money in front of me, but I know we're not rich. Middle-class but barely hanging on, I think. Summer trips to Lake Michigan or rafting in Ohiopyle. We went to Niagara Falls one year. What a pit. But the retro pennant from the Falls still hangs right next to the window that my dad jiggles up and down as he tries to free it. A chilly November breeze rushes in like a cat after a night locked out of the house. I shiver involuntarily; the sleeves of my T-shirt are bunched up at my armpits with my arms tied at this strange, Christ-like angle.

At Melanie's request, Dad turns off all the lights. I'm used to it being dark in here. I usually have just my one little desk lamp on when I'm studying or listening to Spotify or texting my friends. But there's something . . . darker about the light seeping into my room today. It's a cold, blue, November color. Shadows fall across my Dia de los Muertos skeleton masks. The shift in the light makes it look like they're staring down at me, laughing through their lipless teeth. Particles of dust chase each other through the blade of winter glare, making my room look dirty, cramped. Folds in my gray bedsheets breathe in the draft. My mom reaches toward the sheets, but her hand stops and she looks to Melanie.

"She looks cold. Are you cold, Lils?" I nod. "Can I touch her?" she asks Melanie.

"Quickly, please," Melanie says.

My mom untangles the sheets from around my ankles and pulls them up to my chin, lamely tucking me in, looking embarrassed that she can't do more. Are my mom's hands shaking? I've *never* seen my mom's hands shake. My mom is a rock. A rock with a painfully withering glare and an unmatched talent for deeply wounding insults. But she's scared, and that makes *me* scared. She can see the fear on my face. Her tight lips curl into a totally unconvincing smile that doesn't reach her eyes.

Melanie reaches into her bag again and pulls out two large candles in glass jars. Instead of saints, angels, or the Virgin Mary, one label displays a photo of a pristine tropical beach with a single sunbather and the words "Every great dream begins with a great dreamer" in a swirly font. The other candle is covered with cavorting puppies and kittens. She places one on my nightstand, nudging aside a pile of my journals, and puts the other on the floor. I'm reluctantly starting to wonder if this woman knows what she's doing.

Next, she procures a glass bowl and a cluster of dried leaves wrapped in twine. Melanie places the bowl on the window sill and lays the leaves in it. She reaches into the pocket of her long, lacy shawl sweater and pulls out a box of matches. Then she looks directly at me and strikes the match. Her face is lit from below, orange and red, little triangles of shadow above her eyebrows, like tiny horns.

"Lily Emma Resnick, I set fire to remains in order to purge death. The perfume of rot draws out the unclean energy. The smoke carries decay from your being, out of your body, out of your life." Melanie's eyes are half-closed, her voice droning as she recites. She places the glowing match head against the tip of a dry leaf. A bit of smoke, a tiny flash of fire, and the leaf sizzles. Melanie puts her hand on my forearm. "You're going to free yourself of this, Lily. I'm just here to guide you. It's all about you, your strength. Your power."

"Not God's?" my mother asks. She's not particularly religious, but she's seen *The Exorcist* and enough reality TV to know these types of rituals often are.

"This thing preys on *your* fears. On *your* beliefs. A Jewish ritual will call for Solomon's help. For Abraham and David and Yahweh. A Catholic ritual is all about Jesus. Muslims have their version. I know you're Christian and your husband is Jewish, but what's important is Lily's belief." Melanie turns back to me. "I'll call on God . . . if you have faith in God."

"But if the . . . thing believes—"

Melanie cuts me off. "What matters is what *you* believe. You beat your enemy with your strength, not his. Understand?"

I nod, wondering if Melanie can see my lack of confidence. Wondering if *it* can. "Have you . . . changed your mind—about God—since we talked about this?" she asks me. I haven't changed my mind. But I am considering adding a religious insurance policy. But it would know. It would know I'm lying. I shake my head.

Melanie turns to my parents, keeping her hand on my arm. "If you don't think you can handle this, you should leave now. It's not going to be easy to watch. No one will judge you."

My parents don't budge. A sudden rush of affection floods me. Most kids take their parents' love for granted. "Most kids" includes me. The grownups feed and water you. They cart you around to school and sleepovers and doctor appointments. They kiss you and wish you sweet dreams. And maybe you thank them, because that's what they taught you to do. But you don't really *consider* their love. You just accept that this is what parents do. And then, once every couple of years or so, something happens that rocks your world. A broken wrist lands you in the hospital. A distracted driver flies through the red light and launches you into a three-car pileup. A beloved grandparent, or a pet, or—God forbid—a friend dies. And then at your lowest moment, when your head is drowning in why-me's, an arm wraps around you and squeezes. You look up into a face that feels your pain as much as you do, maybe even more. And your insides let go. Waves of hurt flow out because you know someone is there to catch them and put them away.

Melanie continues, "But if you stay, I need you with me one hundred percent. Don't do anything unless I tell you to. Don't talk to Lily. Don't touch her. And whatever you do, don't talk to *it*. Don't engage it. Don't give it any fuel." My father's hand finds my mother's. His fingers squeeze hers. I haven't held my dad's hand since I was eleven. I wish I could hold it now.

I look up and focus on the collage of magazine pages that covers half of my ceiling. Pages from *Rolling Stone, Revolver, Mix*. Major Lazer stares down. Fall Out Boy broods at me. Solange side-eyes me. Spirits of yesteryear, when I spent a weekend on tiptoe on my bed, going through roll after roll of Scotch tape. They used to be my partners, my cheerleaders. Until I lost all my cheer. Now they're just paper.

Melanie turns back to the glass bowl. A glowing orange line creeps along a leaf, leaving ash in its wake. Smoke curls up in ribbons. She gingerly carries the bowl over to me and holds it above my chest with one hand, fanning the smoke into my face with the other. "Breathe deep, Lily." The smoke is bitter and sweet, earthy and sugary. The inside of my nose tickles, the back of my throat feels dry as the smoke pokes around, explores. Melanie waves more smoke into my face. I shut my eyes against the stinging. When I reopen them, the room spins a little before settling back to its original orientation. Melanie puts the bowl back by the window.

"Are you ready?" Melanie asks me. I nod, swallowing.

Melanie looks around the room and raises her chin. Her back straightens, and she clears her throat. "In this room are four souls: Lily Resnick, Julie Rhee, Sam Resnick, and Melanie Godenzi. These are the only four who matter. No one else is wanted, no one else is welcome. This is the only time I will address you, Interloper. You are insignificant. You are pointless. You are *powerless*."

The smoke rising from the leaves drifts toward the window, only to be blown back in by the chill breeze. The sheet covering my legs and torso flutters. The eyes on the magazine pages stare down at me. And then Melanie puts both hands on my shoulders and looks directly at me. "This is *your* body. This is *your* soul. You are in control. You have power. You have agency . . ."

My shoulders tighten, and my upper arms ache from the tension of the straps. My skin is pimpled and pale, bumps rising in the cold. I shift to ease the pain in my back, trying to put more of the weight on my right side, but that just makes my left shoulder flare in pain. My throat burns from the smoke. The dizziness is back.

"I don't feel so hot," I say. My mom and dad both move toward me, but Melanie stops them with a curt shake of her head.

My face is cold, but my scalp sweats against the pillow like a fever's coming on. Melanie's words float by my ears. "Take control." But I'm not sure I heard her right. "Clear your body." I look straight up at my ceiling. The corner of a photo of Drake in black leather comes loose in the draft, flaps against the surface. A few pages away, Jamie xx's face sucks in and out as air slips under it. *Thwick, thwick.* The sheet slips down my body, one side still caught on my shoulder. I shiver.

". . . is yours alone. Tell it to go!"

My body feels trapped. Pinpricks of pain sting my skin. Like something trying to . . . trying to *get out.*

"Can you untie me? I'm not going to do anything." Melanie glances at me and, just as quickly, looks away. "I just need to move. I'll be fine." My dad looks at me with sympathy. My mom grips his hand tighter. *Don't just stand there. Christ!*

I need to move. I kick my legs. Back and forth, riding an invisible bike. The sheets slide down to my knees. Goosebumps run across my stomach. "Can someone please close the window?" I ask. A cloud of smoke hangs thick at the ceiling like foam on a cappuccino. With each breath, tendrils of vapor from the burning leaves drift toward my mouth and nose. I pull at my left wrist, trying to get a little slack in my aching arm. The edge of the Velcro scratches my skin. Above me, another corner comes loose in the breeze, the tape stuttering. In the middle of the collage, a fist-sized bubble of air pushes out, trying to get free.

". . . no hold on you. You're in charge. You decide what . . ."

My hands are shaking. My fingernails have turned blue. Why am I so cold? I usually wear shorts in October, tanks in the middle of winter. My mom calls me her little furnace. But I'm freezing now. My teeth chatter. I look up at the ceiling, distracting myself by naming the individual members of each band. Alex Turner. Jimmy Cook. No, *Jamie*. So cold. *Damn it! Jamie Cook, do something. Play me a song.* Jamie answers by detaching from the wall, flickering with the breeze. Still taped to David Bowie, Jamie and the rest of the Arctic Monkeys push away from the wall. Three or four pages jut out, restrained by the rest of the collage around them. The bulge pops in and out at me, taunting. I start coughing. I can't stop.

"You don't want it, you don't need it." Melanie coughs. "It must listen to you."

I gag on the smoke. My dad whispers to Melanie. I can't hear him, but she shakes her head. He asks her again, more insistent. She ignores him. The layer of smoke is growing. Or is it dropping?

The pages on my ceiling are going blurry. More tape comes loose. Multiple pages detach, barely connected to one another. The center of the collage dips down a foot from the ceiling.

My legs sting from the chill. It can't be that cold in here, can it? The skin on my legs is unnaturally white, with veins drawing road maps down them. They don't look like my legs anymore. The skin is loose and sagging, the knees knobby. Something looks wrong. *Something is wrong.*

"Lily," my dad whispers.

My mom gasps and blurts out, "She looks . . . different. Her face . . . it's . . . that's not . . ."

She's terrified.

"What?!" I yell at my mom. "What's happening?" Smoke drifts everywhere. I can barely see the window behind her.

I hear a rip above me. Another chunk of pages has torn free from the ceiling. The bulge in the collage is as big as my bed. Drooping down over my face, a few feet away. An inverted volcano of magazine pages. A supersized tumor growing from my ceiling. Paper eyes stare at me. White teeth shine. The air pushes the tip of the tumor left and right.

No, *there's something solid under there,* not just air. Something trying to push through. To push through *to me.*

"This is your body, Lily! Tell the Other to leave! Tell it to go! Push it out! Demand that it goes!"

"Untie me! Something's in there! Let me up!" I scream at them. They say nothing. Do they see the pages? Do they see what's happening? Do they even hear me? I thrash my arms, pulling at the straps, whipping them back and forth. The Velcro scratches against my skin, rubbing it raw. I can feel the blood bubble up on my wrists and turn cold in the air. My mom sobs. Tears stream down my father's face. But they just stand there.

"Why won't you do something?" I yell at them as I cough. I lift my legs and slam them into the bed. Over and over. I'm dizzy with pain. "Listen to me! Let me go! Something. Is. Here."

The paper tumor reaches out to me. Inches from my face. Flapping back and forth. Trying desperately to touch me. I shrink my head into my pillow. Push back as hard as I can. I can't go any further.

The tape can't hold it any more. *Riiiiip.* Something pushes through. Razor-thin sharp edges slit my cheeks, my eyelids.

I'm covered in the paper. Something is in my mouth, on my tongue. I hear a scream. There's thumping above me. My parents are shouting. Something crashes. I can't breathe. Hands all over me. Something pressing out *from inside me*. Pressure on my skin, every inch.

I can't breathe.

It feels like every centimeter of my skin is exploding outward, like something rushing out of my body.

Dizzy. Colors fade into gray. Light disappears from the outside of my vision inward. Until everything is black.

"What did you do to her?!"

What did you do to me?!

L ils! Lils!"

"Lily, can you hear me, sweetie?"

"Lily, are you okay? This is Melanie. Can you hear me?"

"I'm calling an ambulance. Julie, keep trying to wake her up."

"Her eyes are opening!"

Suddenly, I can see. My parents are leaning over me. My hands have been untied. My mother sits on the bed, my dad at her side. Melanie stands a foot back, worried. The collage of magazine pages lies in a crumbled heap on the floor, still intact.

"Are you okay, Lils? How do you feel?" my dad asks. I open my mouth, but only a ragged rasp comes out.

"Give her a minute. She'll talk when she's ready," Melanie says. My mom turns and gives her a deadly glare, and Melanie literally steps backward. That's how powerful my mom's stares are.

I open my mouth to tell them I'm tired. I just want to sleep. But nothing comes out. Mom turns back to me, pushing strands of hair from my face. She strokes my forehead like she used to do to help me fall asleep when I was little.

Except I can't feel her hand. It's almost like I'm watching all of this from outside my body. Like I'm in the audience watching a life-size movie.

And then I realize: I can see my parents on the bed. Not just their faces and torsos. Their whole bodies. Their legs dangling off the bed. I can see Melanie's black Converses. I can see my blue rug and the dust bunnies collecting under my bed. *And I can see me.* My whole body. Not just my hands and legs, but my face, too.

I am outside of my body.

I tilt my head down and see what I expect to see: my chest and my arms, my legs crossed under me. I'm sitting in the corner of the room. But I *also* see me lying on the bed.

There are two of me.

I stand. My legs feel weak. My back is stiff from lying in one position for too long. The skin on my wrists is raw and tender. I look at my parents. What do I say? What will they say when they see . . . two Lilys?

"Mom, Dad . . ." I wait. My heart sinks. *They don't look at me.* "Can you hear me?" My heart beats faster. "Please say you can hear me." But they don't turn to me. They don't move from the body in the bed. *My* body in the bed.

I walk over to the bed and look down at . . . at *me*. Me, lying in bed. Eyes open. A shiver runs from my stomach to my chest. I don't understand what I'm seeing. It's like I'm looking into some kind of a funhouse mirror. The girl in the mirror doesn't flex her hand when I flex mine. She doesn't look into my eyes. And her eyes . . . There's something different about them. Something . . . empty.

"Mom, it's me, it's Lily!" I scream. But Mom doesn't look at me. "I'm here! I'm next to you!" I turn to my dad. "Dad. Daddy." I haven't called him "Daddy" since I was twelve. He looks down at the body in the bed. He doesn't look up at me. He doesn't hear me. I put my mouth right at his ear. "Dad! Daddy! Damn it! *Look at me!*"

"Lily, how are you feeling? You don't have to answer. Just nod if you're feeling better." My dad is looking at the thing in bed. And then it opens its mouth.

"Much better . . . Daddy," it says. *In my voice.* It doesn't sound exactly like me, but a recording never sounds right to the person who made it, does it? Is that what this is, a recording of me? A copy?

Upon hearing my voice, my dad's eyebrows knit, his lips purse. Trying not to cry in relief . . . and at the fact that his little girl just called him "Daddy."

Melanie moves closer to the bed, brushing by me as I stand there, and I feel the warmth of her arm. She obviously doesn't feel me. "Lily, do you feel any different?" The thing in the bed looks into space, thinking. Then she looks back at Melanie and smiles a little.

"I feel . . . alone," she says.

"We're here for you, sweetie," my dad promises. He kisses its forehead. I used to love it when he kissed my forehead, but he hasn't done that in years. My mother takes its hand in hers. But I can't feel her fingers wrap around mine. She blinks back a tear. My mother doesn't cry. She doesn't even get close to crying. And now she's trying to hold back the wave of love she has for me. But it's not for me. It's for that thing. That thing has stolen her love. That thing that has stolen my body—my life.

"You're never alone," my dad says.

"Not alone in a bad way," the girl on the bed says. "I feel like . . . it's gone."

"I think we can cancel the call to 911." Melanie smiles broadly.

I watch in horror. I'm *here*. I'm *standing right here*. My parents are smiling at this thing. Loving this thing. And I am right here.

"We thought we lost you there for a second," my dad says, voice trembling.

"That *isn't* me! That isn't Lily!" I scream. "Can't you see? Can't you tell? Don't you know me?"

Someone else is inside my body. And *I've* been exorcised.

And then she—it—looks *at me*.

"I'm back. And I'm staying," it says. Then it smiles. At me. Right at me.

....

Teddy Tenenbaum is a screenwriter and a television writer who, both on his own and with his wife and writing partner Minsun Park, ping-pongs back and forth between horror and comedy, depending on how frightening or laughable the state of the world is at any given moment. In addition to writing work on *The Ghost Whisperer*, *The Grudge* film series, *The Dead Zone*, and numerous studio assignments, Teddy contributed to the New York Times bestselling graphic novel *Love is Love*, in support of and to honor those harmed at the Pulse Nightclub in Orlando in 2016. That makes Teddy a New York Times bestselling author, at least in his own mind. "Interloper" is Teddy's first short story.

ERIK DAY

....

THE LIGHT OF THE MOON

H ey, Bran, there's somebody in your section."

Brandon took a deep breath. It shouldn't have bugged him, but the manager's insistence on calling him Bran was enough to trip him up. "Yeah, thanks. I'll take care of it."

"I need to get out of here, like, right at nine, Bran."

"Right . . ." Brandon bit back an annoyed reply and nodded, bowing to the needs of the Friday Night Exodus. "I'll shoo away the browsing customers."

Other stores could fit inside the tent section of Outdoor Recreational Equipment. Brandon's section included maps, GPS, compasses—all the things people bought but so rarely used.

The final customer in the section was a tall, slender blonde wearing a backpack that looked almost as heavy as her. Unnaturally high cheekbones. Huge blue eyes.

"Hey, welcome to ORE," he said. "We're closing in a few minutes. Can I help you find something?"

The girl looked up. "Can I just look for a moment?" She had a cute accent, though he couldn't quite put his finger on it.

"Miss, if you were just a little earlier, yes. Without a doubt. Right now though, the manager has a hot date and needs to bail."

The blonde blinked a moment, pursing her lips as she processed. She had adorable dimples.

Brandon shoved all that out of his head and glanced at the map book she held. He shrugged toward the registers where his manager was waiting. "We have a pretty good return policy if you want to buy it and look it over."

She shook her head and pulled out a wallet. "My cards don't work here and my cash..." She bit her lip. Her big eyes bordered on tears as she slid the book back onto the shelf.

He glanced at the book she'd been browsing: *Local Hikes*. "I noticed your accent. Where are you from?"

"Cormack."

"Oh, yeah, that's ... uh ..." It sounded like a place he should recognize, but he didn't. "Where is that?"

Something was bothering her, but the words seemed to escape her. She took a deep breath and glanced out the windows. "What direction is that?"

"That's east."

"East. Cormack is east."

"Did you hike here?" He motioned to her pack.

She nodded. "I hiked from the arch to the highway, but by then I was so lost."

"The arch! You hiked from the arch to the highway? With *that* kit? Jesus, that has to be fifteen miles!"

"Yeah," she conceded. "It's pretty heavy."

"And you don't have cash ..."

"Not your cash, no."

"I think there's a currency exchange by the airport. Can I give you a lift?"

She bit her lip and shook her head.

"Are you hungry? Would you like to get a bite? I'll buy and then drop you off wherever you need to go."

She started blinking and looked away. "Oh, could you?"

"Not a problem! I'm Brandon, by the way."

"I'm Elise. It's very nice to meet you, Brandon." The way she said his name made it sound exotic.

"Thanks, I . . . uh, it's . . . thanks."

She touched his arm. "Are you okay?"

"No. I mean, yes. Ha! Just hungry, that's all. Gimme two minutes and I'll meet you out front."

"Thank you."

He clocked out, followed his manager through the door, and found Elise a step away from the parking lot. She'd stopped to stare straight up into the night sky, looking almost paralyzed by the moon.

He glanced toward its full face. "It's beautiful, isn't it?"

"It's terrifying."

"Terrifying?" Brandon chuckled. "I mean, maybe if you're on it without a spacesuit, but—"

"Spacesuit?"

"Yeah, you know, like . . . a suit you wear in space?"

"Yeah! Right! Of course." She nodded, a little too quickly.

"Come on, I'm parked over by the light."

He glanced at her well-worn backpack as they crossed the lot. He'd never heard of the brand, but the frame looked solid and the straps were dialed-in. She looked like a trail pro, but something was off about the whole situation. "So, what's your all-time favorite trail?"

Elise thought for a moment. "The Abbravandaks, hands down."

"The . . . whats?"

"The Abbravandaks! Like, the longest mountain trail in . . ."

"Cormack?" he suggested.

She just shook her head and stayed silent.

"Hey, you've gotta be starving. How does a burger sound?"

"Burger?"

"I'm sorry. You're a vegetarian, aren't you?"

"No, a 'burger' will be great! Thank you."

Brandon opened the car door for her. She sloughed off her backpack and slid it into the backseat.

As they drove, Elise seemed to be taking it all in, staring at the cars and billboards.

"They don't have billboards in Carmack?"

"They have billboards, it's just . . . I've never seen these brands before."

"Huh. Wow."

They rolled through the drive-through, and the small talk was the strangest kind of awkward. All that stopped when she got a whiff of the all-beef patty.

He handed her the to-go bag, and she unwrapped it and held it up like a trophy. "Oh! This . . . *burger* smells delicious. Thank you."

He raised an eyebrow at her. "You call it something else, don't you?"

She grinned. "Was it that obvious?"

"Yeah. Your English is excellent, though. Second language?"

"English? No. It's just . . . I really don't know how to explain it."

"You're having a heckuva night, aren't you?"

She nodded as she took a bite. She closed her eyes a moment, savoring the experience.

"Okay, where to? You got a friend in town? Reservations somewhere?"

She swallowed, glanced around, and pointed into the night sky. "That's east, right?"

"You're amazing."

"Once I get my bearings . . ."

Brandon smiled. "Awesome. Pure awesome."

She crammed in another bite and pointed with the burger. "I'm parked at the arch." A pickle bit spilled out as she spoke, and she giggled as she scooped it back into her mouth. "Sorry. I'm so lady-like. Is that too far away?"

Brandon smiled as he shook his head. "No, not at all."

"Thank you!"

"Sure." He nodded as he pulled onto the highway. "Archway it is."

She reached into the backseat and pulled a plasticized map from her pack. She held it up, found a spot, and traced a line. The whole time she was shaking her head.

"You are beyond lost, aren't you?"

She took another bite before nodding again. "Which is weird because I teach orienteering classes, so I know how to read a map."

"Unlike most people."

"Yes!" She gulped down the final bite of her burger. "That's . . . kinda why I'm really freaking out right now."

"Why?"

"Your maps were . . . I don't want to say they were wrong, but they were very . . . not right. Nothing looked familiar. I think I just have to get back to my car, drive home, and make an appointment to get my head scanned."

"Are you okay? Did you fall? I could take you to the hospital."

"I didn't fall. At least I don't think so." Elise glanced out the passenger window at the moon. "Does it always do that? Just hover there. Staring."

"The man in the moon will do that."

Elise's eyes went wide as she stared up into the night sky. A moment later, her shoulders relaxed. "Oh, that's kind of a face, isn't it? What makes the dark spots?"

"Craters. Look, are you sure you're okay to drive?"

Instead of answering, she undid her seatbelt, rolled down the window, and stuck her head outside. The wind whipped through her hair as she scanned the night sky.

This chick is nuts. Gorgeous, but crazy.

A minute later, she plopped back in the seat and rolled up the window. She rubbed her arms, warming up as she stared up through the windshield.

Brandon glanced at her and turned on the heater. "Okay, I see your brain moving at a million miles an hour."

"Do you know your constellations?"

"Sure. Sorta. I mean, I'm not an astronomer, but I remember enough to navigate."

"What constellations can you see?"

Brandon slowed down as he looked into the darkness. The mountains were a jagged black silhouette, but the twinkling patterns above connected into ancient pictures. For just a flash, he remembered his grandfather teaching him the lore of Ursa Major. "Those seven on the horizon? That's the Big Dipper."

Elise pointed out her window. "Do those three bright ones have a name?"

"South? Yeah, that's Orion's belt."

"Who was Orion?"

"He was a hunter."

She waggled the burger skyward. "Of 'the gods,' I'm guessing."

"Of the Greeks, but yeah. Son of Poseidon, I think."

"The Greeks . . ."

"You know the Greeks, right?"

"Of course! They were . . . Greekish."

Brandon chuckled and pointed a thumb to the back seat. "Okay, so your bag landed on a few of my old textbooks. Grab the one that says 'Anthropology.' "

She stretched between the seats and rummaged until she hauled a once-glossy brick back to the front. She studied its dog-eared pages and tattered spine. "How many times have you read this thing?"

"Not enough."

"Are you still in school?"

"I wish. No, graduated, but I partied too much. I read 'em now to make up for all the classes I coasted through during the hangovers."

"Get out!"

"I should slow down first . . ."

Mile markers flew by as anthropology led them to advertising and back to hamburgers. The sign for the arch caught them both by surprise.

There was a sudden lull in their conversation as Brandon took the off-ramp.

Elise fidgeted as she stared into the moonlit desert. "Please be there."

"What?"

"The arch." Elise dropped her head and smiled. "I know I sound crazy. Brandon, have you ever been lost?"

He shrugged. "Sure. I get lost from time to time, but I always figure out where I am. Even when I want to stay lost."

She gave him a long look, then finally a nod. "It's why we go, right?"

"Yeah."

A breath later, the arch came into view and her eyes lit up.

They pulled into the parking lot and Brandon looked around. "Where's your car? I'll drop you off next to it."

"That would be a challenge. Here is fine."

"Okay . . ." He stopped and she practically jumped out of the car, yanking her pack out and shrugging into it. She looked up at the moon again and whirled around to face Brandon. "What makes the glow?"

"Reflected sunlight."

"Oh." She looked down. "Well that makes sense."

Brandon pointed to the back seat. "You want to borrow the astronomy book?"

Elise grinned and shook her head. "You're so sweet . . . and you must think I'm so weird."

"Just a little." Brandon looked around at the empty parking lot. "So, um, your car . . ."

"I'm parked—" She hesitated. "I'm parked at the other lot."

"Other lot?"

She nodded, dragging a foot through the dirt. "It's on the other side of the arch."

"Right." The other side of the arch was a canyon. There was no parking lot over there. "What do you drive?"

"A Vorgan GTI. She scoots!"

"A Vorgan?"

"You don't have those either." She shook her head. "Listen, I'd love to stay and talk, but I have to get through that arch *right now*."

She turned and jogged up the trail before he could say another word.

"A Vorgan?" he muttered to himself.

"Yes! Vorgan!" she called out from the rocks. "Come see it!"

"You couldn't have possibly heard me from up there."

"Heard you!"

He could just make out her silhouette as she stepped through the arch.

Brandon took a deep breath. *I think it's time to get lost.* He locked his car and ran into the dark after her.

His lungs burned as he struggled to catch up. The trail wound higher, right to the base of the giant red-rock arch. Nearly a perfect circle of stone, weathered from the rocks around it.

Elise sat on the ground, crying, just on the other side of the arch.

"Are you okay?"

She looked up and nodded. "I was just so worried I was going crazy."

"Yeah, I can totally—"

Elise shushed him, her hand on his face. She pointed down the other side of the arch. It was difficult to see in the darkness, but her flashlight caught the reflective lines of a parking lot.

A chill went down his spine as he scanned the lot. *I hiked here just last week. There was no parking lot.* There was one *now* though, and one roadster parked in it.

He glanced behind him, down the hill, and easily saw his car in the moonlight. The parking lot on her side was so much darker.

"No way . . ." he said.

Brandon's heart raced as he stepped through the arch. He looked into a sky with thousands of twinkling stars—but no Big Dipper, no Orion. And no moon.

He hurried back to his side and looked up again. Everything familiar was there, just as it should be.

Elise climbed to her feet. "I'm not crazy?"

He started chuckling as he ducked back and forth. "You're definitely not crazy, not unless I am too."

She threw her arms around him.

"This is . . . *amazing!*" Brandon scanned her skies. "There's no moon here?"

Elise shook her head. "Nothing to hide the stars."

"Do you know your constellations?"

She nodded. "I know *these* constellations."

"Wow. I don't know how, or what, or why." Brandon gestured to the arch. "But I get it."

She let go of him and took one step down her side of the hill. "So, I owe you a burger, but . . ."

"What?"

"You know, that thing"—she edged farther away from the arch—"might close."

"How do you feel about being my tour guide?"

A dimpled smile spread across her face. She nodded as she held out her hand. "I'm going to call them that from now on."

He took her hand. "What?"

"Burgers."

....

Erik Day explores the effects of the extraordinary on everyday life, with magical realism and near-future speculation as his primary tools. Short stories, novels, and scripts become narrative laboratories, and he invites fellow explorers to discover their own new stories at the Burbank-based Quill & Pint Writers' Group. To learn more about Erik, check his writer's site at erikday.wordpress.com.

....

On the Rocks

The last thing Lily wanted to do was celebrate another anniversary.

At first, she had thought it was sweet for her boyfriend to want to commemorate the day they met on the second of each month. But Ryan's meticulous tracking had made her constantly aware of the time slipping by, and her patience had slipped away along with it. The anniversary dates felt so "high school" in Lily's opinion, and the thought of him making this something more made her head ache.

As they sat squished against the bar top at an obscure jazz club on the edge of town for their nine-month anniversary, Lily tried to find some light in the situation. Ryan was wearing her favorite cologne—a mixture of fruity pear and sandalwood—and his black, clean-cut hair shone with just a touch of gel in the dim light. He looked handsome and at ease.

Lily, on the other hand, felt highly self-conscious. She fidgeted with her short black dress, her combat boots clunking awkwardly against the thin legs of the barstool. But from the way Ryan smiled at her, she might as well have been wearing a potato sack, as his eyes never strayed from hers. She wasn't sure how she felt about that anymore.

Everything about the bar felt claustrophobic and foreign. The thrum of the band stuck to the dark mahogany walls like cellophane, the wallpaper shivering with every blast of trumpet or throaty moan of the bass.

"Well," Lily began, looking at Ryan. She nodded her head toward the enthusiasm of the jazz band. "The singer's pretty good!" And she meant it. The singer's voice was the only thing about the band she could tolerate.

As the song reached its climax, Ryan took a thoughtful sip of his Cosmopolitan. He raised his eyebrows, a hint of contempt on his lips. "Yeah, she's okay. But she's pushing her voice too far out of her range, causing her to fall a little off pitch."

Lily deflated. Handsome or not, Ryan was still Ryan as soon as he opened his mouth. "Come on, it's jazz. You can't expect it to be perfect."

"I'm just trying to explain why I didn't agree with you," he replied. Seeing Lily's expression sour, he cleared his throat. "I mean, I'm glad that *you* enjoy her. I wanted to make sure you had fun on our anniversary."

Lily winced. "I appreciate the gesture. But Ryan, can you not call it an anniversary?"

"We've been dating for nine months," Ryan protested. "What else are we supposed to call it?"

"A date. That's it." Lily said.

"Oh. Well, I'm sorry this isn't what you wanted."

Lily tensed. "It's not that I don't want this, Ryan. But calling it an anniversary . . . it makes us sound like we're sixty or something." She laughed, trying to lighten the mood. Ryan relaxed at the sound.

"All right. It's just a date then." Ryan placed a hand over hers on the bar top. "A pretty nice-looking one, too." His eyes glinted dark hazel in the dim light, expectant, but Lily made no reply.

The song ended, and applause rolled through the hall. Lily gently took her hand away, smoothing out the front of her dress as she set her drink down. "I'm going to find the restroom."

"I told you that you shouldn't have had that second glass of scotch already," Ryan teased.

Lily gave him a pained smile and hopped off the barstool. "I'll be back in a few."

"Hurry back," Ryan said, oblivious to her discomfort. "I requested a song from the band that I know you'll love." He winked at her, and Lily held in a groan.

She planted the ghost of a kiss on his cheek as she walked past him. She felt his eyes watching her as she weaved her way through the tables toward the back of the hall. She hoped he hadn't seen the irritation on her face.

R yan twirled a paper straw in his near-empty Cosmo, wondering if he'd done something to make Lily so skittish today. Wasn't this enough for her? They had made quite a trip to the edge of town for this venue instead of their usual bar spot. He'd wanted to make this night special, and Lily had told him that she was tired of all their usual spots.

He'd even dressed for the occasion. His khaki slacks were freshly pressed, his tan loafers shining from new polish. He wore a dark, collared shirt, one of Lily's favorites, on his lean frame. He was even wearing the cologne Lily had picked out for him on one of their first shopping trips.

Well, as long as the jazz band could play Lily's favorite song, that was all that mattered to him tonight. That, and her being there to hear it.

As the singer started up another song, a sudden rush of winter air blew through the venue. Ryan turned around to face the door of the bar, which swung shut behind a bulky figure. The stranger strolled toward the bar top, the studs on his leather jacket shining in the light and catching several women's attention as he walked by their tables.

Ryan tried not to admire the confidence in the man's walk, the way he held his head up high. However, it was hard to ignore the stranger when he took the seat right beside Ryan at the bar.

The newcomer hailed a bartender. "Whiskey on the rocks, please." His voice denoted the colors of a baritone, deep and warm. As the bartender handed him his drink, the stranger turned around and leaned against the bar top beside Ryan, his eyes on the jazz band.

The dark drink in the man's glass shimmered as he took a sip. Ryan glanced at Lily's glass of scotch, which she had left on the counter beside him. Discreetly, Ryan switched out his Cosmo for the scotch, holding it like he knew what he was drinking. The stranger didn't seem to notice, although he was uncomfortably close to Ryan's personal space.

As the singer started up another sultry melody, the stranger nudged Ryan companionably. "Hey, whaddaya think of that jazz singer? She's a stunner."

Now that he was speaking directly to him, Ryan noticed a distinct accent. Irish? "Yeah, she's nice, I guess," Ryan said, not taking his eyes off the stage.

"Oof," the stranger said after another moment. "But she keeps falling flat on those high notes. That's not a good range for her to sing in."

This time, Ryan turned to look at him. "My thoughts exactly." Ryan relaxed a little. "Do you know music?"

"I'm a choir conductor." The stranger's smile spread easily across his face, and he suddenly seemed quite boyish. "I'm Darius." He offered his hand.

Ryan shook it. "I'm Ryan. And actually, I'm a choir conductor, too."

"No way!" Darius beamed.

"Yeah. I teach up at Melody Heights Elementary. It's a private school," Ryan added.

"Ah, well that explains it." Darius took a knowing sip of whiskey.

Ryan paused. "Explains what?"

Darius's eyes glittered like sea glass. "Why yer wearin' khakis at a jazz bar." At Ryan's distraught expression, Darius laughed and slapped his shoulder amiably. "I'm just messin' wicha, bud."

The song ended. A smattering of applause ran through the room. Just as Ryan was about to sip Lily's scotch, Darius nudged him. "Hey, check it out."

Darius gestured toward a pool table crouching in the corner by the front door. The deep green velvet of the tabletop was torn at the corners, but the pool balls sat poised at the center of the table in a promising pyramid. "Want to play a round?" Darius offered.

Ryan glanced toward the restroom. He could just make out the back of Lily's head rounding the corner, out of earshot. He felt a twinge of longing and worry in his chest.

He took a swig of Lily's drink, holding back a cough at the smoky taste of the liquor. The pain in his chest subsided, replaced with the heat of the scotch spreading down his throat. "Sure," Ryan said to Darius. "Why not?"

L ily pushed open the restroom door and entered a dimly lit parlor. The line extended past a large mirror, which hung on the smoke-stained walls above a dark blue chaise lounge. Faded photographs of 1940s jazz singers adorned the walls.

Lily examined the photos. She knew that if Ryan were waiting here with her, he'd explain who all the people were and why they were important. And he'd do it while smiling his sideways smile that suggested she was too simple to understand the intricacies of what he was saying. Typical Ryan. She chuckled dryly.

A restroom attendant, who had been cleaning the mirror beside her, saw Lily's reaction to the photographs. She nodded at them with a smirk. "They're something to look at, aren't they?"

"Yeah," Lily scoffed. "I was just thinking about what a friend of mine would say about them."

"Oh?"

"He'd probably tell me which ones I should like and which I shouldn't, regardless of my own opinion on them."

"Humph. Typical."

Lily turned to look at the attendant. She was squat and elderly, her uniform straining against her doughy figure. But her face illuminated with youth when she smiled, bringing a sparkle to her dark eyes. They shared a giggle.

The attendant gave her a curious look. "I'm glad to see you laughing. You were looking a little pale a moment ago."

"Don't worry. I'm fine," Lily said. The woman raised her eyebrows, and Lily knew she sounded unconvincing. She suppressed a sigh.

A toilet flushed, and Lily stepped forward in line. She glanced once more at the attendant, who gave her a wink and went back to washing the mirror.

D arius sunk a solid red pool ball into a pocket with a satisfying *crack*. Ryan tried not to associate the applause of the crowd with Darius's continued good moves.

"So," Ryan said, "you're from Ireland, right? What brings you to a bar on the edge of Los Angeles?"

Darius twirled the pool stick between his hands as he watched Ryan set up his next shot. "I go to university nearby. Studyin' to get my doctorate. I've heard good things about this bar, so I figured I'd finally come check it out. Lots of undergrads here still, but at least it's got jazz."

"It's not a *bad* venue," Ryan said. He sunk a striped ball, felt a thrill of satisfaction. "I graduated from undergrad a couple years ago, but I definitely haven't missed being around college kids."

There was a *crash* as a beer glass shattered on the floor beside the bar, followed by the gruff laughter of young men. Ryan gestured toward the sound, emphasizing his point.

Darius laughed. "There's a certain charm that only under-grads can appreciate about these places. Especially the women."

His dark blue eyes sparkled with a mischief Ryan couldn't understand.

"That's partly why I brought my girlfriend here," Ryan offered.

"Your girlfriend, eh?" Darius raised his eyebrows and glanced around the bar.

"Yeah. She's in the bathroom right now." Ryan's voice wavered.

"Ah, I see," Darius said. He smirked. "You sure she didn't ditch ya?"

"Of course she wouldn't," Ryan said, indignant. He lined up his next shot and missed.

"Even though you took her to this bar full of undergrads?" Darius prepped his shot. His leather jacket hugged his biceps, which flexed as he made a precise move. Another ball whipped into a pocket.

"She just graduated, so I don't think she minds." Ryan sized up his next shot. "She loves jazz, too. I requested a song for us." Ryan took his shot, but the end of his pool stick skidded on the velvet, missing the cue ball. He cleared his throat, ignoring the prickle of embarrassment on his neck. "Anyway, she should be back any minute now. I'll introduce you."

"I'd be happy to meet her." Darius grinned.

T he sound of a toilet flushing complemented the snare drum as Lily emerged from the stalls. The parlor was nearly empty now, save for the attendant rearranging mints and napkins on the small end table by the chaise lounge.

Lily played with her short blonde hair in the mirror, tugging the strands over her ears. She touched up her lipstick, did a couple of paces around the room, and examined a particularly simple photograph of a trumpet hanging beside the mirror.

The attendant gave her a knowing smirk. "You waiting around until you need to use the bathroom again?"

Lily bit her lip. "Not quite."

Just then, Lily's phone buzzed with a notification. She pulled it out of her purse. *Where are you?* whined Ryan's message across the screen.

Lily texted back, *Long line.*

The attendant tucked extra mints in her uniform pocket, smoothing her skirt. "Looks like we've got some time." She eased herself into a sitting position on the chaise lounge with stiff movements and then patted the seat next to her. Lily hesitated, then smiled and took a seat beside her.

"There we go. You look better already." The attendant stuck out her hand. "I'm Joan."

Lily took it gingerly. "Lily." Joan gripped her hand, tight.

"You've got to have a strong handshake," Joan warned, with a wink. "First impressions mean a lot, you know. Now, tell me. What could possibly be troubling that head of yours?"

Lily surprised herself with a sudden burst of laughter. It began as a low chuckle, but soon small tears pricked the corners of her eyes. "I don't know," she said, trying to catch her breath. "It's about this guy I've been seeing. I've got everything I could ask for with him."

Joan raised her eyebrows. "Like what?"

"Well . . ." Lily paused. "We have a lot in common. He takes me out every week. And he's smart and caring, if a little eccentric sometimes."

"Sounds like a pretty good boyfriend to me," Joan said.

Lily winced. "That's the thing." She struggled to find the words. "He's not *technically* my boyfriend. I mean, yes, he is, but I'm seeing other people too." At the look on Joan's face, Lily rushed to explain. "He knows I am, though. And he's fine with it."

Joan shook her head, but there was kindness in her eyes. "I'm grateful I'm not young again. Dating these days is far too complicated."

"Tell me about it." Lily rubbed a hand over her face. "But I honestly can't commit to any one person right now." It sounded like an excuse as soon as she said it, but it felt like a valid one. "I'm heading out of state to law school in the fall. I'm not going to have much time to myself, let alone to invest in another person."

Joan nodded thoughtfully. "Pardon me for asking, but have you considered a long-distance relationship? If you care about your boyfriend, then this shouldn't be a problem."

"It's not really a 'relationship' I'm after." Lily took a breath. "At least, not with Ryan exclusively." Heat crept up her neck.

A round of applause sounded outside the door, slightly muffled.

A nd now," the jazz singer crooned on stage, "a special request from a thoughtful audience member. Happy Anniversary, love birds." She counted the band in, and they broke into a soft ballad.

Ryan looked around the bar one last time. Still no sign of Lily. He pulled out his phone, and her reply of *Long line* stared at him from the screen. He typed another response. *My song request is up. Hurry back.*

Darius sank another shot and then straightened, listening to the music. A shadow of something tender flickered across his face. "This is her favorite song," he said.

"Yeah, I know," said Ryan, staring at his message a moment longer. He deleted it. "I requested it for our anniversary."

Darius chuckled. "No, no. I meant *my* girlfriend's favorite song."

"That's funny. Are you two pretty serious?"

"Well, I haven't seen her much since she graduated." As Darius lined up his next shot, he took his time moving the pool stick forward and back between his fingers. "But I like spending time with her. We have a lot of fun together." The cue hit two balls into separate pockets with a loud *crack*.

"If you have . . . *fun* together, you should try to see her more often," Ryan said carefully. "Isn't that what a relationship is all about? Spending as much quality time with her as you can?"

Darius took a sip of whiskey. Small droplets of liquid shimmered in his trim beard. He shrugged. "I guess for some people. But the thing is, I don't think a relationship is what she wants from us." He took another shot, missed. The eight ball and one of Ryan's striped balls remained. Darius leaned against his pool stick. "It's not really what I'm wanting, either."

Ryan hit his last ball into a pocket. "I get that."

Darius raised his eyebrows. "Oh, do you?"

Ryan nodded. "My girlfriend is seeing other people too. But that doesn't stop me from trying to see her." He lined up the cue ball to aim for the eight. His vision blurred at the edges as the final verse of Lily's song floated toward his ears, and he blinked rapidly. "I'm sure it's what she wants."

A smile crept onto Darius's lips, like he'd opened a particularly fascinating gift. "My girl doesn't let people tell her what she wants. That's what I like about her."

Ryan hit the cue ball sideways. It bounced around the table walls, missing the eight completely.

"Looks like I've got this one." Darius swaggered across the table. He lined up his final shot, taking careful aim.

"Where did you say you go to school, again?" Ryan asked.

"I didn't."

Lily's jazz ballad ended to a round of applause.

W hy don't you tell me a little about these men you're seeing," Joan asked kindly after a moment.

Lily shifted in her seat. "They're both involved in music, which is what I love about them. They're very passionate people. But one overthinks everything, and the other never thinks past the next ten minutes." She glanced around the restroom, as if worried she'd see one of them walk through the door at her summons. "One takes me out on dates, and the other . . . we have great chemistry." Lily blushed.

Joan chuckled. "Sounds like they complement each other very well."

"Together, they make the perfect boyfriend," Lily explained. "Or, almost perfect. One of them wants to commit to me, and . . ."

"And you want the other one to commit to you."

Lily huffed. "Well, I don't want to commit to Ryan. But the other isn't necessarily commitment-worthy either. Both of them alone are . . ."

"Are what?" Joan prompted.

". . . unsatisfying." Lily felt an invisible weight lift from her shoulders as she said the word. She'd been holding it in so long, she'd forgotten what it was like not to have its pressure. "Sometimes I feel like I'm just going with whatever I have time for in the moment. But the thing is . . . I honestly don't know what I want."

"There's something to be said for that," Joan said, thoughtful. "It either means you haven't discovered what it could be yet or that you're so afraid of being wrong that you don't even try."

Lily could just make out the end of the lyrics to the latest song playing out in the hall—her favorite song, undoubtedly the one Ryan requested for her. The round of applause echoed off the guilt nestled in her ribcage, hollow.

Maybe Joan was right. Lily couldn't commit because she was afraid of making mistakes. After all, dating lots of people at the same time was new territory for her. There was no rulebook to tell her how she should feel.

The thought made her perk up with sudden realization. "There aren't any rules," she murmured, thinking. "All this time I've been so worried about my choices that I haven't actually thought about how I feel." She let out a small laugh.

Joan nodded, chuckling. "That's more like it."

Lily stood with a flourish. She paced the room, running a hand through her hair. "The only mistake I've been making has been *choosing* to be unhappy." She stopped, putting her hands on her hips. "And my happiness doesn't involve two half-perfect men."

Joan stood up beside her slowly. She offered Lily a mint in her open palm. "You're worth all of their attention. No matter what."

Lily took the mint. "Thank you."

"Anytime, hon. Now, go get 'em."

Lily turned and walked toward the door, where a new round of applause roared just outside. She took a shaky breath, popped the mint in her mouth, and walked through the doorway.

In that moment, she knew exactly what she wanted.

G ood game, bud!" Darius laughed approvingly as he shook Ryan's hand.

He wasn't sure if it was the conversation or the scotch, but Ryan was beginning to feel an odd kinship with Darius. "You surprised me," Ryan said, playful. "I didn't know a choir conductor could pull off a leather jacket."

"I'll drink to that." Darius held up his glass, and Ryan clinked his against it.

As Ryan took a sip of his drink, he saw Darius's eyes flicker toward someone across the room. Darius choked on his drink mid-sip.

"Hey, you alright, man?" Ryan moved to Darius's side.

Darius coughed and took a deep breath. "I'm fine, I'm fine." His eyes flashed back toward whatever he had been looking at before, and this time Ryan turned to look. People had begun to leave their seats, and they crowded the common space as the band packed up their things, the stage dark. The back door behind the stage swung closed.

"Where the hell is Lily?" Ryan said, an edge in his voice. He searched the faces of the people around him, all glittering eyes and white teeth and dark fabric.

"She just left. Out the back door," Darius said, a sigh in his voice.

Ryan blinked. He turned back around, glaring at Darius. "How do *you* know? You've never met her." His hands clenched at his sides, his heart pounding.

Darius placed his empty glass on the edge of the pool table and stood up beside Ryan, looking out at the crowded bar. "Oh, bud." A soft, pitying smirk hung on Darius's lips. "I think I can recognize my girlfriend when I see her."

As Darius adjusted his jacket, Ryan caught a whiff of a familiar scent—pear and sandalwood. The pieces clicked together in his mind. "Oh."

He kept his eyes on the back door, willing it to open. It didn't.

....

Anastasia Barbato is in her final year as a Narrative Studies and Sociology & Social Change double major at the University of Southern California. Writing has been her passion since the second grade, and she desires to bring stories to life in the realm of interactive and immersive entertainment experiences as a career goal. Nature is her happy place, as are singing in choral ensembles and traveling across the world to learn as much as she can about the different landscapes, cultures, and people to be found there. This is her sixth consecutive story published in the NaNoWriMo anthologies—the first when she was only seventeen years old—and she's inspired each year by the voices of her generation in their pages. You can follow her writing at sincerelystasi.weebly.com or find her on Instagram @staz_mahal.

....

ALONE

T he day before her parents left on their trip, Nina hid outside their study to eavesdrop. When she pressed her ear flat against the door, she heard Father saying that he wanted to leave for the airport early, while Nina was still asleep.

"We should at least say goodbye," Mother said. "I'm worried about her, Charles. We've never left her for a night, let alone a whole week."

"She'll be fine," Father said. "I'm more worried about you. You're sure you can be away from her for that long?"

"Don't be silly," she scoffed, but Father was right. While Mother was anxious about leaving her only child, Nina couldn't wait to have the house all to herself.

Not that Nina wasn't sad that her parents were leaving. She was! And a little frightened, too. But a brighter feeling shone through the patchwork of dread, because she would finally be alone in their towering Victorian home. She imagined the two floors and the attic completely empty of anyone but her, her dolls, and the mice that scuttled within the walls. Her friends often refused to come over, saying they were too frightened of the shadowed corners, the creaky stairs, and the doorknocker shaped like the face of a goblin. But those things didn't frighten Nina. They lit her imagination on fire.

Nina's reverie was abruptly cut short when she heard the next words out of her father's mouth.

"I know it bothers you that she hasn't met the nanny yet, but Harper comes highly recommended," Father said. "I'm sure the two of them will be inseparable by the time we get back."

E arly the next morning, the doorbell echoed through the house. Nina's parents were due to leave in five minutes, but Nina refused to come out of her room. She didn't want to meet the nanny. Why couldn't she stay home by herself? She was seven, after all, and she knew how to cook. Well, she could pour a glass of milk, anyway. Finally, after Father lost his patience and threatened to ground her, Nina huffed and stomped down the stairs the way a monster might, hoping she would scare the nanny away.

The nanny wasn't frightened. Instead, she smiled. Nina had imagined someone imposing and gray, but this woman was quiet, polite, and decidedly colorful. She wore a long green skirt and a thick scarf the color of raspberries. The only thing gray about her was her gleaming silver hair, but when she stepped in front of the stained-glass window, the light made it look lavender.

"Nina, this is Harper," said Mother.

Nina cocked her head at Harper, who mirrored her.

Mother gave Harper a small smile. "She's shy around strangers."

"No, I'm not," said Nina.

"That's okay," said Harper, as if she hadn't heard Nina. "I'll make sure we have a lovely time."

"She's also very independent," Father said. "Loves to play on her own."

Harper smiled. "Of course. I'll give her all the space she needs."

Harper was true to her word. The second Nina's parents left, Harper said, "Nina, I need to get settled in my room. Why don't you stay in the living room for a few minutes, and we can play a game when I'm done?"

Nina agreed, and Harper ascended the stairs with her suitcase, disappearing at the top. Nina crawled onto the worn floral couch and waited, kicking her feet, wondering when her legs would be long enough to touch the floor.

A few minutes went by, and Harper didn't reappear. Nina kept an eye on the clock, which she'd just learned to read at school. When ten minutes passed and there was still no sign of the nanny, Nina closed her eyes and pretended that she was truly alone. She took a deep breath, listening to the soft sounds the house made as water moved through pipes and wind pressed against the outside walls. She walked to the stained-glass window in the front of their living room and passed her hand through the light, stirring the dust motes. Then she sat on the windowsill, watching the staircase with unblinking eyes.

Perhaps Harper wasn't coming back. Maybe the house had swallowed her up. The idea made Nina giggle.

Five more minutes, she told herself. *Then I'll have some fun.*

After she reached the end of her countdown, Nina almost leapt from her seat. It was easy to convince herself that Harper really was gone, but she knew it wouldn't last forever. Sometime soon, Harper would come downstairs and make Nina do something boring, like math or cleaning. While she had the opportunity, Nina decided to do all the things her parents had told her never to do.

In her mother's office, she used the dark cherry bookshelf as a ladder, climbing high enough that she could tap the ceiling. In the kitchen, she pulled herself up onto the counter, balancing on its edge with her arms outstretched and her front foot pointed as if she were a gymnast. She ate half a plate of chocolate cookies, licking the brown crumbs from the tips of her fingers. All the while, Harper stayed upstairs, quiet as a ghost.

When she was tired, Nina lay on the floor of the living room, staring at the ceiling. The fullness from the cookies had worn off, leaving Nina's stomach growling. She could pour herself that glass of milk, but milk didn't sound very filling. She was suddenly quite glad that an adult was here to prepare food.

"Harper!" Nina called. "Can you make me soup?"

No answer.

Nina walked over to the stairs. "*Har*-per!" she called again, drawing out each syllable so that it echoed up into the dark landing of the second floor.

Still no answer. Nina strained to listen for any sign of Harper's presence, but the wind had picked up outside. On the front porch, her mother's chimes danced against each other, sending up their fairy twinkling.

Nina put her foot on the first stair. It creaked as it always did, but this time there was another sound behind her, almost like a sigh. Nina gasped and whipped around, but nobody was there.

"Hello?" she called.

Somewhere deeper in the house, a door whined as it opened. Was it coming from the kitchen? Maybe Harper had come downstairs after all, and Nina just hadn't seen her.

What if *this* was the game Harper wanted to play? Nina didn't like games unless she knew the rules, but she wasn't one to back down from a challenge.

She stepped carefully off the staircase and rose to the balls of her bare feet, tiptoeing toward the dining room. She sidled along the wall like a character in a cartoon, listening all the while for sounds in the kitchen. A pot and a pan brushed against each other, and there it was again: that sigh, light and voiceless.

Nina grinned. If Harper thought she could scare her and get away with it, she was in for a surprise. Nina crouched and counted silently. On three, she sprang around the corner.

"Boo!" she yelled, hands up and fingers curved like claws.

Nina was good at scaring people. Her parents told her so all the time. She'd hoped to make Harper scream or even drop the can of soup she was about to prepare for lunch.

But nothing happened, because Harper wasn't there. The kitchen was empty.

Nina's smile faded as she lowered her hands and looked around. "But I know I heard . . ."

She stopped. Across their long kitchen, the pantry door was moving. It rocked almost silently back and forth, like someone had ducked quickly inside.

Nina held her breath as she took one step closer. The door stopped swinging, but Nina knew someone was on the other side. Her chest felt tight, and the hairs on her arms stood up.

"Harper?" she said.

No answer.

A thought struck Nina, making her stomach clench: What if it wasn't Harper in the pantry? What if it was someone—or something—else?

Her plastic toy tools were on the counter, and Nina grabbed the hammer as she took slow steps across the kitchen.

"Please come out!" she called. Once again, her words were met with silence.

Slowly, she reached for the doorknob. Just as she was about to grab it, the door flinched almost imperceptibly toward her.

Nina screamed and abandoned the kitchen, running straight for the stairs.

Normally, Nina didn't feel small. She preferred to think of everyone around her as giants. But as she tried to run up the stairs two at a time, she felt tiny and helpless, like a trapped rabbit. She stumbled and dropped the plastic hammer. Floorboards creaked behind her, but she didn't let herself turn around to see who followed. She ran into her room, with its pink walls and handmade dollhouse in the corner, slamming the door shut behind her.

Nina pressed her ear to the door, trying to quiet her own breathing. One of the stairs creaked, and Nina gasped and reached for the lock.

All too late, she remembered that her bedroom door didn't lock. Only the attic door could be locked from the inside, but it was at the very end of the hallway. It seemed too far, but what would happen to Nina if she stayed in here? Surely, whoever—or whatever—was following her had heard her go into her bedroom. It was only a matter of time before they caught her.

She had to try.

Nina threw the door open and ran from the shadow at the top of the stairs, never looking directly at it. Her feet barely touched the floor as she pushed forward, going so fast that she slammed into the attic door before she could stop. She opened it just wide enough to fit through and then pulled it shut.

But it wouldn't close all the way.

Nina tried again, pulling the door toward her, but she couldn't close it. When she looked down, there was something in the doorjamb.

It was a foot.

Nina screamed and fell onto the stairs. She scrambled backwards, her limbs fumbling and heavy. Finally, she managed to get to her feet, and she turned before whatever was waiting for her on the other side of the door could be revealed.

The furniture in the attic was sparse, which also meant there were few places to hide. She dove toward her mother's trunk and opened it, shoving aside some half-finished crochet blankets before she hopped inside and closed the lid as quietly as she could manage.

After a pause, footsteps climbed the stairs. Before, Nina had wondered if she was hearing things, but there was no question that these footsteps were real. She pressed her eye to the trunk's keyhole, but all she saw in the dim light of the attic was a shadow moving about the room.

Nina pressed a hand to her mouth to muffle her breathing. Her heart beat rapidly in her chest. She found herself thinking about birds. Her teacher said their hearts could beat more than one thousand times per minute when they were flying or when they were scared. Did their hearts hurt the way Nina's did now?

The shadow moved around the attic with purpose, stopping to check all the corners and lift the sheets off old armchairs. As it approached the trunk, Nina looked for a way to keep the lid shut, but there was nothing. She would be caught. A sob escaped Nina's lips, and soon she began to cry in earnest.

"Nina?"

The lid opened, and there was Harper. Her hair was disheveled and her eyes were bleary with sleep, but they seemed to focus when she saw Nina curled up and sobbing.

"Oh, Nina! What happened? I've been looking all over for you, dear." Harper leaned down and pressed the back of her hand to Nina's cheek, wiping away some of her tears.

"You tricked me," Nina said between sobs. "Your game isn't any fun."

"Game? What game?"

"You were hiding from me!"

"What? Oh no, Nina, no . . ." Harper knelt on the ground next to the trunk. "I was in my room. After I unpacked, I sat back on my bed to rest my eyes, and . . . oh Nina, I fell asleep. I'm so sorry to do that to you. It won't happen again."

"You were sleeping?" Nina said. "But there was someone in the kitchen."

"You saw someone?"

"No, but I heard them."

Harper shook her head. "Your house is very old. It must make all sorts of noises."

"But someone kept me from closing the door to the attic! They used their foot."

"Well then, let's look." Harper straightened up and headed back downstairs. Nina crept out of the trunk and over to the top of the stairway, wringing her hands. At the entrance to the attic, Harper was looking around with her hands on her hips.

"Ah!" Harper grabbed something off the floor and came back upstairs. At first, Nina thought Harper was holding the very shoe she'd seen in the doorjamb, but when she blinked the tears out of her eyes, it was only an old wooden car.

"Look familiar?" Harper said, kneeling down so that they were once again at eye-level. "Goodness, look at your face. Didn't I tell you to come get me if you needed anything?"

"You never said that," Nina said between sobs, though she wasn't sure. Everything from the last few hours seemed warped. Had there really been someone in the kitchen and on the stairs? At the time, Nina would've said yes, but now that she was with Harper, she felt silly, like a cat scared of its own shadow.

"Come here," Harper said, pulling Nina into a hug. "You have to promise to stay by my side from now on. No more scaring yourself."

Nina gave in, wrapping her arms around the woman's middle and burying her face in Harper's scarf.

A gust of wind made the house groan. The empty rooms below no longer called up images of the adventures Nina could have. Instead, the house felt full of secrets she never wanted to learn.

"I want my parents," Nina said.

"I know," Harper said.

Nina had the sudden urge to twist away from her, to check the stairway and the pantry, to make sure there wasn't anything hiding. But Harper held her too tightly, and Nina couldn't move.

"You poor thing," Harper said, stroking Nina's hair. "It's scary, isn't it? Being alone?"

....

Alyssa Villaire is a writer and nonprofit-er living in Los Angeles. She spends her evenings writing books and her days working at a foundation where she's up to her elbows in public policy and community development. Originally hailing from the Midwest, Alyssa loves LA's eternal summer but really misses autumn. When she's not reading, going to concerts, or hanging out with her friends, she daydreams about owning a dog. "Alone" is her first published story.

....

LOST AT SEA

emind me again why we're out here, Cap'n," came the lilting voice of Adawalai from behind her.

Captain Jessica Lynch stared out beyond the bow of her ship, one hand rubbing the tarnished golden locket on her bosom. A thick fog had rolled in over a day ago and forced them to hoist the sails. Now they bobbed on the water, at the mercy of the current until the fog cleared and they could navigate again. "Because the ship needed repairs, the crew needed food, and we all needed work."

Adawalai, a small, dark-skinned woman and first mate of the ship, joined Jessy at the bow. "Aye. I thought the bosun was gonna have to use the lash if the men came back drunk any more mornings. Only the cabin boy had his wits about him."

"And when a passenger offers us a chest full of gold to ferry him around, it's not like I can turn it away. It's that or we all start looking for a new line of work."

Adawalai smiled. "I'm not cut out to be a pirate, Cap'n. Or a privateer. Honest sailing is more my style."

"You and me both." She rubbed her locket once more before dropping her hand to the railing. "Damned fog has us going nowhere. It's nearly afternoon. It should've burned off by now."

The smile on her first mate's face faded. "It ain't natural. Fog never lasts this long."

"Now don't start getting all superstitious on me. We're only four days out from port with another two months to go. I need every sailor with a level head. Especially you." Jessy sighed. "Come on, let's go check with Navi." She turned on her heel and marched across the deck and toward the wheelhouse.

"Captain?" The smooth, cultured voice came from her left. She turned toward it and spied their passenger. He was dressed in his usual attire, an outfit similar to what the crew wore and completely at odds with his otherwise well-groomed appearance. When he had first arrived, his gait and stance on board showed his familiarity with ships and the sea. Jessy was grateful to finally have a passenger who wouldn't leave the cabin boy cleaning sick off the deck the whole trip.

"Yes, Mr. Powell?" She stopped her stride and turned to face him. "What can I do for you?"

"Quite the fog we have, eh?"

"Indeed. However, I'm sure it'll be gone in no time and we can continue on our way."

An easy smile graced his features through the stubble he had grown while aboard. "I'm not worried. I have faith that you'll deliver me precisely where I need to be. Your reputation says so as well."

"The sea may be fickle, but God protects us, Mr. Powell. You'll get to your destination if I have to get the crew to start pushing."

He chuckled. "That's hardly necessary. I'm not on a strict time frame. Whenever we make it to port is fine."

"Yes. Now if you'll excuse me, I must speak with my navigator."

"Of course, of course. I shall bother you no longer." He patted a book he had tucked under one arm. "I came up on deck to enjoy some reading. And yes, I'll stay out of the way of your crew."

She nodded to him, turned, and climbed the stairs to the wheelhouse. "Report, Naveen. What's going on?"

Navi was hunched over a small table next to the wheel. The wheel itself had been lashed into place, and the brass spoke that indicated a straight rudder pointed toward heaven. No need for active steering when they weren't going anywhere. "Nothing good, Captain," came his reply. He gestured for her to come over. "Look here."

She glanced down at the table, where a sea chart was unrolled. A compass sat next to it, its needle pointing roughly west. "What's the problem?"

"For one, the fog. It's thick and unnatural. Can't see more than a few meters off the side of the ship. A whole fleet could be passing right by us and we'd never know it. For another . . ." he trailed off. "Captain, I have no idea where we are."

"How so?"

"Well, before the fog rolled in, I had a pretty good idea of where we were. But now?" He tipped the compass back and forth. The dial rotated first left, then right, before settling on north-northwest. Another jiggle and the movements repeated. Now they were apparently headed back east. "I can't get any kind of straight reading off of this thing. Either we're going in circles, or something's just not right here."

"Is the compass broken?" She picked it up and gave it a gentle shake. After a moment, the dial indicated that they now sailed south despite the lack of any feeling of the ship making a turn.

"This is the third compass I've tried, ma'am. They're all doing this. I doubt every compass onboard broke at the same time. So only God knows where we've drifted to now." He flicked his wrist and closed the compass with a click. "Once the fog lifts, I can get us back on a proper heading and course, but until then . . ." He shrugged. "I'm at a loss, ma'am."

"Keep trying your best. And don't tell the rest of the crew. Everyone's on edge over this fog. No need to add even more superstitions to their fears."

He nodded. "Aye, aye, Captain."

Jessy gave him a pat on the shoulder. "Come, Ada." She descended the steps to the deck and entered her cabin with her first mate in tow. While not decorated as finely as some cabins she had seen, it still had a few luxuries such as a large bed, a desk, and a table around which she and her officers met. She took up her position in the chair at the head of the table, Ada sitting by her right-hand side.

"I told you, ma'am. This fog is the Devil's work."

"I'm inclined to agree, though we can't let the crew know."

"It's the Devil's work. He's testing us."

Jessy sighed and placed her palms on the table. "Ada, you know I value your counsel and wisdom. Being a female captain of a ship has made for many difficult times over the years, but I would hardly call this the Devil's work. I'm a pious woman myself, as much as I can be. This fog may be odd, but it's still just fog. We've always pulled through in the end, and we will do so again. Just have to pray a bit harder for it to lift soon."

Ada withdrew her rosary from beneath her clothes and rubbed its beads. "And what do we do if it doesn't lift, ma'am?"

"Then we set the best course we can and start sailing. We'll hit land eventually."

"Unless we sail in circles." The two of them lapsed into silence, and Jessy's hand returned to her locket.

"Captain!" came a cry from outside.

The two of them rushed out of the cabin. The fog was rolling away. For the first time in days, they could see the blue sky and the sea around them.

"Ship off the port side!" cried the lookout from the crow's nest. Jessy looked up to see one of her crew pointing off into the distance. "Captain, she's running pirate flags!"

Indeed, a ship had appeared no more than a few hundred meters away. Ada handed over a spyglass. Through it, Jessy could just make out figures scrambling across the deck. Gunports opened, revealing cannons. Up at the top of the mast, a black flag with a skull and crossbones flew.

"Navi! Get us out of here. Bosun! Get those sails lowered. Catch the wind and let's be gone." She shouted her orders, hearing booted feet rush to carry them out.

"Belay that order!"

Jessy lowered the spyglass. "Who dares countermand me?"

Mr. Powell strode forward. "Captain, if you'll indulge me for a moment."

"I don't have the time to indulge you, Mr. Powell." Fortunately, her crew knew better than to listen to a passenger over her, so they continued carrying out her orders. "I have no intention of being captured or sunk by pirates today or any other day. Not again."

"I'm aware of the stakes, Captain." His voice indicated no sign of panic or fear. In fact, he seemed quite calm and controlled. "I'm offering to help with your pirate problem."

"How in the nine hells are you going to manage to do that? We're an unarmed ship. So unless you're packing a brace of cannons in your luggage, I don't see how you can be of much help."

He smiled. "Then perhaps you should keep an eye on the enemy ship, Captain."

Suppressing a groan of frustration, she turned back to the ship, raising the spyglass once more. She could see that the pirates were turning to head right for them. No doubt they wanted to board them rather than waste the cannon shot and risk destroying any precious cargo.

"All I see is slavery or death approaching, Mr. Powell." She turned to look at him, surprised to see his grin had only grown wider. For a moment she feared she'd brought a lunatic on board. Or worse, a collaborator.

"What in God's name is that!?" the lookout in the crow's nest cried out.

Jessy snapped back to look at the pirates. It took her several seconds before she spotted it. When she did, her jaw dropped as readily as her stomach.

Rising out of the water was a monstrous head. It looked akin to the head of an eel, complete with sharp teeth and a fin on top. But eel heads weren't half the size of a ship. The head, with its gray skin and large, protruding eyes, continued to rise out of the water. It rose and rose until it was looking down at the ship from above the top of the main mast. It had to be at least fifty meters out of the water, and still there was no sign of any end to its body.

All around her the entire crew froze, staring at the sea beast. Not even the bosun shouted at them to move faster—he was as stunned as the others. No one dared speak a word.

Her heart thudded as the creature eyed the pirate ship. Then its head darted toward the pirates, slamming into the main mast. The sound of splintering wood carried over the water as the mast split and fell. One part of Jessy's brain mused that there was no way the pirates could hope to catch her ship now. The rest of her brain was too shocked to acknowledge anything else.

From the other side of the pirate ship, something else rose out of the water. A tentacle erupted forth and wrapped around the center of the ship where the mast once stood. Jessy raised her spyglass and watched the pirates, armed with swords and pistols, try to dislodge the appendage. They may as well have been hurling harsh words and insults for all the good it was doing. Their swords and pistol shots could only be a mere annoyance to something that size, if it felt them at all.

The pirate ship shuddered. Jessy imagined the creaking and groaning of the wood as it tried to hold on. The tentacle appeared to be tightening its grip around the center of the ship. With a snap and a crash clearly heard across the water, the tentacle crushed the middle of the ship, leaving two halves upended in the sea. A cry rose up from her crew, equal parts exclamations and prayers to God. Beside her, Ada had fallen to her knees, rosary beads gripped in her hands.

The creature appeared to stare at the remains of the ship. Another tentacle rose out of the water and flipped something up into the air. Jessy could just make out a flailing human before the jaws snapped shut around it. Another pirate met the same grisly fate a moment later.

She dropped the spyglass and summoned the will to turn away. "Get us out of here!" she screamed. She drew the knife she kept at her side and slashed at one of the lines holding up the mainsail. The sail dropped, unfurling and crashing into the mast with a massive thud. They would have to run a new line through the rigging later, but if they were still alive to do so, it would be worth it.

The crash of the sail snapped the rest of her crew away from the spectacle of the feeding monster. Everyone scurried about, lowering the rest of the sails.

"Naveen! Get us moving!"

"I'm trying, Captain!" came the shouted reply. "But she don't move without any wind, and it's deader than those pirates out here."

Sure enough, the sails hung listlessly. On a dead sea, they were a sitting duck for that monster. Not that Jessy had any illusion about outrunning it; she just hoped they could get away while it was distracted.

She swore, turning back to the beast. To her sheer horror, the head was looking right at them. It lowered until it was barely out of the water, then came right for them. The creature was as quick as she'd feared, closing the distance between the sinking wreck of the pirate ship and their own in moments. She looked up into a face with teeth larger than she was as eyes with slitted pupils gazed down at their next meal.

Just as she was planning on joining Ada in kneeling down for a prayer, a man's voice rang out across the silent deck.

"*Zuul! Lok tii krosis ahkrin.*" The language sounded guttural, unnatural to her ears. Mr. Powell, forgotten about in the chaos, strode across the deck and over to the railing in front of the creature. *"Nu faras denek kul monahven."* The giant head lowered until the nose was just even with the railing. With a smile, he reached out and stroked it with a tender touch. "Very good, my friend."

The crew stared at him in horror and amazement as he turned back to face them. "As I said, Captain, all you had to do was indulge me for a moment."

It took a few breaths before she found her voice. "That thing is yours?"

He chuckled. "She's more like my partner."

"But . . ." She struggled to find the words.

"It's a long story. Suffice it to say, she's been quite helpful when I'm out at sea. So helpful, in fact, that I'm in need of a business partner. One with a ship."

Ada looked up at him. "We would never partner with the Devil."

"Are you sure? There's riches involved. More than you could ever hope to spend in a lifetime." He gestured, speaking once more in the guttural language. A moment later, a tentacle appeared over the railing. It extended and gently set something on the deck, receiving a loving pat from Mr. Powell as it retreated back into the water.

The object in question was a chest. With a flourish, Mr. Powell kicked the latch, and it popped open. Inside was a trove of gold coins and gems of all colors. "There's plenty more where this came from," he said.

Jessy could hear her crew muttering around her. That was more money than they had ever seen in one place. Far more than they'd earn in ten years of ferrying people and supplies around the ocean.

"My friend has other uses. She can make sure you always have clear skies and a good wind." A thump drew Jessy's attention upwards. The sails were no longer hanging limply but were full of wind. The ship lurched as it started moving, and the monster's head kept pace with them. "Plus, you can move farther, faster. Check off the bow."

Jessy looked toward the setting sun. At first she saw nothing but the sea, but then on the horizon came the unmistakable sight of land. The sailor in the crow's nest was too surprised to utter the customary cry of "land ho!"

"Impossible," she said, finally finding her voice. "We're not due to reach port for quite some time yet."

"Another of the many benefits my friend brings to the table. Voyages will take much less time to complete. She's quite helpful." He reached out and stroked the head of the creature once more. It lidded its eyes, seeming to nuzzle against his hand.

"And you just want my ship? Why not buy your own?"

"Because I need someone with expertise on the sea, really. I'd need to find an experienced crew. Why go through the trouble when you already have one?"

"And what do you get from this . . . partnership?"

"Well, she does need to feed. But if it helps, think of it as a service, ridding the seas of pirates and whoever else you want."

"Why did you pick us?"

"I asked around in port. You have a reputation for running a reliable ship. Only one unfortunate incident five years ago. Other than that, a spotless record. I say your record makes you the perfect partner."

Jessy looked from Mr. Powell to the chest of gold . . . and then to the creature. Then she gazed off into the distance. It was a lot of money. And if they rejected the partnership, Mr. Powell would probably see to it that they'd never make it to their next destination.

"Cap'n," Ada whispered, "surely you're not thinking about consorting with the Devil. What about your eternal soul?"

"What makes you think we'll survive our next voyage if we refuse?" she replied just as quietly.

"Then we die in the good grace of God and will be seated beside Him in Heaven."

Jessy chewed her bottom lip, her hand on her locket out of habit. "Mr. Powell, if I refuse, can you guarantee the safety of my ship and my crew?"

"Of course. My friend and I would harbor you no ill will. You can even keep the chest. Consider it a sign of friendship and for a job well done."

"Then . . ." She continued to chew on her lip as she thought. "I accept your offer."

Ada gasped.

Mr. Powell clapped his hands together. "Excellent," he said. His attention turned back to the creature. "*Nehvokiin rotmulaag.*" The creature slid into the water. Jessy looked over the railing but saw nothing besides the rolling waves. "We'll speak more once we get to port. I must prepare a few things." He strode across the deck and disappeared below.

"Everyone, get to your stations and prepare to dock." When no one moved, Jessy barked, "Now!" The crew jumped into action, leaving her alone with Ada.

"Cap'n . . . why?" The look on Ada's face was one of betrayal.

"You know why, Ada. This is too good an opportunity to pass up. And I can finally do what I've been looking to do for five years now." Her hand went to her locket, continuing to slowly trace over the design and wear it down.

"I know what it is you seek with your family's deaths. But can you do that and remain in God's light?"

"How do we know this isn't part of God's plan? Are you sure this is the work of the Devil?"

Ada seemed to think for a moment. "I'm not sure. I only know what I feel." She shook her head. "I'm sorry, Cap'n, but I refuse to be part of this. I'll take my leave once we reach port, find work on another ship."

"Ada . . ." She dropped her locket and reached out to hug her first mate and friend.

"No." Ada brushed away her arms. "Your mind is made up, and so is mine." She walked away, leaving Jessy alone at the railing.

Jessy looked down at her locket one more time. With a practiced motion she opened it up, revealing a portrait of a clean-shaven man on one side and a baby girl on the other. She lightly ran her thumb across both portraits. "I made you two a promise, and now I can keep it. I'll get the ones who killed you." She closed the locket and looked out over the sea. "Even if it means dealing with the Devil."

....

Brad Ray is a writer and gamer by day and a chef by night. He's a cat lover who enjoys playing his guitar and searching for the perfect burger. His steak seasoning is classified Top Secret. He can be found musing on topics on Twitter @BradRay44.

S P E N C E R   H A M I L T O N

....

THE WORMHOLE IN EDWIN'S CUBICLE

Edwin McCabe was thinking vague, gray thoughts of committing suicide on the day he discovered a wormhole at the office.

The elevator ride up to the eleventh floor hadn't been enough to derail his thoughts (which in that moment had revolved around deep, dangerous elevator shafts), and neither had the long walk across the entrance's black marble floor before that, nor his passage through the revolving doors at the front of the building before *that*. He'd kept contemplating how he'd do it— kill himself, that is—throughout the long subway ride, with its collage of thundering tracks and flashing light, then dark, then light again, and jostling strangers who scared Edwin to no end. He'd kept his eyes fixed on his black loafers and refused to look up even when one of the strangers boxing him into his tiny corner of the subway jostled him. He'd tightened his hold on the railing above his head and tried not to jostle them back. He'd read once that diseases were transmitted via these subway railings. Maybe he'd contract hepatitis and die that way. He'd be okay with that. Before that, when he'd stood waiting for his train to arrive, his eyes had been glued to the tracks leading into that dark tunnel. All it would've taken was one step and he'd have fallen onto the tracks. Whether he met his end at the spark of that dreaded third rail or at the wheels of the train itself, it would've made no difference to him. Before that, his walk from his apartment building to the subway entrance hadn't interrupted his suicidal thoughts—in fact, the gray, overcast sky and rainy drizzle may have even turned up the volume, like a moody score in an indie film. The thoughts hadn't started as he'd left his building, or before that as he'd got ready for the day with his single cup of black coffee, or before that as he'd dressed in his gray suit, or as he'd brushed his teeth, or even as he'd woken up inside his tiny, badly decorated studio apartment.

Now that he thought back, Edwin couldn't remember the genesis of these thoughts. They'd slipped seamlessly from his dreams to his waking, and who knew how far back they went before that? But today, those thoughts came to an abrupt stop, as if he'd pushed them in front of an oncoming train, the moment he entered his firm's floor and rounded the corner to his cubicle.

He stopped in his tracks, still five cubicles away from his own.

Edwin didn't enjoy his coworkers and went out of his way to avoid social interactions with them—including arriving at work at least thirty minutes before they did. So no one else had arrived yet to see the blue glow surrounding his cubicle, stark in the dim lighting. No one else had yet seen the dancing blue glow or Edwin frozen in place, staring at it.

The sphere of blue light almost perfectly encapsulated his gray cubicle. But "blue" couldn't possibly describe the hue, he decided. Cerulean? Azure? It was a shade of blue that reminded him of . . .

Childhood.

Not only the shade, but the vibrancy of it. It appeared to be alive, and the glowing sphere of blue danced and *thizzed* in the air as if it were conducting an electrical current.

Whatever the case, Edwin decided he'd stood there for too long already. What if his coworkers started showing up? He'd have to interact with them.

He approached his cubicle one step at a time, but he returned his eyes to his black loafers. They reflected that strange azure hue more and more with each step. He ticked off each cubicle in his mind as he passed them. He didn't know the names of most of his coworkers, but the final cubicle before his belonged to a very loud man named Stan. Stan acted as if he and Edwin were best friends, and no matter how much Edwin ignored him, he refused to stay at his own desk. He'd peek his head over the cubicle walls and tell Edwin about his weekend's romantic "conquests"; sometimes he'd even come into Edwin's cubicle to "pick his brain" about some work-related problem or other. Edwin had considered requesting a new cubicle almost every day since meeting Stan—but that would require going and talking to his boss. That was just too much.

Edwin closed his eyes for the final three steps past Stan's cubicle. He stopped, eyes still closed, and pivoted ninety degrees so that he faced the inside of his cubicle. He could feel the light in front of him dance against his closed eyelids. That dancing scared him. He didn't trust things that wouldn't hold still.

At first, he thought maybe he wouldn't open his eyes. Maybe he'd just retrace his steps, go home, and spend the day in bed. That sounded nice.

But no. Just minutes ago, he'd been entertaining thoughts of suicide. If he couldn't simply open his eyes right now, how would he ever build up the nerve to kill himself?

He opened his eyes.

Before this moment, Edwin would have thought he was different from most people. He would say that most people would exclaim their awe, that most people would find beauty in such a thing as this, but that he was different. He didn't see beauty in the world—only pain and drudgery. But perhaps Edwin had been living in the darkness and the rain and the cold for so long that something like what was in front of him, inside *his* cubicle, was just too much for him to ignore.

The entire back wall of his cubicle had vanished. No calendar, no kitty-cat-dangling-from-a-tree *HANG IN THERE!* poster (a present from Stan), and none of the other useless things Edwin's cubicle had accumulated over the years. In its place was a circular, swirling mass of blue light that bathed his workspace in an electric azure wash of color. The light felt warm on his skin, like UV rays. Edwin once read that ultraviolet sunlight was good for a person's endorphins, and therefore a natural antidepressant; but he'd also read that ultraviolet radiation caused skin cancer. Perhaps *that* was how he'd kill himself.

He stepped to the edge of his cubicle entrance. His new, blue, dancing companion didn't reach his desk. Tentatively, he stepped inside, sat, and swiveled his office chair to face the source of the blue light.

What was it?

He hadn't the slightest idea.

The elevator *ding!*ed and the susurration of his coworkers' conversation broke the silence like a wave.

He sighed and muttered, "Better get to work."

E dwin had been ignoring the blue thing in his cubicle for over an hour by the time Stan showed up. He was one of those employees who seemed to get away with showing up late to work every day. This always perplexed Edwin, because Stan was startlingly loud when he entered the office—drawing attention to his tardiness and disrupting the other workers. Wasn't that enough for the boss to step in? Apparently not.

"Ay-yo!" came Stan's daily arrival call. Edwin dreaded hearing that non-word shouted across the office each day. It was like a countdown to their inevitable interaction.

Edwin sat rigidly at his desk, his back to Stan. He'd been able to ignore the massive glowing blue wall just two feet away, after all; maybe today was the day he ignored his aggravating coworker and Stan finally got the message.

"Eds, my boy!"

Edwin shut his eyes and braced himself. He hated that nickname. Nobody called him *Eds* before Stan was hired, and certainly nobody had called him a boy. Not since . . . he couldn't remember when.

"Eds, there's someone here I want you to meet."

Edwin opened his eyes. This was new. Meet someone? Maybe it was a replacement. Yes, Edwin was being fired and he could go home and never look at the glowing thing in his cubicle again.

Despite his earlier convictions, he turned toward his cubicle's entrance. There was Stan, tall and smiley and gelled and stuffed into a starched button-up shirt a size too small. Next to him was a man Edwin had never seen before: fancy three-piece suit, Rolex watch, tanned skin . . . definitely not a cubicle worker.

"Eds, this is Charles. Charles, Eds."

Edwin was immediately uncomfortable. Should he stand? Shake the man's hand? He gulped and stayed seated, managing a small nod up at the man in the expensive suit.

"Charles is the new district manager," Stan was saying. "He's just informed me things are gonna start changing around here, for the better. Lots of shake-ups, and an overhead you can be proud of."

"That's right," Charles said. Just like his clothes, his voice sounded rich. It came from a mouth of perfect white teeth, too.

Edwin sat awkwardly staring up at them. Something seemed off. What was it?

Edwin blinked. Of course. Neither of the men standing at his cubicle entrance seemed to have noticed the glowing blue wall next to Edwin. But how could they not? It was bathing them both in light so bright he was surprised they weren't squinting.

Stan was talking. "I was telling ol' Charles here, 'You know who you need to meet? You need to meet my cell mate, Eds.'" Stan laughed at this, and Charles joined him, but Edwin only managed a weak smile. "And so here we are, making the rounds. Why don't you fill Eds here in on what you were telling me, Charles?"

"I'd love to," Charles said. "But first . . . cat got your tongue, Eds? Or do you not like being called Eds?"

Edwin immediately liked this man far more than he liked Stan, which was none at all. It had taken Charles all of two seconds to figure out that a grown man probably didn't appreciate being called *Eds*.

"Ed . . . Edwin," he said, clearing his throat.

"Edwin," Charles repeated, nodding. "Fine name. And I'm glad to hear you can speak. Got anything else to say?"

And then Edwin surprised himself by actually having something else to say.

"Yes," he said. "I'd love to talk more, but . . ." He gestured at his computer. "I've got work to do, you see."

Charles laughed, taking Edwin aback. "Stan said you were a hard worker. Said he barely got five words out of you a day, you were that focused on work."

Stan laughed with him. "Hang in there, Eds, my boy!"

I'm not a boy, Edwin wanted to say. But instead he just nodded and turned back to his computer.

And, amazingly, they left.

Edwin smiled at his reflection on the computer screen, which, thanks to the new glowing wall next to him, was tinted blue.

E dwin decided it must be a wormhole.

He wasn't familiar with what wormholes were, exactly, but it sounded right. In Edwin's mind, wormholes were like doorways, or tunnels, leading to only God knew where.

Actually, he thought a *slide* was a better simile.

He thought back on the days of his childhood spent on playgrounds—by himself, of course. He remembered how he would sit atop the slide, the breeze playing with his hair as he looked over the vast expanse of the playground and the park surrounding. It was breathtaking, how the world would steal the words from his mouth every time with its unspeakable beauty. Then, anticipating the butterflies which he knew would flutter in his tummy, he would push off the top of the slide and *swooooop!* down he would go. The breeze in his hair would strengthen and sting his eyes, and the ground would rise up to meet his feet, and suddenly he'd be in a new world: the park ground. Gravity would take hold once more.

That sounded nice. Perhaps that was what this wormhole was like.

Deciding it was impossible to work with a literal wormhole beside him, he opened an internet browser and began searching for answers. Most of the articles about wormholes went over his head, but he was electrified to learn that they could be visualized as tunnels.

Or slides, he thought.

Even better, wormholes were said to connect two points of the *spacetime continuum.* Edwin didn't have the slightest idea what this term meant, but he loved when they mentioned it in the old sci-fi television shows he liked to watch. *Space* and *time* together in one word? Edwin wasn't sure why, but it seemed almost romantic to him. *Spacetime.*

Apparently nobody knew whether or not wormholes actually existed, but he was pretty sure that if they just paid his cubicle a visit, they'd change their minds. The possibilities thrilled him—the idea of visiting different universes, or different points of time.

Despite his growing excitement, or maybe somehow because of it, suddenly his thoughts returned to that dark elevator shaft

. . . that noisy subway tunnel with the high-voltage third rail . . . those disease-infested subway trains stuffed full of jostling strangers . . .

And then all of those images vanished, replaced by the memory of that playground slide and the breeze and the view of the park and the blissful feeling of being the only person in the whole wide world.

Edwin closed the internet browser and pushed away from his desk, swiveling his chair as it rolled back so that it came to a stop with him facing his spacetime continuum slide. Its vibrant swirl reminded him of when he'd visited the carnival as a child. His father had lifted him up so that he could see how the confectionary made the cotton candy. It had swirled just like the wormhole before him did now—soothing, almost hypnotizing.

"You going to lunch, Eds?"

Edwin ripped his gaze away from the blue swirl. There was Stan, peeking over the wall that joined their cubicles. Edwin returned his gaze to the wormhole. *His* wormhole.

"No," he said. "I'll stay inside."

"Predictable Eds," Stan said, laughing. When Edwin didn't laugh with him, Stan said, "You gotta get a sense of humor, Eds, my boy."

But Edwin wasn't listening to Stan anymore. His mind had drifted into that cotton candy swirl just inches in front of him.

Unprompted, he thought again of throwing himself into that dark elevator shaft. *Why* did he want to kill himself? He wasn't sure. Was he really so unhappy that he wanted to just give up? He wasn't sure of that, either. Where had the boy on the slide gone? The last handful of years had been gray and lifeless. Gray sleep, gray suits, gray cubicle.

But here, today in his cubicle with his wormhole . . . he saw *color*.

Would he die if he stepped into that color? Scientists weren't even sure if wormholes existed, so they were probably clueless about what would happen if somebody tried to enter one. Maybe he would simply bounce off the shimmering ball. That would sure be a letdown. Maybe he would fall down the slide forever, and would then have to wait until he starved to death, and even then his dead body would just fall and fall and fall and . . . that actually sounded a lot like his life here, inside his cubicle. Maybe the wormhole would take him to another dimension, or an alien planet, or back in time, or some combination of all three.

But what sounded most likely to Edwin was that his body would be torn to bits the moment he stepped into the sphere. He'd read once that black holes were so incredibly dense that a human simply could not exist inside one. Maybe that was how this wormhole functioned. He'd step inside and just stop being Edwin. His last conscious moment would be filled with this beautiful, childlike swirl of azure blue.

That sounded wonderful.

He paused. Edwin might be the only person able to see this wormhole, but maybe everyone would *feel* it if he touched it. Maybe attempting to enter it would cause it to explode or implode and kill everyone in his office. Though Edwin didn't know any of his coworkers except for Stan, and he didn't *want* to know his coworkers (especially Stan), he didn't want them all to die because of him, either. The possibilities of the wormhole crumbled at this thought.

But wait . . . why was it so quiet?

He stood up and lifted onto his tippy-toes (one hand on his desk for balance, lest he trip and fall into his wormhole), and scanned the office floor. From what he could tell, he was the only one here. It seemed everyone else had gone off to lunch.

He sat down heavily, his head once more dizzy with possibility.

On the day he found a wormhole in his cubicle, he also happened to be the only person inside during lunch. That couldn't be a coincidence . . . could it?

He decided it couldn't.

In a burst of action, he stood back up, his office chair spinning out from beneath him and coming to a crashing stop at the cubicle across the way. He stepped back so that there was a little breathing room between him and his wormhole. His *slide*.

And for a moment he was back at the top of that childhood slide with the entire park spread out before him. He could almost feel the breeze in his hair, and the butterflies filled his stomach just like they did as a kid. The breeze at the subway tracks had reeked of garbage, but this breeze was fresh, new, invigorating. And there'd been butterflies in his stomach as he'd contemplated that dark elevator shaft, but those had been more like moths, not exciting at all and filled with an empty dread. These butterflies seemed to lift him up, making him weightless. Fluffy, like cotton candy.

"Come on, Eds, my boy," he said. "Just push off."

Though he'd always hated it when Stan called him that, somehow it felt right in this moment. It was, after all, a childlike name. Fitting for a boy about to launch himself down a slide on a bright and sunny day. Fitting for a boy about to taste a thick swirl of blue cotton candy.

Edwin stepped forward. His right loafer touched the worm-hole's blue boundaries and then slipped in without resistance. He stepped through the portal as easily as gravity pulled him down the slide.

E dwin McCabe didn't get torn to bits that day or any other. He also was never seen again at the office. And by the time his coworkers returned from their lunch, the swirling blue mass in Edwin's cubicle had vanished.

Over the following months, as Edwin's coworkers accepted the theory that he'd finally had enough and abandoned his life at the office (and they weren't wrong), Stan would often peek over the cubicle wall at his boy Eds's old office. He would often wonder where Eds had gone off to, and why Eds never said goodbye. But Stan liked to imagine that his good ol' pal Eds had gone off to find a little adventure in his life.

Stan wasn't wrong.

....

Spencer Hamilton was born in Los Angeles and currently lives in Austin, TX, where he and his cat run a freelance editing business at www.NerdyWordsmith.com. "The Wormhole in Edwin's Cubicle" is Spencer's fifth story to be published in the LA NaNo anthologies, three of which he has contributed to as editor.

....

B O Y T O N   C A N Y O N

The door of his shared office opens with a whoosh, and Tanner steps inside. The spacious room is packed with desks and small, comfy couches, and every seat in the place is full. It's mostly quiet, save for the occasional conversation and the keyboards of countless laptops clicking away.

Tanner makes a beeline for the automatic espresso machine. He needs his caffeine fix for today's big event—Planet Rock is finally making the offer to acquire his startup, LoveIT.com. He's been working years for this payout.

An attractive girl in front of him pushes buttons on the machine, finally selecting a Columbian blend cappuccino with almond milk. He decides immediately that they'd never get along. If you're not going to froth real milk, why bother?

The machine takes entirely too long, and by the time Tanner's Ecuadorian super-blend, double espresso starts to pour, he's tapping his foot. He cranes his neck toward the corner where his startup occupies two offices containing one white board and up to seven people. He doesn't manage to catch a glimpse of any of them, though.

Tanner gives the LoveIT.com silver bracelet on his left wrist a rub for good luck. He's worn the bracelet since the company gave it to him to celebrate their Series A funding eighteen months earlier. Could be a collector's item soon.

Grabbing his mini espresso cup just as the pour completes, he charges toward his office in the corner but stops short in the doorway, confused. The only one inside the two offices is Melody, his boss. The office is empty except for her gray backpack. No LoveIT.com logo on the wall, no clever gift box accessories on the bookshelf, no printer and office supplies tossed in the corner. There's only one black dry erase pen at the whiteboard, and its lid is missing.

Melody looks up at him, a pained smile on her unmade-up face. Then she looks down and fusses with some papers in front of her. "Hey Tanner," she says.

"Hey . . ." Tanner says, barely audible.

"I might as well cut right to it," Melody says, clearing her throat and looking up but not exactly into Tanner's eyes. "It's over, Tanner. LoveIT.com is over. No one wants our gift boxes anymore, and Planet Rock bought the competition instead of us. We've been drop-shipped out of here. We were running on investor fumes as it was. Pete and I will be cleaning out the warehouse tomorrow."

An awkward silence follows. Tanner's heart sinks to the floor. He fidgets his hands in his pockets and looks around, but all the other shared offices are business as usual. Only his has this empty feeling. He doesn't say a thing.

"So, that's it," Melody says. "Sorry to drag you in here, but I had to give you your last check." She hands it to him and glances at his espresso. "Damn, I'm going to miss the almond cappucci-nos here!"

Tanner just stands there, tapping his foot uncontrollably. He's crushed inside and can't move. This place has been his life for the past three years.

Melody finally breaks the silence. "Oh, and I'll need your key card."

*K*nock-knock. *Knock-knock-knock.* Several more raps on the solid door, this round of knocking louder and more determined. Still no response. The sound of fumbling keys follows, and then the cadence of turning tumblers. Tanner looks up just as his girlfriend, CeCe, opens the apartment door. She stops in her tracks, and he idly wonders if it's because of the look or the smell of the place. Probably both.

His apartment is piled high with dirty laundry, empty fast food containers, and other random debris. He realizes he's sprawled on the couch in a heap of mess, but he really can't muster himself to move.

CeCe huffs. "Tanner, it's been three weeks. The only reason I've tolerated this mess so far is you've been telling me this slump of yours was temporary. I'm worried about you now. Don't you think it's time to clean up and move on?"

"It's not *that* bad," Tanner mumbles. He'd been half sleeping, half not.

"Not that bad?" CeCe gestures around the room. "Tanner. It is *that* bad. And I can't believe you'd just sit there while I'm undoing that bank vault of a door! You're in deep, Tanner. You need help."

Tanner lets her words wash over him. On the couch, he finds a lost potato chip from God knows when and puts it in his mouth. The light is behind CeCe, so he can't tell from her silhouette exactly, but he's pretty sure he's just disgusted her further.

"Look, Tanner, I've got to shoot some videos for my page this afternoon. I thought maybe you and I could grab some breakfast first. Anyway, I don't have time for this. Go crawl back under the couch and look for old M&Ms for dessert. I'm leaving." She pauses, but he really doesn't know what to say. "It was just a job, Tanner. We all lose jobs." CeCe lets out a long sigh at his continued silence. "Just call me when you're feeling better. I miss you."

CeCe walks out, and Tanner notices she doesn't bother to fumble with all the locks again. He sits alone in the dark, unconsciously toying with the LoveIT.com bracelet on his wrist. His self-loathing is fueled by CeCe's reaction, and he knows he'll probably lose her if he's not careful.

Maybe she's right that it would be good for him to get out. CeCe's video shoots are always fun. He likes seeing that side of her.

He rummages through his open dresser and finds a pair of jeans that seem clean enough. He smells under his arms, applies a liberal amount of deodorant, and changes his T-shirt. He even surprises himself by managing to find his car keys under a fast food container. He grabs his wallet and phone and heads out. The day is looking a little brighter already.

Tanner fires up his Mini Cooper. CeCe's shooting downtown, only about six or seven miles away, but his tank is dangerously low. He fills up at the corner station, using crumpled bills and a lot of change to pay.

Back behind the wheel, he remembers that Lori, CeCe's manager, will probably be at the shoot. Last time she told him to look up "fashion" in the dictionary; she's never really nice to him. Craig, the photographer, will be there too. He'll likely spend the whole time telling CeCe how lucky she is to have found such a "gorgeous man." That's uncomfortable. Tanner wonders if he's really ready for this. The cloud that barely lifted over him starts to sink a little lower again.

The off-ramp for downtown comes . . . and, almost unconsciously, he passes it. He skips the next exit, then another, and another.

Something tingles inside Tanner. Doesn't this freeway go all the way across the country to Florida? He's suddenly thrilled by the idea of having that much road in front of him.

As the distance between himself and downtown increases, so does his desire to just keep driving. Another off-ramp speeds by on the right. His mind snaps to a decision, then he flips on the radio and starts singing along. He's going east, as far as his gas tank will take him!

T he phone on the seat next to him starts to buzz, shaking Tanner out of the driving daze he's been in for several hours. "Jay" is displayed in the caller ID, and he decides to ignore it. He dials CeCe instead.

"Tanner? Is everything okay? I went by your apartment after my shoot to apologize for being so grumpy this morning, and you were gone. Are you alright?"

"Yeah. Yeah, I'm alright, Ceese." In the long silence, he drives by a road sign for Blythe, Arizona. "Umm . . . this is kind of weird, but I was going to meet you at your shoot today, so I got in my car and . . . well . . . I just sort of kept driving. I just entered Arizona."

"What?" CeCe's voice is soft, not angry like this morning. "Where are you going?"

"I honestly don't know. I thought of Florida first, but I think I could turn north and make it to Vegas. I'm not really sure. But all this driving is clearing my head. It's a good thing, I think."

"Okay." CeCe's voice has that tone that makes him feel safe. "You keep driving then, Tan. You drive and you clear your head. That's good. Just call me when you know what your plans are. If you're going to go north, maybe stop in Sedona. It's magical there."

"I could use some magic," Tanner says.

An unfamiliar buzzer rings in Tanner's ear. He opens his eyes and squints at a small digital alarm clock next to the bed. Beside it, as if placed there to jog his memory, is a card that reads "Enjoy Your Stay At The Sedona Inn."

In the bathroom, his new T-shirt reflects back to him in reverse letters: "There Are Two Types Of People In The World And Neither Are From Arizona." He'd kept driving until he'd begun falling asleep at the wheel, then he'd stopped to buy gas and find a place to stay. Since he hadn't packed, he picked up a T-shirt and some toiletries before he maxed his Visa.

He wanders outside the hotel and finds a decent-looking coffee shop amidst a number of souvenir and crystal stores. He orders an Americano with regular milk, frothed, then sits down at the high counter. A few minutes later, a twenty-something woman with long blonde hair and a pastel blue top sits next to him and orders a cappuccino with almond milk. The waitress tells him his card was rejected just as the woman gets her cappuccino. His face reddens and she notices.

"Happens to me all the time," she says. "Hate that."

He smiles at her and hands another card to the waitress. "Thanks."

"First time to Sedona?" She smiles at him, amused.

"How'd ya know?" he asks, sincerely curious.

"That T-shirt, dead giveaway." She chuckles and then holds out her hand to shake. "I'm Emily, by the way." She sips and savors her drink.

"Tanner," he says, offering her his hand.

"You gotta go to Boyton Canyon," she says. Tanner gives her a quizzical look. "You're here for the energy vortexes, right?"

"Energy what?"

"Oh my God. What are the vortexes!? They are like these ley lines in the earth that only occur in certain places in the entire world, and this is one of them. Boyton Canyon has the couples' vortex, one of my favorites. You've got to go there!"

Emily sucks in another breath and continues. "These vortexes are outright magical."

"There's that word again."

"What?" Emily's eyes glisten with curiosity.

"Oh, nothing . . ." Tanner shyly answers, only just realizing he spoke aloud. "Sounds interesting."

Emily's eyes squint before she continues. "You're clearly here for a reason. Look, let me do a tarot reading for you. No worries, I'm a professional. I do it all day next door at the Psychic Eye."

She pulls out a tarot deck, shuffles, and starts drawing cards. "You're in a transition, like a job change. But it's affecting other areas as well. Do you have a girlfriend? Of course you do. Says so right here. She's a good one, you'll wanna keep her. She's a little thrown by you right now though. Are you aloof? Never mind, of course you are. You need to just let go. Oh my God, you're holding on to the past and it's keeping you from your future."

She slowly turns over another card.

"Okay, that's it. That is clearly it!"

Tanner hangs on her words. "What?"

"You have got to go to Boyton Canyon. Here . . ." She pulls out a pen from her purse and starts scribbling lines on a napkin. "You go down 89—we're on 89 if you didn't know—and you just turn right"—she draws it—"here. You'll know it because of the crystal shop on the corner. Then down and over and right and voilà!" She finishes the drawing by writing "Boyton Canyon" with little hearts where the o's should be.

Then, as if shaken from her trance, Emily looks at her phone, scoops all the cards back into her purse, kisses him on the forehead, and says "Namaste" before leaving in a cloud of patchouli scent. Tanner waves belatedly.

Stunned, he just sits there for a while, thinking of the "magical" vortexes Emily mentioned. On impulse, he hops back in his car and follows the lines on the napkin. To his surprise, they actually lead him right to Boyton Canyon.

There, a hiking trail leads from the parking lot into the foothills in front of him. Hills of giant red spires and rugged, steep cliffs crowd him on either side, commanding to be seen. Tanner, mesmerized by the giants, hikes for about two hours before stopping to rest. He then wanders off the bigger path onto a side trail.

He stops to wipe the sweat from his forehead and looks around for some shade. A shady nook carved into one of the cliffs grabs his attention. The cliff is steep, but he's a pretty good climber. Might be rough, but he can make it there. He starts up.

The red rock gets looser under his feet as the trail gets steeper and steeper. He climbs for a bit in a daze. Suddenly he stops in his tracks and looks down, realizing he's clinging to the cliff face with both hands, feet slipping, a scary distance above the gravel below. He's not sure how it happened, but he's stuck—it's undeniable.

Sweat beads his forehead and drips down onto his shirt. He's drenched, and now his sweaty palms make it hard to keep his grip. He's actually scared he might slip and fall to what could be some fairly bad injuries, or worse. Concern becomes outright fear in seconds. His grip tightens, and he's at a total loss for what to do next.

"Quite a predicament you've gotten into, young man," says an unexpected voice from somewhere below him. He looks down and sees an older man, over fifty for sure, at the bottom of the cliff. He has long, dark hair with braids and wears nothing but an old pair of tan shorts.

"Good thing I came along," the man below continues. "You could have a nasty fall if you're not careful!"

All Tanner can muster in response is: "Help?!"

"First thing we've gotta do," says the man, "is calm you down. Stabilize you. You've gotta forget everything and be right here. Right now." He pauses and Tanner struggles to keep his grip. "Breathe. Slowly. First one breath, then the next."

Tanner forces himself to take slow, intentional breaths.

"Okay, good. Now, slowly lift your right foot about six inches and put it on that ledge. That one there." Tanner follows his instructions.

"Good," says the man. "Now this is a little trickier. Swing your left foot all the way around to the ledge next to the right foot. You're going to face outward from the cliff. May be scary, but it's what needs to be done."

Tanner feels suddenly much younger than he is. "I ... I can't," he mutters.

"You can. And you will. Just take all those voices in your head—the one saying that you can't, the one insisting that you'll fall—take them all and make them listen to your gut. Your gut knows how to survive. Your gut knows what to do next."

"I'm ... I'm s-s-sc-scared," whispers Tanner.

"Let's put your mind on something else then," says the man below. "What do you do for a living?"

At this, Tanner's left foot slips completely. He slides down the cliff several feet, skinning the palms of his hands as he grasps for something to stop his fall. He's seconds from crashing to the gravel below when he barely catches hold of a protrusion. Tanner anchors himself to it, shaking and sweaty.

"Well, that wasn't the right question, obviously," says the man. "Don't think about work. Think about now. You. Here. On a cliff in Arizona. Hanging on with everything you've got. This is all that matters. Right here. Right now. Let go of the past."

Tanner closes his eyes and takes another deep breath. Then he braces himself and looks down. It takes a second to realize that his slip has put him only three or four feet above the older man.

He feels the laughter first in his gut, then it rises up into his chest and bellows out his mouth. It all seems so silly all of a sudden. All of the worry, all of the holding on. What is he so worried about? He positions himself, laughs some more, and lets go.

He slides right into the arms of the older man.

The man lifts an eyebrow. "Did I miss a good joke?"

"You've made my day!" Tanner says, taking a step back to look up at the cliff. "It was hairy there for a minute, but now I feel light as air." He pumps his fist and mouths a silent "yes."

"Well now, that's the spirit!"

Tanner is just happy to be alive and uninjured. To be out of danger and able to go back to any life feels like a blessing now.

He looks down at the LoveIT.com bracelet dangling at his wrist. He slips it off and hands it to the man. "I want you to have this. I don't need it anymore."

"Nonsense," says the man, waving off the gesture.

"No, you don't understand," Tanner says, "by giving you this I get rid of my past in a way. You'll be doing me a big favor."

The man takes the bracelet and offers a proud grin in return.

T anner watches the sunset as he drives back to the hotel, the sky as red as the hills on the horizon. He's mesmerized and pulls over to take it in, wishing CeCe was there to share it with him. Now that the cloud of emotion has lifted he realizes he could have treated her better. On impulse, he pushes speed dial on his phone, and she answers.

"Hey Ceese! I'm going to stay here another day or two, but I'll be coming home by the weekend. I wanted to let you know."

"You sound . . . different. Having a good time?"

"Magical. I'm ready to move forward with my life again, Ceese," Tanner responds with a certain sparkle. "I may just take a fire hose to my apartment when I get home."

"Save me some chips!" CeCe says. He can hear the smile in her voice.

The next morning, Tanner is awakened by the now familiar buzz. He opens his eyes to discover the alarm clock is still unplugged from yesterday. It's his cell phone buzzing on the nightstand with "Jay" on the caller ID. He decides to answer.

"Where have you been, dude?" Jay asks. "I've been trying to reach you for days!"

"What's up, my man?"

"We're crushing it!" Jay rambles on excitedly before Tanner can even ask a question. "Look, I don't care what you're doing with that company of yours, I need you over here with us! What can I do to convince you?"

"Well, anything's possible." Tanner tries to keep a grin off his face, but it's hard.

"You gotta do this!" Jay responds. "Can you come in today or tomorrow?"

"Well, no. Not exactly . . ."

"Man, don't play hard to get. I promise to make it worth your while. Don't say no. Just take a couple days, whatever. Think about it. But come in next week and let's talk!"

T anner dresses, checks out, and gets in his car. As he pulls out of the motel parking lot, he wonders where to go next. He looks at a thin tan line on his wrist where his bracelet once lay. He passes the coffee shop and the Psychic Eye and smiles about his encounter with Emily yesterday. She was right, after all. About everything, including Boyton Canyon.

He thinks about the old man in the canyon and how calm he was when Tanner panicked. His dad had been like that when Tanner broke his arm as a kid. It made him feel a little braver because the world wasn't as scary after all.

He listens to the voices in his head. One voice is dreaming of all the possibilities of this new job and thinking of CeCe. Another voice is wondering if he's good enough for it. Still another voice is afraid Jay might change his mind, and . . . and . . .

Then Tanner ignores the voices and puts his hand on his gut. *What is my gut saying?* he wonders. His heart calls for home and yet stays open for whatever adventure he might find along the way.

"Keep moving forward," Tanner says aloud to the open road ahead of him.

....

Jonathon Barbato is the Co-CEO of Best Ever Channels and is committed to making sure important stories find their audience. His themes generally revolve around the odd juxtaposition of spirituality and his roots in the entertainment industry. He was Head of Marketing at MGM TV and Starz Movie Channel, among other things, and currently lives happily ever after with his wife and two children in Los Angeles, CA.

MEGAN MCCORMACK

....

THE LEGEND OF THE WATER SEEKERS

L ong ago in the days of old, there was a little village in the middle of a vast desert. It was a journey of three days on camel to the next town, a journey of intense heat during the day and freezing winds at night, of sand blowing through the sun's rays and beneath the moon's glow. For centuries, the people of the village survived on the bounty of a sacred spring, but every year, the spring shrank slightly, until one year the villagers found that their spring was hardly more than a puddle.

Panic spread throughout the village, and so it was decided by the chief elders that the people should leave the land of their ancestors to search for water, stopping first in the neighboring town. But just as they had made this decision, an old woman with gnarled hands and a face full of wrinkles appeared in the village. She approached the elders and spoke to them.

"In my days I have learned to bring life to the desert," she said. "If your villagers come to my tent and tell me a story, I will give them water in return."

The chief elders were skeptical of how this could be, so they decided to test the old lady. The matriarch of the village, a regal woman who was the daughter of a blessed bard, volunteered to go to the old woman's tent. She told a story from her childhood, about the first time she had ever ridden a camel and how it had gotten lost in a sandstorm while she had clung fearfully to its back. When the matriarch emerged from the tent, she held a jug full of water in her hands. She recounted to the elders how, after she had told her story, the woman disappeared behind a curtain, made some strange noises, then came back with the full jug. The chief elders were amazed and still somewhat suspicious, but they agreed to see how the newcomer would fare under the demands of the entire village.

The villagers did not wish to leave the land of their ancestors, so they went willingly to the woman with their stories, returning with the water their families and crops needed. They did not concern themselves with the strange noises that came from the woman's tent nor with the growing lapses in their memories once their stories were told. The village continued on in this way, days turning to nights that turned back again to day while crops and children grew taller and stronger.

There was at this time a man who roamed the desert alone. He was known to the villagers as a wise man, yet he never stayed in the village long. No one knew why he came or where he went, but the matriarch always met with him when he arrived and before he left. So many years had passed since his last appearance that the matriarch could barely remember his last visit, yet when she saw his face, leathery from the sun, it was as if he had left only the day before. The old man stood grave in front of the matriarch.

"Your village has changed since I last rested here," he said. "The children grow, the past fades, water dries up, and new villagers come to settle. Villagers with magic and water." He paused, and the matriarch saw in his face an uneasiness she had never seen before. "There is a tale of an evil spirit who appears to those in the desert who need water but cannot find it. It is said that little by little the spirit empties the minds of its victims while filling their bellies with a poison only it knows how to create. This is done so that the spirit can remain immortal, for once an infected person dies, the spirit collects and feasts on its victim's soul." He paused again. "It is said to be a slow poison, one that can even take a lifetime to finish its work, for emptying the mind is a long process. But in the end, the spirit comes and collects the soul all the same. Yet not all stories are true. Perhaps this one is not. Some truths you must figure out for yourself."

The matriarch thanked the man for his wise words and invited him to rest from his travels, providing him with the small amount of water and food he always requested. To herself, she vowed to find the truth in the old man's words, for the sake of her village.

The moon shone brightly that night as she went to the tent to question the old woman. A sudden fear gripped the matriarch as she thought of the old man's tale, and she decided to walk around to the back of the old woman's tent. Through a small flap she saw the old woman at work.

A fire crackled without emitting smoke, and on a table lay a human figure, translucent like a ghost, and shimmering in the firelight. Where skin should have been, images instead flickered across the figure's surface. The matriarch realized that she recognized faces in the images, faces of several of the villagers, but these were their faces as they'd looked many moons ago.

A scene played out across the ghost-figure's body. Four children peeked inside a crowded tent, and the matriarch was startled to see her father's face appear among the people seated inside. As if from far away, she could hear faint, childish giggles and the familiar rumble of a low voice. She knew, somehow, that she was looking upon the story a villager had given up to the old woman. And the old woman, in her magic, had coaxed the story to take solid form.

The old woman picked up a knife, plunged it into the figure's chest, and twisted. The images of the memory swirled angrily, and the matriarch heard the childish giggles turn to sobs. Hefting the shimmering figure onto its side, the old woman set a jug on the ground beneath the table to catch the water spilling out from the wound. The story in human form groaned and groaned as the images began to seep out, turn clear, and trickle into the jug. The old woman paid the figure no heed. After all the images drained and the figure could hardly be seen on the table, she picked up the jug and disappeared to the front of the tent. Shortly after, a villager walked out with a jug of water.

And so it was that the matriarch learned the truth. The old woman emptied the mind by taking their stories, and she filled their bellies with the poison of dying tales.

The matriarch raced back to the village center and found the old man where she had left him with his eyes closed, resting. He was so still that for a moment she wondered if he was not human, but a rock that had been buried in the sand for thousands and thousands of years.

"I fear the old woman is as you say," she said, shaking him. To her relief, his skin was warm, his limbs pliable. "What can we do?"

The wise man opened his eyes. "It is said," he said, "that an evil spirit may be banished by mixing the blood of a camel calf with its mother's milk and sprinkling this mixture in a circle around the spirit's dwelling place. Then you must summon the spirit by name and declare it banished forever. Sit here, and I will speak its name to you."

And so the matriarch learned its name. The sun began to rise as she slaughtered the baby animal, its cries echoing through the still cool air. The matriarch willed a coldness about herself as well. If she wanted to save her village, sacrifices must be made.

She mixed the blood of a camel calf with the milk of its mother and sprinkled this mixture around the old woman's tent, and then she summoned the spirit by name.

And the old woman appeared in her true form, a spirit flickering between the human realm and that of the next, as the tent dissolved into smoke in the summoning ring.

"You thought to trick the people of my village and collect our souls," the matriarch said, "but I will not let that happen."

The evil spirit laughed. "It is too late for your village," it said, "for you have all been infected by me through the stories you delivered to my care. I will always have a part of you, and you will never be able find water without betraying any stories you have left. You will be cursed to give them up, even distort them, if you wish to live."

"Quiet!" the matriarch commanded with a shout. "You will lay no more curses on my people. I banish you from this place forever."

The evil spirit cackled. "You believed that old fool? How do you think he knows my name? Why do think he roams the desert? How many years has he come here, telling stories and then disappearing again? He has tried to rid himself of me so many times, but he is as infected as any of you."

The matriarch's head began to throb painfully, and her vision blurred as if she might faint.

Now when the matriarch had summoned the spirit, villagers had heard her shouts and emerged from their tents. After learning that the old woman was really an evil spirit, they began to whisper amongst themselves, creeping ever closer to where the spirit floated in front of the matriarch. But as they approached, they began to lose all sense of time. They found themselves gripped by hallucinations of pristine lands where water and food were always abundant and where they wanted for nothing. They heard voices that told them those places were real, that they could remain there forever if they desired, but only if they were willing to truly join the spirit.

Driven mad by desperation to live in their hallucinations, one by one the villagers killed themselves until only a dozen remained. The matriarch, in a haze, seemed to see both the horror in front of her and the alluring paradise. The voices beckoned her, but another voice whispered in her mind as well. *Some truths you must figure out for yourself.*

The matriarch screamed the evil spirit's name again, a cry so piercing that the spirit shuddered, and it once more took on the guise of an old woman. Though weakened by their delusions, the remaining dozen found a final strength to set themselves upon the spirit. They hacked her to pieces with their knives, flesh mingling with the camel milk and blood, and flung her remains far from the corpses of their fallen clan.

The matriarch and her dozen villagers wept and prayed and thirsted until the sun set. There were too many dead to bury, so they instead laid sand over the eyes of all those they had lost. Then the villagers packed up their remaining belongings and left. In the chaos, the old man had disappeared once more.

Shocked by what had happened and ashamed of how easily they had allowed an evil spirit into their lives, the villagers felt they could not burden their nearest neighbors, fearing they would spread this curse to every village they approached. And so at last they left the home of their ancestors.

It is said that the evil spirit lingers on the outskirts of that abandoned village to this day. Yet other tales tell that the spirit scattered, shattered in as many pieces as its earthly body was cut into and blown away by the wind in all directions, to islands and forests and villages on continents far away, reforming a hundred times over. And this is why stories still die, because the evil spirit continues its work wherever it lands.

The thirteen survivors wandered through the desert for many years. As time passed, they found it easier and easier to give up their stories, desperate to quench their unquenchable thirst. Some say that, even now, you can find a band of wanderers in the desert, asking for nothing but water in exchange for the tales they have to tell.

....

Megan McCormack graduated from the University of Notre Dame in 2017 with varying levels of mastery in English, creative writing, French, and art history. She recently moved from LA to New York in order to pursue her childhood dream of working in publishing. When not reading, she enjoys eating copious amounts of peanut butter and/or baked goods.

....

THE REPLACEMENT

S weating inside my pressure suit, I placed one last rock on the shallow grave. Then I laser-burned in the details: Julio Manuel Martinez, April 17, 2029–November 5, 2054.

He'd left my underground farm's pressure early to walk the power line and hadn't come back. I'd followed in the rover and found him dead five klicks west. He'd have found the valve leak if the fool had run his checklist.

And it had been the first nice day in three weeks. No dust, not a breath of wind. I'd been looking forward to finishing chores early and getting some sleep. Now I was stuck west of Valles Marineris, forty klicks past any other homestead, with just myself to work the farm and face the Martian spring dust storms. I had a quota to meet by autumn—two person-years each of oxygen and food. Without Julio I'd be lucky to stay alive.

It served me right. I'd gotten greedy and took a cheap new lag instead of hiring an experienced hand. *Stupid, Leticia. Is this how* Abuelito *taught you to run a business? No.* He'd always said, "Never hire anyone who won't respect you." He was so right.

Few prisoners survived a year on Mars. Lags who lived got a homestead once we'd served our time—but nothing else, *nada* except a bare pocket of rock and a connection to a small automated nuclear reactor that served fifty other farms. Most sold their claims back to the Consortium.

Not me. I'd worked my ass off and bought a full homestead kit. At least the Consortium started claims in fall so homesteaders had a chance.

No chance now. No money left. Too much work for one person.

Comm antennas had been disconnected for spring; storm static played hell with gear. At the farm I could connect an antenna and try a high-energy compressed burst—but unless I was dying, it would be a silly risk of my equipment. Only the distant Consortium security station would be listening, and might not hear it even so. No, I'd wait for the mail rover. With luck, I'd get a replacement for Martinez in a few weeks.

Otherwise, I could sell out like the other losers and go back to the mines.

Dammit, run your checklist and get home. Stand here feeling sorry for yourself and you're freeze-dried like Martinez. You won't live to sell out.

B ack in my rover, I rubbed my eyes and yawned. When was my last full night's sleep? Three days ago? I couldn't recall. I glanced at my displays and saw a blur to the southwest—another storm on its way. Northwest, a puffy trail meant a rover was coming. *What in hell?* There wasn't anything in that direction but rocks.

When I zoomed in, I saw a "pill"—a cheap prisoner transport shaped like a gel cap—hauling ass toward me. I didn't blame the driver. Pills had few reserves, and the duster had built fast. But it was twenty klicks away on the plateau leading to Olympus. Why was a pill out there?

As I watched, the pill disappeared. A puff of water vapor meant it'd lost pressure. My emergency beacon alert started blatting.

Oh, shit.

I had to check out the wreck. There would be salvage; there might be survivors. Besides, Consortium security would pull my rover's tapes and know I'd heard. If I didn't go, I'd be back in the mines faster than you could say "busted parole."

Dammit. I'm going to miss milking time. My poor goats!

While crawling up the plateau, I calculated. An hour there, a little more than an hour back, what with angling to catch the power line markers in case the storm caught me. I had plenty of battery—how about air?

The driver and guards might survive—Consortium personnel got quick-sealing suits. But the lags . . . screw-down faceplates took too long. Say three survivors, tops. I could put two in the cargo bay and scavenge some extra air bottles for them.

The popped pill sprawled on its right side in a shallow crater. From a small rise, I paused and followed its tracks from the northwest to a large boulder. The left track disappeared, the right swerved, then the debris trail led to the pill.

Damn. They must've been movin'.

I scanned the debris trail, but nothing registered as warm.

To mark a salvage claim, I had to visit the wreck anyway. I sighed and wiggled out the airlock.

The pill's vehicle plate showed it was sixteen standard years old, though I'd thought everything older than twelve years got recycled. The pill looked beat-up enough for sixteen years, though—it was all patches. *The Consortium's getting stingier.* I stuck my salvage beacon next the plate, then climbed into the cockpit. I counted three pressure suits. Thermal signatures were below freezing. The nearest faceplate was open. I didn't look close; I'd already seen the red-tinged frost on the walls. So much for driver and guards.

The lockdown door was open. *Huh?* Maybe the guards had tried to be nice and warn the lags to seal up.

The lockdown was a mess. I counted eleven suits, but pills were built for ten prisoners—why were they running heavy? The suits were patched and as old as the pill. *All new lags, then.* I saw two heat sources: the engine and one more in this compartment. I hurried to the possible survivor.

The small pressure suit was crumpled across two seats, with some white frost at one corner of its sun shield. When I flipped up the shield, I found a teenager—small, blonde, and unconscious. Her med readouts showed healthy, although her air pressure was down and decreasing. I screwed the faceplate knobs tighter, and the pressure stabilized.

She must have been tried as an adult and transported, poor kid. She was okay for now, so I checked the rest of the lockdown. I confirmed no more survivors, then carried her outside.

A glance south revealed a much bigger storm blur. *Dusters don't move that fast!* I dragged the girl through my airlock and into the spare seat. I ran a range to the duster edge—it wasn't moving faster than normal. *¡Gracias, Dios!* It was just so big it was like a moving mountain range. Creepy.

I started the rover on autopilot so I could I check the girl out. Air pressure was still steady, and her vitals were decent. Her ID pocket was empty. Figures. I opened her faceplate for the trip.

I'd salvage the wreck later. The girl might be coming off assignment, so I could hire her. With luck, she'd make up for losing Julio.

I could barely see the power line markers through the dust. The weather was so clear that morning that I'd pulled the rover's inertial guidance for maintenance and navigated on MGPS. Now I couldn't use inertial to get home, and MGPS wouldn't operate through the duster's static. *Well, that was stupid.* The dust got heavier, and I told the rover to anchor herself. While waiting for the storm to ease, I started filling out my rescue and salvage claim. Dust hissed against the hull, which shuddered as the gusts hit.

My passenger moaned, and her foot twitched.

"Hey, *chica.* I'm Leticia Montes. And you are . . . ?"

She tried to get up. "Where am I?"

"You're halfway between your crashed pill and my farm."

"You blew up the bus! You kidnapped me!" She started screaming.

I grabbed some patch tape from the breach kit and strapped her arms down before she could try anything. I ignored the screams and waited. When she calmed, I said, "Listen, *chica.* I'm a farmer, a lag like you. I saw your pill crash and came to help, but everyone else died. Now, you did good. You closed your plate like an old hand. But you got no ID. What's your name?"

She stuck her nose up. "I'm Lizzie *Chandler,* I'm not a *criminal,* and my ID is in my purse."

"Lizzie, lags don't have purses."

"You *stole* it, didn't you? I had five hundred nitrogen chits! My dad will call the FBI! He'll *sue!* You—"

Well, she was feisty enough. Delusional, too. Kidnapping!— as if anyone would bother. More money in her purse than a prisoner earns in Consortium scrip in a year! When I came out of suspension, I thought I'd been captured by Nazis. I even hallucinated the coal-scuttle helmets. It recurred for weeks.

I closed her plate again, got some sleepy gas while she screamed and struggled, attached it to her suit med port, and pushed the valve. Quiet arrived. I typed her name into the claim.

Damn. I hoped the storm would blow out so I could get home before she woke up again.

I thought we'd roll to my farm in a bit over an hour. Instead, it took five. When the dust wasn't so bad, we crawled along because I could barely see thirty meters to the next marker. When it picked up, I anchored, wrote my report, managed air bottles, and checked Lizzie's vitals. I didn't dare fall asleep or I'd miss a break in the dust. When I saw the tunnel to my airlock with the RANCHO ALEGRE sign next to it, I could've kissed it.

First things first. I carried Lizzie in, put her on Julio's old bunk, and gave her another dose of sleepy gas. Getting her out of her suit was going to hurt.

Besides, I didn't want to deal with hysterics again.

It took half an hour to free her from the ancient suit, but it turned out she was in decent shape. Lots of bruises, a swollen wrist, but nothing broken. I taped her wrist, put a cold pack on it, set a timer, and hurried off.

Two hours later, I'd started dinner, milked the goats—that took a while because the poor things were sore—checked the chickens and the crop chambers, hooked the rover to the power station, and set air tanks to refill. I also changed the cold pack on Lizzie's wrist twice, letting her skin warm up in between.

There was plenty of work left, but I heard movement from Julio's old room and stepped in. Lizzie had pulled herself up on one elbow and was looking around with a puzzled expression.

"Hey, *chica*." I kept my voice soothing. "How you doing?"

"I'm sorry. I don't remember your name."

"Leticia Montes."

"Are you a doctor?"

"Nah. But I got a medic cert."

"I'm Lizzie Chandler. But I think I told you that." She paused a moment. "Where are we?"

"My farm. *Bienvenido al Rancho Alegre, señorita.* Supper's cooking. I noticed that no one else in the pill closed their face-plate. What's up with that?"

"I heard a recorded message that said we should close our faceplates as a precaution, but the guide didn't bother to close his. I guess no one took it seriously."

"No one but you," I said, grinning at her.

She gave me a little smile and settled back.

"... and I'm going to a new school anyway, so when Daddy invites me I go, 'Why not?' ... You're not listening."

Sleepiness was making my eyes water. I rubbed them and said, "I heard you. Your mom pulled you out of school. You don't like her new boyfriend. Your daddy's a bigwig starting a new rover factory here, and he invited you for a vacation." I yawned. "Have some flan."

She scooped some onto her plate. "You don't believe me," she pouted between delicate little spoonfuls.

A vacation? To a prison colony? *A four-year round trip?* "I believe you about the boyfriend and getting pulled out of school." I took a bigger scoop of flan and shoveled it into my mouth. I still had chores waiting. Around the custard I said, "Hey, it's one of the better suspension delusions I've heard." I washed the flan down with cold tea.

"Why don't you *believe* me? Just call Daddy." The whine in her voice put my teeth on edge.

"Nobody's calling anyone. Comm is down until summer. No voice, no internet, *nada*. Besides, you know how to tell if a new lag is lying?"

"Um . . . no?"

"Her mouth's moving. You wash up."

"What?"

"Wash up. Do the dishes."

"Why should *I* wash dishes? You don't even have a *dish-washer* At home, Conchita did that."

"Oo-o-oh. 'Conchita did that.' Listen up, *chica*. This is my farm. My only hired hand just died. You're eating my food, breathing my oxygen. You damn well work."

"My dad will *pay* you to get me back to High Tarawa. More than this *stinking* farm is worth."

I lost it. "This farm don't stink. I build it! Me, Leticia Teresa Montes! I work two jobs besides my prison job, buy my home-stead kit! Already produce more than quota in just two years. People depend on *me* for their food, their air! *¡Caramba, loca!*"

Deep breaths, Leticia. "Now, look. I . . . I send my report with the next mail rover. I'll ask for a new hand, and the Consortium may assign you here." She might drive me nuts, but it'd save them money and I'd make my quota. "You'll get better wages than the mines."

"I'm not a criminal!"

She started sniffling. *Jesus. Here come the tears.*

"If your story's true, *chica*, when the Consortium sees your name, you'll go home with the next rover. We'll both be happy. Now get in there and wash dishes."

Lizzie burst into tears right on cue, ran back to her room, slammed the door, and rammed the bolt home.

Madre de Dios, *don't let me break her stupid skull.* "You don't want to work, fine!" I yelled. "But you don't work, you don't eat, crazy lag."

"You *bitch!*" She sobbed loud enough for me to hear through the door—on purpose. I shook my head and stomped off to do the chores before I fell over from exhaustion.

I started mucking out the milking pens, shoveling harder than I needed to. *Dammit, she's just like Ronnie.*

Veronica was my baby sister. Eight years younger than me, she'd never acted older than two. She'd act cute, she'd act charming, and if that didn't work, she'd pout and cry. She'd gotten her way—from *Mami*, from *Papi*, and from me.

I'd been home on leave from the Marines. She wanted me to pick up her gangbanger boyfriend in Torrance. I thought it was a bad idea—no telling what Tony was carrying. She whined, she cried, then *Mami* and *Papi* started in on how little it would cost me, don't you care about your sister, blah blah blah.

Long story short, I caved and picked him up—from committing a bank robbery. One of the bank guards died of his wounds. So I was convicted as an accessory, discharged from the Marines, and sent to Chino on a murder one conviction.

Ronnie had the gall to visit me in jail afterwards and blame me for her *boyfriend* being jailed.

The lights flickered as I dumped the last of the goat crap into the composter and slammed the lid. *Dios.* The flickering was why I'd sent Julio out to check the power line. In the chaos after, I'd forgotten.

I checked the status in the control room. The reactor power voltage was fluctuating near 75% of normal, as it had been this morning. The problem wasn't the reactor, though. If a meteorite big enough to take out a hardened reactor had hit, I'd already be dead. So the problem was with my connection.

The solar cells hadn't been producing well—not enough light coming through with all the storms. At least my emergency batteries were full.

I was too tired to think straight. The storm would die in a couple days. Then my solar cells would produce full power and I could go fix the main connection.

The dishes still needed washing and I had to put the day's milk in the dehydrator. It was just past midnight. I folded my arms and put my head down on the nice warm battery case, just for a minute . . .

The power alarm's shrieks startled me awake. *Jesus.*

Only the emergency lights were on. The readouts showed no power from the reactor and no systems except human life support. I glanced at the clock.

0207. Dammit. Two hours gone.

226

I switched the alarm off and turned systems to the "solar-only" setting. The lights came back. Then I ran and pounded on Lizzie's door.

"Lizzie! We've lost power! I need help with the livestock!"

"Too damn bad! I hate you!" she screamed. More sobs floated through the door.

"Lizzie! It's your neck, too!"

"Some emergency! The lights are back on already. Eat shit and die!"

Why bother to force the door? With her attitude, I'd get more help from the chickens.

I'd managed to move the goats to a spare compartment. Then I ran around chasing chickens in their increasingly cold and stuffy pasture. What in hell was I going to feed them?

The remains of your freeze-dried crops, that's what.

I got two of the chickens into crates and was carrying them to join the goats when the power alarm went off yet again. I dashed to the control room with the panicked chickens still in my arms.

How can Lizzie ignore this?

I killed the siren and strobe again. The solar panels' readout was blinking red—it was an hour after sunrise, and the panels weren't producing power. Not a single nano-erg. I checked my outside cameras—totally black.

Madre de Dios. No light at all meant a continent-size storm, maybe planetary. If absolutely no solar energy was reaching the surface, there would be at least a week of darkness. My batteries would run down. We'd freeze in six days without grid power.

What the hell could I do? I couldn't go out in the storm—I'd get lost. Reflective stakes marked the power line, but only at thirty-meter intervals. In my suit, without MGPS or inertial guidance, I'd never find the first one. From the rover, I'd never spot the break, not with heavy dust and static interference.

A soft chime on the alert system made me check my readouts. My livestock panel was flashing orange. I stopped the chime and started turning off all stock alarms—after all, the animals were in the house—when I saw the error message.

Oh, no. No, no, no. It was my egg incubator temperature warning. It had lost power with the rest of the livestock areas. I'd just bought it last month—it wasn't on my emergency check-list. And I had chicks due to hatch any day. They were probably already dead.

I sat down on my tatty chair and cried. *Madre de Dios, please, I need help. I'm too tired. I'm making stupid decisions. And my only possible helper has tantrums like a two-year-old . . . Just like Ronnie.*

I hate whiners. I hate spoiled brats. And here I am babysitting another one, who'll help me when Hell freezes over. What am I going to do?

I heard the sound of breaking glass and a scream of pain from the kitchen. *Dios mío.* I ran through the tunnels.

In the kitchen, Lizzie was still screaming. Her left hand was mottled red, a plate was in pieces on the floor, and steam was rising from the sink. I got ice water and stuck her hand in it. "There, *mi hija.* It's going to be fine. Calm down, we'll get it taken care of. I can handle a scald easy, no problem . . ."

What kind of idiot doesn't know how to wash dishes without getting scalded?

The kind who's never done more than start a shower with a safety valve, that's what. Madre de Dios. *She really is a rich kid.*

It fit. The pill hadn't been a Consortium transport but a tour. The Consortium had contracted it out, and the contractors had run it as cheap as possible. They'd even run one junked pill overloaded instead of buying two junked pills. Hell, Lizzie's purse with its five Cs was probably still aboard. Like my sister, she was a spoiled brat who got her way by whining and having tantrums when she couldn't buy her way out.

Unlike Ronnie, she wasn't hopeless. She'd had the sense to close her faceplate. She'd tried to do the dishes.

I needed to start teaching her teamwork. Fast.

There now, *amiga*. You won't blister," I said as I finished her bandage. I took a deep breath. "I'm sorry. Look, I believe you about your family and the money."

"Thanks." She looked away. "I'm sorry, too. I should've washed the dishes." She paused. "When the lights stayed out, I decided you were right. But I guess I suck at washing dishes."

"That's okay. We got bigger troubles, *amiga*. I need ideas."

I quickly told her all of it. As I sat down at the table, she said, "Wait. You left the chickies to *freeze?* Where are they?"

I told her, and added "But they're already dead." She rushed off anyway. I put my head down—just a minute . . .

I jerked awake when she came back. "I got the incubator running in the control room."

My mouth dropped open. "You know how to run an incubator?"

"Chicks were a school project. Anyway, I took out five dead eggs, but the rest are okay. Three have hatched and need food."

"Let's feed them after we figure out how to stay alive." I gulped cold tea and started scrambling eggs. "Any clues? I got *nada*."

"Ms. Montes, if we found the break, how would you fix it?"

"Call me Tici." I toasted two tortillas, then sipped more tea while thinking. "I'd have to use the portable clean chamber."

"What's that?"

"A clear box with gloves sticking in, a filter on one end and a vacuum pump on the other. You clean the air inside by running the vacuum. It would be a pain in the ass, with all the dust."

"Right. You said the power line's underground?"

"Shallow trench, not well-hardened."

"Can you feel the edge of the trench?"

"If it's not under too much dust, yeah."

"What about . . . no, I guess not."

"What? Tell me, *amiga*."

"Well, trying to get through the dust . . . it sounds like rock climbing, only horizontal, you know? But we'd need climbing equipment."

"You know rock climbing?"

"Well, yes," she said, like it was obvious.

"I have climbing equipment." It was in my homestead kit, in the back of the emergency container. I couldn't figure out why they'd included it until now. "Maybe we can make this work."

The plan was simple. After rolling fifteen minutes to Julio's grave, Lizzie would go outside, tethered by her climbing rope and a hard-wired comm line. She'd have to crawl—the dust was less dense near the surface—so that a flashlight would let her see about a meter ahead. Every time she got to a marker, I'd let the rover move up slow, walking outside to unclip the carabiners like she'd shown me.

At least we'd both gotten some sleep before we left. Still, the rover only had five hours of air for two, and all our air bottles combined had about four hours—two each. We'd spare the air bottles by keeping me in the rover. If the operation turned bad and we had to walk back, it might be tight.

"So seriously. Why'd you come to Mars?" I asked.

"Mom married Frankie the Boyfriend. Dad cut off alimony after she did, so she pulled me out of boarding school. Frankie kept hitting on me. Mom didn't believe me. Meanwhile, Dad offered to take custody. I said yes." She shrugged. "But he got married while I was in transit."

"And your stepmom doesn't like you?"

"Hell no. She's only five years older than me. She wants me to go back."

"Your dad's rover business must be booming. Must be expensive to bring you here."

"He's doing okay, I guess. He's too busy to talk much."

"And Evil Stepmom is jealous of the time he spends with you."

She nodded. "I wish I hadn't come. But I can't go back with Frankie."

"Well, that sucks. But . . . you're sixteen, right?"

"So?"

"So if you have a job, you can ask to be declared adult. And, I know it's not what you're used to, but I sure could use someone who's good with chickens . . . well, if we don't die out here."

"Wow, I dunno. I like chickens . . ."

"And of course, you'd get wages. Your own money with no strings." A chime and a blinking panel got my attention. "We're coming up on Julio's grave," I said. "Your time to shine, *amiga.*"

I t's weird out here. There are sparks every time I drive a piton."

"Careful then, *amiga.* Keep your flashlight well away."

According to plan, I followed her in the rover, occasionally getting out to free up her lines. We crawled on for what seemed like forever but was only an hour. I was waiting for Lizzie to tell me she'd reached another marker when I heard some really loud static, followed by a scream.

"Lizzie? Are you okay? Lizzie?"

"It's not *fair!*"

I breathed—if she could complain, she wasn't dead.

She went on, "I just put down the stupid flashlight, and a spark took it out! I can't see anything! We're gonna *die* out here!"

"Lizzie, we don't have time for this."

"What, we don't have time to die? We worked so damn hard. It's not *fair!*"

Yelling at her wouldn't help, but soothing wouldn't either. I had to get her back on task.

"You're right. It's not fair," I said in a matter-of-fact voice. "You nearly died in a wreck, a crazy farmer wouldn't drive you home and forced you to do dishes, and now your flashlight's dead." I heard nothing, so I continued.

"I offered you a job. I think you're worth more than a new lag. I'd rather have you than a hand I don't know. I want you to survive. Breathe, Marine. What do you need?"

Silence. Then, "I need to see."

"Let me dig around. I don't have another flashlight that strong, but I have some spares."

I crawled out with the spares, hooked myself into the comm line, and had a look around. "*Amiga*, you need to be careful. Back up. The spark that melted your flashlight came from the raw power line end." A tiny meteorite had struck and left a crater a half-meter across. It cut a third of the way through my power line. The cable had melted the rest of way.

"Holy crap! That was close."

"*Verdad*. You see it, there?" I pointed with the spare flash.

"Yeah."

"You set up these lights to shine on it—real careful. I'll go back and get the tools."

It was my turn. After we'd shoveled out the trench, I deployed the clean chamber, loaded in the tools and parts I'd need, and started it running to filter out the dust.

"You called me 'Marine.' Were you a Marine?"

I bit my lip. " 'Once upon a time, in a galaxy far, far away.' "

She laughed. "Do you think I can learn goats?"

"Sure. Goats are easier than chickens."

"I accept your offer, Ms. Montes."

"Welcome to the firm, Ms. Chandler."

The telltale on the clean chamber finally turned green. I stuck my hands into its built-in gloves and picked up my tools. "Come on," I said. "Stick your hands in those other gloves. I can't do this by myself. Let's fix this mother and go home."

....

S. F. Lakin is a former aerospace and software engineer whose work has varied from teaching to medical data mining to development of rocket ships and ray guns. Really. Ms. Lakin is excited to be publishing fiction, a lifelong dream while figuring out why rocket engine parts break, dealing with students, and troubleshooting apps. She lives in Tarzana, California. Please look for her other work at http://sflakin.com/books.

JENNIFER ROBERTSON

....

THE NIGHT HAS EYES AND TEETH

The townsfolk spoke in whispers of the thing that slept deep in the forest to the north, snippets carried on the wind and gone before young ears could hear more. To the children of the town, the creature was like looking through shattered glass, fractured and incomprehensible—a thing of many eyes, or many arms and legs, or many mouths, or all of them combined into one great, horrible beast. With its eyes, the monster spied through children's windows and selected its prey. With its arms, it plucked them from their beds, and with its legs, it chased down those few who ran away. And with its mouths, it gorged on each stolen child without fail.

Candice Clearwater had grown up with the creature's fragmented image lurking in the corners of her mind and haunting her dreams. Countless nights she'd fallen asleep staring at the bricked-up window in her bedroom. Years before, the monster had snatched her older brother through that very window. She'd been just five years old then, and Adam's face was now a great blur, a sketch with the barest hint of features. Sometimes if she focused hard enough, she caught a soft

"Candy" on the wind or the whisper of a warm hand rustling through her curly black locks.

She did, however, remember with perfect clarity the change in her parents after Adam's disappearance. They lived in fear, and they never spoke to her of him. All signs of him were locked away until he was no more than a ghost inhabiting their home. Without the few conversations she had overheard during visits from her concerned aunt, she might not have remembered his name. Candice sometimes felt like she was nothing but a shadow of someone long gone.

The week after she turned fourteen years old, older than her brother had ever been, a boy on the other side of the forest went missing. She had never met Seth Haverford before, but she had heard about him from her younger cousins, Rachel and Jonah. Although he was a year older, he would follow them with big doe eyes and no questions wherever they went when he visited their cottage. And now he was dead.

No one would do anything about the disappearance, she knew, except bring the children inside earlier and hold pointless meetings where everyone talked and talked and never did anything. Though the creature only woke from its sleep for a single week once every three years, a hunting party had never been sent out, not even while the beast slumbered. Candice knew it was time to do something before any more children met the same fate. She would find the monster, and she would slay it herself.

When her parents fell asleep that night, Candice snuck out into the darkness without stopping to change out of her night-gown and slippers for fear of getting caught. She paused only to grab a knife from the kitchen before making her way to the forest.

The woods sprawled around her, and the trees were so tall that she couldn't see past them to the open sky. What little moonlight pushed through the canopy turned the world a muted gray. There came a sound from afar, a scream or a howl, it was impossible to tell. The cry struck her deep, paralyzing her by the entrance to the monster's wood. She wanted to turn back. But in the next few days, any one of her friends—perhaps even she, herself—would be lost to the gaping maw of the monster forever, another ghost to haunt the woods. So she ignored the cry—and those that came after, mocking her—and carried on, marking her path by carving arrows into tree trunks with her knife.

The farther Candice walked, the colder it grew. The gnarled tree trunks did nothing to keep the breeze from whispering through the woods and cutting through her thin nightgown. On she went as the chill settled deeper into her bones. It wasn't long before all she could feel were the knife clutched in her hand and the uneven terrain beneath her feet.

Although the world around her remained the same, shadowed gray, Candice knew she must have been traveling for hours. She continued in as straight a line as she could, never coming across one of her path markings, and still the trees extended forever. Soon enough, the girl lost all sense of direction except forward. She nearly gave up and turned back, wondering if perhaps fifteen would be the right age to hunt monsters and not fourteen, but something caught her attention. The lack of something.

The forest had grown quiet. The chirping of the birds gone, the rustle of rodents in the bushes frightened still, and even the cries which had followed her from the entrance died. Candice fell silent too, her breath catching in her throat as she listened to nothing. The only sound was the brittle *shh shh* as the girl's feet trod upon the autumn leaves. Then the sniffling of muted sobs started. Gripping her knife tighter, she moved closer.

At the base of a tree sat a boy, his face buried in his knees as he cried. Candice kicked a stone—flat and brown and large enough to skip across the packed earth with heavy thumps—to get his attention. "What are you doing here?" she asked. "The woods aren't safe, especially not now."

The boy lifted his head, and big green eyes stared out from his blotchy face. He looked a few years younger than her, with tears and snot running down in pitiable streaks. "It grabbed me out of my bed and nearly ate me in its den," he said between gasping breaths. "I ran away when its back was turned, but I couldn't find my way home."

"You're Seth Haverford," Candice breathed.

He nodded.

"I'm so glad you're safe! I'm Candice Clearwater. My cousins have told me so much about you."

"Why are you out here? Aren't you afraid it'll eat you?"

"I went looking for you," she said. The young boy's gaze turned to the large knife in her hand. "And I'm here to make sure no one else goes missing."

"What if you go missing?" Seth asked.

"You made it out alive, didn't you?"

"It was luck. But you're going after it with only a knife as protection."

"Then I hope luck's on my side, too."

"You don't know what it's like. I saw it!" He shuddered, his whole body shaking with the motion. "You don't stand a chance."

Candice dropped to her knees before him. "What did it look like?"

"It was terrifying."

"Does it look like they say?" At the other child's hesitant look, she elaborated, "Uncountable heads and arms and mouths and everything else."

"I only saw three heads," the boy said, slowly, "but the arms . . . too many to count."

"Can you tell me where to find it?"

The boy's eyes widened. "You're going to fight the monster all alone?"

"This is my only chance before someone else is taken. If I don't go now, that death is on my hands."

Seth stared at her, long and hard. "I'm going with you," he said, at last.

Candice frowned at him. "You should go home. I've been carving arrows into the trees as I go. If you follow them, they'll lead you into town."

He shook his head. "I got away," he said, "but the next kid might not be so lucky."

She took in his shaking shoulders and ashen face. Tears still streamed down his cheeks, but they didn't cut through the building determination in his bright gaze. There was no convincing him. "Okay," she said at last, voice soft. "Let's go."

I don't think I've ever met anyone who lived farther than my aunt, and even she only comes once every few weeks," Candice mused as she stopped to etch another mark on a trunk. The trees had once more blurred into one another until they all appeared the same in the unnatural quiet.

"There's not a lot of us on the northern edge anymore, and it's a long way to town," the boy said. His sniffling had ceased, but he still carried the solemn hush of one who had cried himself hoarse. "There used to be a village up there, but most people moved away years ago. They knew better than to stay."

This rang familiar to Candice. There were no more than a few dozen families left back home. Only those who were too stubborn—or, in the case of the Clearwater family, too broken—stayed.

"All Mother does is stay," Seth continued. "She doesn't like leaving the house for too long, even for supplies. We make do with what we can, and your aunt's a great help." His eyes widened. "This is the furthest south I've ever been."

Candice didn't know what to say. The two fell silent. They continued that way, subdued and as quiet as the forest around them.

They hadn't gone much farther when she spotted a large, flattened stone, smoothed into a neat rectangle. She was almost certain that it was the same one she had kicked toward Seth when they first met. On a hunch, she decided to test her idea without worrying her companion.

She clutched at her side and grimaced. "Let me rest for a second," she said, laboring her breath. "I've been walking for hours." Seth look at her, concerned. "Don't worry, I'm not giving up that easily."

He nodded.

Candice made her way over to the tree nearest the stone, but instead of engraving her mark as she normally would have, she rested against it in feigned exhaustion. She kept quiet about her suspicions, hoping to prevent whatever might be watching from knowing she had noticed anything. She wondered if it was right not to let Seth know.

The girl toed the stone over with a dirty slipper, rolling it back and forth as she examined her companion. His cheeks and the rims of his eyes still bore the faintest red tinge from his earlier crying fit, but he otherwise appeared fine. The earlier distress had left him, and strength had taken its place. He seemed comfortable with the forest, almost as if he didn't have to worry about tripping like Candice so often had. He seemed confident now—perhaps overconfident—something she didn't remember from Rachel and Jonah's stories about him. Would telling him her doubts break through that calm veneer?

"Ready to go?" he asked. His green eyes bored into her with a look almost like hunger. She shivered and pretended it was from the ever-present cold. Was he really so sure they could defeat the monster?

"Yeah, I'm feeling better now." She kept her gaze away from the brown stone now resting against muddied bark.

The gray of the forest made it impossible to know how long they had been walking, but it couldn't hide the brown rectangular stone resting at the base of a tree, staring out in warning. Candice turned to Seth, but he hadn't noticed, continuing forward with assurance. He looked more relaxed with every step, the tears and snot long-dried and his voice stronger than ever. His ease had grown increasingly more unsettling to her, even as they circled back for the third time to the same place they had first met. Where was the meek boy her cousins had told her about?

"How much farther is it? Are we getting close?" She struggled to keep her voice calm as the knife handle dug into the sensitive meat of her palm.

"Oh yes, it's not far now." There was no fear or doubt in that voice. "This all looks familiar."

"How do we know it will still be there?"

"Hmm?"

"The monster," she said. "It's been hours now, almost the whole night. How do we know it will be where you saw it?"

"I was taken to the creature's den," he said. "His home."

Candice paused. The boy said *his home* as if the creature was anything other than a monster. Seth hadn't once faltered in his steps, navigating the dimly lit forest as if he knew it by heart, yet the stone's reappearance proved they were going in circles. She still hadn't heard a single creature since they met, but the hair on the back of her neck rose as if something dangerous was watching her, waiting for her to grow tired and weak. The only eyes she met were Seth's—so green and calm and hungry.

She resumed her earlier pace, falling a step behind as she steeled her nerves. One last test to stay her doubt once and for all. "You know, if we get out of this alive, Elijah and Rebecca will be so excited to see you again. The twins don't really know what happened—they're too isolated from the town's gossip to have heard much—but they know *something* happened."

"Well, I can't wait to see them too—"

Candice stabbed him in the back before he could react. The blade, long and serrated, stuck through to the other side of his body. Blood glistened its way down to pool at their feet. "My cousins' names are Rachel and Jonah."

The boy looked at her in shock. In betrayal. Her heart pounded as it hit her that she might have been wrong. But then he smiled, his teeth sharp and slick with black ooze. "Clever, clever. At last, the act is over for us both." His hands reached up to his stomach, coated in the same oily black. Curious fingers explored the tear spilling him open. "Just in time. I had begun to grow bored of this game."

Seth's body began to change before her eyes. His skin and bones shifted as his face split in two, then in three, and his limbs stretched and multiplied into grotesque hybrids caught somewhere between arms and tentacles, an unholy mix of muscle and bone and rubber. The child's body elongated until it was far taller than her father. Countless glowing eyes stared down at her in vicious amusement. Gone were the round cheeks and flaxen hair, replaced by three waxen approximations of faces which had melted in the missing sun. The carving knife slipped from the monster's form as the meat around it slithered into its new shape. The description he'd given as the boy imposter had been right: the monster was terrifying.

Candice dove for the knife at its feet, and the creature laughed. Her hand shook as she pointed it at the rising heads of the monster before her.

"The real Seth made it almost too easy. He never even tried to flee. His legs froze on the spot as if he'd forgotten how to use them. Nothing like your brother," the thing said. "He ran. I liked it. Made the blood flow faster and the meat juicier." It licked its six sets of drooling lips, the number growing as Candice watched. "I wonder if you'll be the same."

A tentacle shot out at her, but Candice saw it coming and jumped away, ducking behind a tree. There was a crash, and the trunk trembled from the blow. The tentacle reached out around her sanctuary, and Candice took her chance. She swung her arm up, and the knife cleaved through the tentacle in one clean motion. As the remaining tendril writhed, the girl ran from her spot to another tree. The monster was too busy wailing to notice. The screeches pouring from its mouths echoed around them and beat into her head.

"That wasn't very nice of you!" the creature hissed out. "Why don't you stop hiding so you can apologize to me, face to face?" Another bang came from where she had just vacated, and there was a belated thud as a branch plunged to the ground.

Candice ran to the next tree over. Perhaps she could attack the monster from behind. She peered around her perch and stumbled back as a tentacle came too close for comfort. A stick cracked beneath her feet, the sound cutting through the angry cries. All three heads snapped in her direction, their green eyes gleaming at her in hunger and hatred. She froze.

The tentacle rushed forward, encircling her unmoving body and jerking her toward gaping, salivating mouths. Desperate, she slammed her blade into the thick meat holding her captive. Its grip weakened, so she stabbed again. And again and again. Tears trembled down her cheeks, but she didn't stop until her knife's work was done and another limb dropped to the forest floor.

The monster howled. She looked up at the beast and noticed a jagged scar, puckered and painful-looking, on the chest directly below the middlemost head. Candice knew she had found her target. A stubby, bloodied tentacle flew at her and flung her back into one of the trees. Even as her head smacked against the ground, hope bloomed in her cold-numbed chest. She grabbed the knife from where it had landed and brandished it in front of her, chin held high.

"That's enough! No more playing with my food," the three heads bellowed in unison. The leftmost attacked, its green eyes promising violence as its jaw unhinged wide enough to swallow her whole. Candice's eyes squeezed shut—she couldn't help it—but her weapon stayed, unwavering as she swung wide. Fanged teeth grazed the shoulder of her nightgown, and something warm spattered against her face. Nothing more. She opened her eyes to see the head rear back, two of its eyes slashed through and weeping black ichor onto the dead leaves and packed earth at their feet.

The monster struck again, but it was slower this time, more hesitant . . . afraid? Candice's determination grew as she ducked. The rightmost face slammed into the tree behind her, and the girl stabbed upward, lodging the serrated blade into the throat bared above her. The head gurgled and withdrew, heavy and barely conscious, to join the others. With one head half-blind and another choking on its own blood, the monster was a shivering shadow of the towering beast it had been. The tired, bruised girl struck a final blow and the creature fell beneath her. Her knife pressed below its heads, halfway submerged into knotted scar tissue. It tried to buck her off, but her weight was too much for it to dislodge.

With the last of its energy, the monster changed again, taking the form of a different boy—one around Candice's age with her same curly black hair and almond eyes. "Candy, please don't do this! It's me! It's Adam! Have mercy on your poor brother."

Candice hesitated.

"You remember my brother better than I do," she said, the truthful words bitter on her tongue. "If you hadn't said so, I'd never have known." She plunged her knife deeper into the creature's chest, embedding it between his ribs. With a shriek, the monster transformed back, her brother's face once more lost to her forever. The body jerked under her hand as she jammed the knife in deeper. There was a gasp and a word she didn't catch, but she didn't much care what the monster had to say. She let go of the blade, and the body dropped to the ground with a muted thud. It didn't move.

All at once, the sounds of the forest returned. Birdsong whistled all around in burgeoning triumph. Animals rustled through the brush and called to one another that it was safe to return to their homes. And all too loudly, the girl heard the labored huffs of her breath as she struggled—and failed—not to collapse to the floor and cry.

When her tears had run their course, Candice gave one final glance at the form laying crumpled at her feet, its faces staring wide-eyed up into the endless black of the canopy, before leaving it and her knife behind. She followed her arrow markings mile after mile until there was a break in the unchanging gray. Early morning sunlight shone down and broke through the deep chill that had settled inside her the moment she'd stepped into the forest.

Covered in bruises and stained in blood and ichor, she trudged forward until she caught sight of her family's cottage at last. She broke into a run, a wide smile across her face. It was a smile untouched by fear, one she had never allowed herself since her brother's death. Adam's ghost was finally free, and so was she.

....

Jennifer Robertson grew up on scary stories and Scooby-Doo and is an ardent fan of monsters and the macabre. She recently received her BA in English Literature & Writing from the University of California, San Diego, where she served as an editor and regular contributor to the bi-weekly student publication *Revellations*. In her free time, she writes about the supernatural and tries to figure out how her sewing machine works.

....

THE OBSOLESCENCE OF MEMORY

First Instar*

T he doppler ping of her self-sustaining capsule was first close by, then distant, then silent. Milja bobbed on an ocean of hands. When the sickening movement stopped, her head continued for a while. Eventually, her eyes cracked open and a slate-blue world swam into view. She found herself in a steamy room, on a spongy mat on a yellow floor. Warm, astringent water rained over her skin, melting away the funk that had crusted between her skin and the null-gee suit during the year of speed-cap transit. A medic gently shaving off her matted hair unintentionally nicked the thick scar on her scalp. Milja gasped.

"Apologies," the woman said. "How did you get such a long scar?"

---

* Instar *n*. A postembryonic stage of development between molts that an insect undergoes before it reaches maturity. From Latin *instar*, likeness, resemblance

"Don't know," Milja murmured. An urgent thought levered the weight of exhaustion. "How is Yee?"

The medic leaned down and said softly, "We are so sorry. Lead Exobiologist Celia Yee did not survive transport. You will lead the investigation of our potential biome."

The fear that had weighed in Milja's chest expanded, broke, and flowed out of her eyes.

"You could stay." Milja hung her head, unable to face her teacher. Dark hair curtained her expression.

"If I didn't want to go, I'd refuse," Yee said. "But I do."

"How can you be confident that—"

"I'm not. I know my chances. If I survive speed-cap, Vesper is where I want to spend my autumn years."

She swallowed salt and mucus. She understood her mentor's choice, but couldn't accept it. They had come to Vesper to discover the possibility of life; instead, it had taken hers. Milja vomited and fell back into unconsciousness.

Second Instar

The heavier gravity of Vesper protracted Milja's acclimation to the planet. She wished she'd paid more attention to her mother's work helping newcomers to the lower-grav orbiter adjust to the new forces in their environment, but they hadn't been close since they left their home planet, Rhea. After two weeks in the denser air of the controlled environment of the habitat, Milja was able to resume normal activity, and the medic cleared her to prepare for the enterprise ahead, with the caveat that her breathing might remain labored for another

week. But the heaviness in her chest was more than environmental.

Over those restless days reconfiguring the work for a single
explorer, Milja felt her grief moldering in the vacuum of Vesper's
yellow habitat. She could ping her mother back on the orbiter,
but *Umma* was irritated by Milja's emotional need to reach out,
especially to *Iskä*, who hadn't replied to his daughter once in
thirteen years. She had expected to celebrate her mentor at
home, among friends on the orbiter years from now, but no one
on Vesper knew her. And no doubt Yee's colleagues on the
orbiter had held their own memorial for the field's matriarch,
honoring her legacy with anecdotes of her achievements and
personal moments in the field. Scientific pursuit was all that was
meaningful to Yee. So Milja would honor her mentor by taking
up the mantle of lead exobiologist and do the job well.

But first, she broke her own promise and unsealed Celia Yee's
dark green travel pack. In a small zipped bag, she found a set of
polished black rings on a thin cord: her mentor's only piece of
jewelry. The largest ring was of ebony; nested inside it was a
slightly smaller ring of black coral, and within that, the smallest
ring of rossbium, a mineral from the first exoplanet Yee had visited as an exobiologist. All three were organic and buffed to a
seemingly identical black shine, though they were, respectively,
vegetable, animal, and mineral. She slipped the cord over her
head, tucked the rings under her shirt, and zipped the bag shut.

A flash of pale purple among the neutral garb caught her eye.
She slammed the case shut. Yee only wore a splash of color for
joyous occasions, and had last worn that periwinkle blouse at
Milja's postdoctoral party. The elderly scientist had likely

planned to wear it in celebration, were she to survive the transit to Vesper.

Milja wiped her swollen eyes and went in search of the geologist who would drive her to the site of the potential biome in the morning.

Gabelius, the lead exogeologist, drove them across the barren terrain in a nomad stocked with storage for geological samples and emergency gear. The dull gray-blue of Vesper's atmosphere was mirrored in the deeper hues of the rocky landscape. A patina of Prussian-blue acid, caused by a reaction between compounds in the air and a mineral abundant in the planet's crust, coated every surface with a sickly, sweat-like sheen.

"I've read the reports," Milja said as they rode toward the broken hillside. "Your account includes a sighting of certain dust particles that the others' don't."

Gabelius nodded. "After an unusually strong windstorm caused an avalanche in the region, I went out to survey the slope and saw rock had broken through the roof of a hole. Vesper doesn't have any recent signs of water, so I went down to see if it had been a gas pocket caught underground when the crust was formed. It would be an insightful discovery. But instead, the structure of the depression corroborated what we know of cover-collapse and caprock doline sinkholes: at some point in the past, water flowed under the soil here, taking sand and dirt with it until only a huge, hollow pocket was left. In fact, there's a huge fissure at the bottom of it, possibly a conduit system where the water drained away. I could see bright particles of dust circling near the crack, which might indicate air circulating from the other side."

"And if the water that formed the sinkhole still exists somewhere farther down the system, there could be life."

"I hope not. No offense, but it took me four years to get this assignment. To come all this way to a new planet and not get to finish exploring it?" Gabelius jabbed a finger at his temple through his helmet. "Shoot me now."

The memory pierced her like a gunshot.

"But if you don't survive, you could have spent those years here on the orbiter, studying the samples I'll send you."

Yee speared her protégé with a glance. "Looking through a distorted lens at specimens I can't touch myself, forever taking someone else's word—even yours—as the truth? Torture. I'd kill myself first."

And in a way she had. Milja's heart squeezed.

"We're here," the exogeologist said.

Milja nodded.

Whatever signs of life—or prebiological phosphorylation chemistry—might exist in this rocky subterranean environment, it would most likely be found in the soil. Yee had therefore specifically designed cleated biolanalyzers that would gather all relevant data they came in contact with as she walked and display it at her right hip. Milja stepped into her "striders" now, snapping them onto her suit's boots. On her left hip was a topography display that would map her path as she explored. She strapped on a pack of sample corers and slid out of the nomad. She pinged the geologist over the comm.

Gabelius gazed at the jagged blue maw of the sinkhole. He pinged back, then said, "I'd give my left testicle right now to spelunk that sinkhole."

"If you can cram an advanced degree in exobiology and exploration ethics in the next five minutes, Gabelius, come along. Otherwise, I'll be back in four hours."

He snorted. "Copy. And call me Gabe."

After a slow 280-meter descent, Milja reached the lightless bottom of the sinkhole. The striders' probes sent a flurry of data to her green-lit right hip display. The incandescent glow of her headlamp and strider lights cast a soft white sphere that gave her a view of the blue boulders and dry, mineral-flecked rock that caught her headlamp as she swiveled it across the sloped sinkhole floor. It shone on the triangular gap.

"I see the fissure."

"Copy."

She picked her way between the broken rock downhill to the jagged fissure in the wall. A few mineralized dust particles sailed into the passage through the edge of her incandescent light, glinting copper before disappearing into the black. Air flow. Milja felt a stir of excitement, hoping there might still exist some liquid at the other end; that would be the best potential location for life.

Her throat caught. She wished Yee were here to carry out this last expedition together.

Milja headed slowly into the fissure, broken rock and debris crunching under her striders. She pulled out a vacuum-sealed sampling auger. The tube had a pointed coring blade attached to the blood-red seal at one end, which she slowly pressed into the soil at her feet. When it reached the bedrock a few centimeters down, she shoved straight down, breaking the outer seal. *Snick!* The vacuum within the tube sucked the auger and its bored contents inside, and the gel-coated seal congealed into a new cap, like blood platelets sealing a wound.

She sifted a few grains of silt between her gloved fingers to see if the air flow had changed. The dry, gray silt dropped straight down; but when she turned to look back the way she had come, she could see more glints of copper flowing toward her as they caught her radiant suit-light.

Milja continued down the rock-strewn channel, one hand on the surface overhead. Every fifty meters, Milja paused to take samples of the soil banked against crevices and turns, absently watching the occasional mote float through the beam of her headlamp. Her path was monotonous, the same rock above, the same crunch below as her cleats sank into the dry silt, all looming out of the darkness for brief seconds in her suit-light and gone again behind her.

After an hour, her eyes were mesmerized by the same featureless view. Discouraged, Milja eased herself to the floor of the channel and propped an aching leg on a hunk of rock to stretch. Hoping to find evidence of life on the first day of exploration was ridiculous, she knew. And yet, she wanted reassurance that Yee's death wasn't for naught. Not once had her right hip blipped with organic data. She stared at her thick-gloved hands resting on her leg.

"Halmuni, my mother's mother, had passed by the time we'd arrived at the orbiter," Milja said as they packed essential supplies in the lab.

Yee nodded. "I imagine that loss might have brought your parents back together."

Milja shook her head. "He didn't even say goodbye when we landed. For the life of me, I can't remember why. But I haven't seen him since."

"Will you now? Before we go? You won't get another chance for years, if you even return."

Milja shook her head. "I already did. Or at least I sent him a ping like I do every week, letting him know I love and miss him. He never answers. Really, you are all the parent I want."

Yee covered the younger woman's hand in her own warm, shriveled one, and held it.

The sensor at her right hip blipped.

Her heart lurched. Organic matter! Yet she hadn't moved her feet from where they were propped for minutes. How had her striders come in contact with organic matter? Unless it was floating in the air. Her eyes rose toward the brilliant orange motes sailing past.

Milja rested a hand over the spot where Yee's nested rings lay, between her coolant undersuit and the outer shell. Three identical rings of vegetable, animal, and mineral, all of which were organic. Each of which "grew" in its own way. Was this a copper-mineral life form? If she were able to get a sample . . . Otherwise, a single blip, data notwithstanding, might be considered a misread by her equipment.

Milja pushed on, wanting to prove that the organic compound that had registered on her readout wasn't a mistake.

Ahead, the charcoal-gray tunnel loomed into her suit-light then drifted into darkness behind her, but whenever she paused, she saw more of the bright particulates. Though the mineral glint was copper-colored, Milja found herself thinking of methanobactins' high affinity for copper ions. With a high methane atmosphere, could methane-oxidizing bacteria exist in these underground pocket-biomes?

In the next step, the channel bent to the left, then ended, though motes continued to flow through some crack in the rock wall. She gasped. She knew that the channel might eventually narrow too tight to follow, but she had hoped to pursue it farther today. Either way, she could take a key sample back to test her hypothesis about its similarity to methanobactins.

Milja snagged a sample tube from her pack and snapped the coring tool from the tube into the stream of fiery dots as they whipped around the edge of the tunnel and disappeared. The broached tube resealed itself, and she held it up to her visor. Inside, the sample tube held three copper particles, floating in circles as if riding their own air current. Satisfied, she stowed the sample in her pack.

Following the glittering aerial path, she touched what she expected was the dead end of the tunnel. Instead, she found her suit-light had played an optical trick. A wall of rock jutted out from the right nearly across the width of the tunnel. Just beyond it, another wall of rock jutted from the left, forming an *S* curve.

Elated, she navigated the narrow twist.

The tunnel opened down into a subterranean nightmare. The low walls of the sunken, wide cavern were dotted floor to ceiling with dozens of gaping, round holes.

Blood drained from her head in a rush of apprehension. Her skin broke into a cold sweat. Each black hole was roughly fifty centimeters across—wide enough for her shoulders to jam into. The holes stared at her, waiting. A whirl of bright particles passed her and zoomed into one of the upper holes, then back out, corkscrewing into a low hole a meter from the cavern floor.

Milja crossed the cavern floor, sundered by two forces: the scientist in her, exhilarated at the particles' movement, which seemed to confirm it as an organism with autonomy—a higher order of animal than merely organic particles blown by the wind; and her inner twelve-year-old girl, filled with dread as she realized that she would have to gaze into the hole to observe the particulate organism. She hesitated. Impossible as it seemed, the hole felt like death, waiting.

Struggling to overcome her unnamable terror, she bent to peer into the opening without touching the wall. But the hole curved like a throat. She would have to insert her head into its maw to shine her headlamp inside. She was a scientist, she reminded herself, and Yee would have disapproved of emotions clouding observation.

So Milja thrust her head into the hole. Particulates danced at the edge of her light, and she pushed forward, determined to observe what she and Yee had come so far to understand.

Blazing in the glow of her headlamp, the swirling mass of copper particles resembled stirred flakes of glitter in a jar of clear mineral oil. To her excitement, these flakes stirred themselves. By what method they propelled themselves, she would examine later in the lab.

The more cogent question was: To what purpose did they move? Primal instinct, like mosquitos to moisture? Or something even less cognitive, like coral polyps that were carried by the ocean's eddies?

She watched the organism—for she was now certain it *was* a form a life—rise like a dazzling tiny tornado. Tiny glints bounced off her helmet. More of them streamed over her visor, gathering at the edges where the polycarbonate pieces fitted together, then swarmed over her communication pad and back up to her visor. Her vision cleared as the stream of copper dashed off to the left, out of view. She shivered.

At the back of her helmet, a sharp squeal of pressurized air escaped. Her breath was sucked away. The sound of sand trickling through an aluminum tube accompanied a frisson of cold down her spine. Her suit's containment alarm triggered.

"Purge valve breach. Purge valve breach. Purge valve breach."

It's inside the suit!

Milja reared. Her arms wedged at her sides and her pack jammed against the smooth, gray ceiling. She choked, and the dark hole swallowed her.

Her knees slammed against the cavern wall as she tried to lever herself out. Familiar pain. She tugged but couldn't dislodge herself. She was caught, *had been caught*, would always be caught in this nightmare hole.

"Breach sealed," her suit announced.

The cold frisson rode back up her spine. Copper glinted at the edge of her vision, dancing among dark-brown strands of hair, caught in the tear film of her eye, trickling through her duct into the external nasal vein, riding the great cerebral vein through the blood-brain barrier. The tickle of cold entered her mind. Milja stopped struggling. Copper filaments continued their dance inside and outside her helmet.

Third Instar

The part of her brain that still belonged to Milja the exobiologist examined the invasion.

The part of her brain that belonged to copper-infested Milja wondered why there was a remodeled scar on the back of her head without remembering the circumstances in which it had happened; those images were not in the hippocampus. But some of the bridges from the hippocampus to the neocortex had been cut, cauterized, bypassed. *How, and by whom?* The infestation repaired the gap with a bright new bridge of copper-colored conduction.

Excited electricity explored regions lost, disconnected. It reconnected them. It found not only that the scar had six stitches, but also that the bearded medic who sutured her had had a dour, disgusted look on his face and had quit the room the moment he was done. He had been replaced by a different medic, a woman who had asked her to lay back—even though her backside hurt—because the micro-gamma knife she inserted through Milja's nose would take away the pain.

But the gamma knife had not taken away the pain, had only cleaved away the reason for it so that her pain swam in a confused haze without context. Later, a new context was told and repeated by *Umma* until it made its own home in her neocortex. The new context was a fairy tale of parents who argued and grew apart, of a resentful father who had disappeared into the orbiter, never to be seen again, and a mother who resented the failed partnership and saw Milja as a daily reminder of it.

The copper connection bridged the fugue to the old context— the truth. She had witnessed but not understood that the disgust on the bearded medic's face was not for her but for *Iskä*, who had been caretaking but not taking care of her when she split her scalp on the inside of a filter tube. *Umma*'s job as a cardiology acclimation medic was needed as much on the transport as on the orbiter. *Iskä*, who had been a proud atmospheric geoengineer on Rhea, became a glorified janitor, maintaining the transport's filtering systems while in space; he resented menial tasks below his advanced degrees—especially that of watching his child.

The eleven bitter years the transport had taken to reach the orbiter had only held tiny pockets of relief and one moment of release. Through copper-colored memory, Milja-the-infested watched *Iskä* drag eleven-year-old Milja with him on his maintenance rounds where he had to empty filters and scrub the tubes. As her body reached puberty, his resentful glare became a soft, pleased gaze. It was the same pleased expression he had worn when she danced and capered in exaggerated fourteen-year-old mimicry of adult swagger, and his bemused approval encouraged her to continue. If she had noticed that the hand petting her backside lingered, she had thought it a gesture of familial fondness.

Then a day came when Milja grew too big to slide headfirst down the smooth filter tubes *Iskä* had polished, and she got stuck. Her top half jammed inside and she panicked, wedging herself more firmly, forearms trapped between her ribcage and the tube walls. At her cries for help, *Iskä* had wrapped his arms around her, pulled and pushed, twisted and tore at her clothes to create wiggle room. Proud *Iskä* abhorred asking for help; he tried and tried, sweating so profusely he had pulled off his own clothes. The push and pull at her waist, his bare skin against hers, became so sharp that she screamed, battering her head until it split against the clean, polished filter tube that she would never go near again, and, unable to draw breath in the compressed space anymore, she passed out.

The copper-infested brain that belonged to Milja realized that *Iskä* had traded away his fulfilling planet-bound career for obsolescence on an orbiter and could blame no one but himself. Saw that this was a choice he had made, subconsciously perhaps, but entirely his own. Saw that *Umma* had bowed to the decision to cut away Milja's memory, since the damage to her psyche would anchor her in pain and distrust, betrayal and fear. Saw that it tortured *Umma* to witness her remodeled daughter act as if *Iskä* had not maimed her, to witness her daughter worship the rapist who would remain in isolated quarters until they landed, to witness her daughter vilify the mother who kept *Iskä* from visiting.

Milja's copper-conjoined brain simultaneously saw both the images as they had originally imprinted on her neural pathways and the same images through her mind as scientist-self. Felt her sliver of outrage before the bridges had been severed, and the dust-dry outrage of old wrongs too late to right. Felt the absence of fresh outrage as a cheat. Wondered if processing his assault and her loss without the deserved fury would heal more cleanly. Wondered if it *had* healed. Wondered if it would ever heal.

The copper continued to pave bright roads to images and sounds long since laid to rest while Milja extricated herself from the hole. *A lilting harvest festival song in* hangul *that* Umma *had sung when Milja was two.* Her bruised knee ached, and her scraped forearm tingled painfully from twisting inside her suit.

She checked her time. She had spent nearly three hours in the hole and was now low on oxygen.

"Gabe? Gabe, copy?" she called over the comm. As she strained for a hint of reply, her breath seemed to thunder in her ears. Fragments of reconnected memories washed over her.

Breathing amniotic fluid and listening to the comforting stutter-step of her mother's heartbeat while she talked her patient through the physiological acclimation from his home planet to Rhea.

Milja turned back toward the entrance. The low-ceilinged cavern did resemble the air filtration unit of the transport ship her father had had to maintain; when her father had ejected and scrubbed all the filters in one section, the emptied wall of tubes lay open from floor to ceiling like a honeycomb of dark eyes. Would the similarity have eventually bridged those cut connections to her trauma without the aid of the copper life form? Perhaps. But this gave her access to so much more than that.

Milja fished out the last sample she had collected. Three glints wafted inside the tube. With a snap, she cracked the tube against the edge of the hole. The fused quartz shattered. She dropped the broken tube in the silt, knowing the copper would find its way. Iskä *raging in Finnish, a crash of glass waking her from a sound sleep in the next room, pressing herself back against* Halmuni's *until he stopped. Her father had been belligerent even before their journey to the orbiter.* Milja didn't know Finnish, but were she to learn, the copper would help her recall his words.

Darkness swallowed the cavern as she left.

Light-headed, she turned off the empty-O_2-tank alarm and retraced her footsteps through the twisting fissure back to the open sinkhole, puzzling over which Milja was authentically her:

the stunted, fractured self that had walked into the cavern, or the gasping, copper-laced, fully-restored self that emerged into the slate-blue sky from a black hole that had opened up beneath her. The last molecules of oxygen dissolved.

Fourth Instar

The jostling of the vehicle over the rocky terrain brought her to. Milja reached up and discovered Gabe had taken off her helmet and strapped her into the seat. When he saw she was awake, Gabe said, "Why didn't you return when we lost communication?"

"I had to follow a trail before it disappeared," she muttered, disoriented. What was the last thing she remembered?

"Don't do it again. We're going into the nomad's air reserves as it is."

She shot up in her seat. She had to warn him about what she carried. But, turning toward him, Milja saw a glint disappear into his nose. He scratched his nose with a wrist.

"You found something, you said?"

"A life form, yes. It's . . ."

He glanced at her. "What?" He glanced at her.

"Invasive. But also benign, sort of."

The exogeologist's quizzical expression smoothed as the vehicle drifted to a stop. His eyes shifted back and forth, following the waking memories, long buried or forgotten, as they unfolded in his mind. Eventually he turned to her, face twisted in surprise and anger.

"You knew this would happen," he said, accusing. "You didn't even pretend to be surprised."

"You unsealed my suit. Then it was too late."

"You should have followed containment protocol and stayed out of physical contact! What the hell do we do now? We can't bring this back to everyone else!"

"I wasn't ready to die. Are you? As you said, we only have enough oxygen to get home."

Gabe howled, pounding the dashboard until he was breathless.

"Ping the habitat and tell them to quarantine us," Milja said. Gabe raised his head. "It won't do any good. But they'll believe we didn't expose them deliberately until . . . well."

"Lie to them?" he growled.

"Yes. Whatever this is isn't fatal, as far as we know. But it does seem to be unstoppable. So we go home, study ourselves, and eventually—"

"Quarantine the planet."

"For those like you and me who were never likely to leave, it won't be much different."

"I won't do it."

"This is who we are now, Gabe. Whatever this life form is, it hasn't hurt us; it's made us more completely ourselves. Are you really ready to die today, rather than risk this change?"

He stared at her in silence.

"Neither am I," she answered.

Resigned, Gabe resumed driving them toward the habitat.

For the first time, she couldn't imagine what Yee would tell her to do in her circumstances; Milja was treading unknown waters. Old memories continued to fall in place like paved paths cleared of neglect's overgrowth while the domed, white exterior of the habitat bloomed on the horizon. With time, she could mine her memories for her mother's work in physiological acclimation to help Vesper's inhabitants deal with this new metamorphosis. Surely, when all of them could reach into their pasts, they would emerge with a much greater body of knowledge—and, hopefully, wisdom—with which to build their new future.

....

Joy Park-Thomas is a freelance reality television story producer on shows including *Top Chef*, *Project Runway*, and *Rock of Love*. Her first love is her husband, Chris, but her second love is creating feminist science fiction. She is currently editing her urban fantasy trilogy about a prostitute-turned-priest who must stop the Eight Fates from destroying humanity in their quest to save the planet. "The Obsolescence of Memory" is her fifth short story for the Los Angeles NaNo Anthology series.

....

T H R O U G H   A N O T H E R   D O O R W A Y

I f I had just listened to my intuition, everything might have been different. At least I would have been prepared for some of it. For months I'd suspected that Ashley was cheating on me. I'd also guessed things weren't going well for my parents. And some part of me knew from the start that there was something very unusual about the girl on the trail.

A week before Thanksgiving, Ashley moved out without any warning. I decided that spending the holiday with my parents would be better than laying around on the couch, bingeing shows and wondering what the hell I was doing with my life. I tried to throw a positive spin on it: as a newly single freelance artist, I could even move back to Virginia if I wanted.

After only two days at home, I regretted coming. From the moment my parents picked me up at the airport, they were strangely quiet and tense. Though they talked with me, they didn't say a word to each other during the hour-long drive. But the next day when Mom suggested I join her and Dad for a walk, I pushed aside the nagging suspicion that I'd be better off skipping it. Sure, I'd go. Why not?

It was a crisp autumn afternoon with sunlight filtering through the leaves, but I only had a few minutes to enjoy it before my parents were at each other's throats. I'd made the mistake of asking if they had any trips planned, and then down the rabbit hole they went: Dad bemoaning Mom's love of cruises, Mom asking why he'd gone for early retirement in the first place.

I considered trying to calm them down or distract them, but it was easier to act like I was a kid again and let them ignore me while they fought. As their volume increased, a young couple with a stroller passed by, heading the other direction. Right behind them, a small boy toddled along, pulling a red wagon.

About twenty yards back stood a little girl in a faded yellow sundress. She looked about seven years old, judging by her height, but I found myself squinting at her. Something about her face made me think more of a teenager—both her petulant expression and her rather angular facial shape. Her straight blond hair fell nearly to her waist, and she wore the tiniest pair of cowboy boots.

"Hey, look!" she called out to the family who'd passed me. "Do you see it? Hello?"

They didn't respond, paying as much attention to her as my parents paid to me. I wondered if they knew that she was lagging so far behind.

I turned to Dad to mention it, but Mom was launching another volley his way. "Don't you start this again," she began. "I cleaned the kitchen for years before you'd even put your dishes in the sink." I tuned her out, shaking my head.

"Hey," the girl yelled again. "It's behind you!"

Something about the way she said it made my neck prickle. We passed her a few seconds later, but she didn't even glance at us. Curiosity got the better of me, and I stopped to see what she was talking about. My parents kept bickering their way down the trail, oblivious to the fact that I wasn't with them.

Beside the girl stood a scarlet bush covered with little black berries. She appeared to be pointing at something on the ground beside it, but I couldn't see anything there. Her back was to me, her attention fixed on the little boy with the wagon.

Suddenly the girl spun around and gazed up at me with this unnatural intensity. Never having spent much time around kids, I wasn't sure if that was normal behavior, but it creeped me out. "You go away right now," she said to me, eyes narrowed. I didn't know what to say, so I turned around and hurried to catch up with my parents.

"Well, if you wouldn't leave them there, they wouldn't get knocked over!" my dad yelled.

"Okay then," I said, projecting my voice over theirs. "This has been a lovely walk. It's really been great to get some fresh air with you two, just like old times."

Dad looked away and Mom gave me an abashed look, and I worried I'd overdone it.

"I'm sorry, Nate," she said. "We're sorry."

Without a word, my dad turned and headed back toward home.

"He's probably not going to speak to me until the weekend now," Mom confided.

I didn't know what to say without appearing to have taken sides, so I just nodded. As we turned to follow Dad toward the house, I realized that the girl in the yellow dress was gone. She'd been only a few steps behind us, but now there was no one.

The boy with the red wagon was nearly cresting the hill on our route home, but the girl wasn't with him. The trail between us was empty, with no obvious place she could have run to, unless perhaps she'd sprinted over the hill ahead of him.

"Something wrong, dear?" Mom asked me.

"Uh, no . . . I'll be right back, okay?"

I jogged past my dad toward the family, catching them at the top of the hill. Looking down the far side, I saw no one on the path ahead of them.

"Excuse me," I said, feeling awkward. The woman stopped pushing her stroller and cocked her head at me. "I'm sorry to bother you, but did your little girl run off somewhere?"

The woman gave me a funny look. "She's right here." She pointed to the little cherub in pink tucked beneath a blanket in the stroller. "She won't be running anytime soon."

I laughed. "I'm sorry, I meant your other daughter."

She shook her head. "She's my only girl. You must have me confused with someone else."

I almost let it go at that, but I knew it would nag at me later. "Did a little girl in a yellow dress come running past you, by chance?"

"Why, no, I don't think so. Did you see one, Jack?"

"Not a one," the man said, frowning at me.

"She was calling out to you before," I said. "At least I thought she was. Asking if you'd seen something?"

The baby started fussing, and the mom had a concerned look in her eyes that I was pretty sure had nothing to do with her child. "I don't think so," she said.

"I'm sorry, I—I must've been mistaken," I said, realizing how crazy I must sound.

I turned back toward my parents as the couple headed onward. My dad stormed past me, scowling. Mom followed seconds later, a puzzled look on her face.

"Why'd you run off like that?" she asked. "Do you know those people?"

I shrugged. "Mom, do you remember passing a little girl in a yellow dress? Just a minute before we turned around?"

"I wasn't paying attention, Nate. Your father's been making me so mad lately."

I sighed. "Yeah, I can tell."

The next morning, I stayed in my room until I heard the garage door signal my parents' exit for church. At least they couldn't argue there.

I made some toast and helped myself to a cup of coffee. On a whim I decided to enjoy some fresh air without the arguing from the day before.

It was cooler out, with a brisk wind that made me wish I'd brought my jacket. Tree branches swayed above me, carpeting the sidewalk with their brilliant leaves, and a wonderfully earthy smell was in the air.

Without thinking about it, I found myself at the place where I'd seen the girl. The scarlet shrub she'd been standing by marked the location beyond a doubt. No one was nearby to wonder if I was nuts, so I walked over to look where she'd been pointing.

I spotted the object so quickly that I wondered how I'd missed it before. It looked like some sort of engraved, metallic box. I reached out for it. The second before my fingers made contact, I heard a shriek behind me: "Don't!"

But it was too late. My fingers closed on the box, and a massive shock coursed through me like a bolt of lightning.

I woke up on the ground, surrounded by a thick fog. It was dusk, and the darkened trees loomed overhead as if bending down to inspect me. Had I spent an entire day unconscious on the trail? Surely someone would have called an ambulance.

I sat up carefully, expecting pain or broken bones, but I just felt numb and disoriented. Tendrils of fog swirled around me.

A sudden scream of fury erupted from behind me: "You destroyed it!"

Heart racing, I jumped up and spun around, nearly falling over as a wave of dizziness hit me. I blinked and found myself facing the girl in the yellow dress, fists clenched and hatred in her eyes.

I took a step back, hands in the air. "I'm sorry. I'm leaving."

"It's too late!"

Had I stepped into a nightmare? I turned and ran toward home, sparing only a moment at the top of the hill to confirm she wasn't following me.

My parents' house came into view, and relief flooded through me. The lights weren't on, which seemed odd. Perhaps my parents were out looking for me.

I felt for the house key I'd slipped into my pocket before leaving, but it must've fallen out on the trail. I reached for the doorbell instead—and my finger slid right through it.

I yanked my hand away as if it had been stung, and another wave of dizziness hit me. Clearly I had some sort of head injury. I reached for the handle on the screen door, but it passed through my fingers too.

Blood roaring in my ears, I sat down hard on the front steps. Something was wrong with me, but I couldn't puzzle it out. I'd been fine running home—the path hadn't disappeared beneath me—and the porch steps supported me well enough. I rubbed my temples and felt my fingertips against them. It had to be a visual disturbance, I decided—some problem lining up objects in my mind.

I walked to the door, closed my eyes, and reached forward. I hit nothing, no resistance. I opened my eyes and saw my arm extending halfway through the door.

I screamed. The sound died away without any response.

"Fine, okay, fine. Just a little bump on the head," I said.

Without really thinking about it, I closed my eyes, took four steps forward, breathed in slowly, and opened my eyes.

I was standing inside my parents' foyer.

I spent a few seconds there, convincing myself I'd opened and closed the front door as usual. Sure thing, totally normal, nothing to see here.

The microwave started beeping from the kitchen, and I jumped. "Mom? Dad?" I called, making my way down the hall to the kitchen.

Despite the gloom outside, the windows were wide open and the kitchen lights were off. My dad sat at the table eating a bowl of oatmeal and reading the Sunday paper.

"You need a light, Dad?" I asked.

He didn't answer. Mom carried over her own bowl of oatmeal and sat at the table. I grabbed the chair next to her to sit down—and, of course, my hand slipped through it.

"Mom . . . ?"

She looked up at my dad and then back down, her lips tightening.

I reached out to touch Dad's shoulder. I couldn't feel the fabric of his plaid shirt, but I felt a distinct warmth.

He set down his coffee hard enough to slosh it over the side and groaned.

"Lucas?" Mom said. "Are you feeling all right?"

My dad reached his left hand up to his chest, bent forward, and then crashed to the ground.

"Lucas!"

I spent the next half hour huddled in the corner of the kitchen, watching the paramedics arrive and carry Dad out on a stretcher. They'd gotten him stabilized, but that was all I knew for sure. I wanted to follow them to the hospital, to give Mom a hug—anything.

But I didn't dare touch anyone.

By the time everyone was gone, the kitchen clock read 11:12 a.m. I watched another ten minutes tick by before standing up. It was almost noon, and yet the dusky sky outside hadn't changed.

I wanted to crawl into bed, but I wasn't sure if it would hold me, and I was afraid to find out. Maybe it would swallow me up whole, or maybe I'd drift off to sleep and never wake up. Perhaps that would be preferable to whatever was actually going on.

It finally dawned on me that the only one who might have some answers was that hateful girl on the trail. When no other options came to mind, I walked to the front door and grabbed for the doorknob, without effect.

"Whatever," I said, exhausted.

I walked right through the door and down the front steps to the path.

I found the girl sitting next to the scarlet bush, her head resting in her arms. Though she looked harmless enough, I was careful to keep my distance.

"Hey," I said, my voice as calming as I could make it. "Whatever I did, I'm sorry."

She raised her head, and I was shocked to see her cheeks were wet with tears. Was this some kind of bizarre trap?

"It took me a year to get that box ready," she said, sniffling.

"Ready for . . . ?"

She pressed her lips together, and I caught that strangely adult look on her face again. "I have to catch a child."

"Why would you do *that*?" I asked, horrified.

She surged to her feet, screaming. "Because it's the only way out of here! Get it? Do you think I want to *stay* here?"

I backed up, my arms making soothing motions. "Okay, okay. Who told you that?"

New tears flowed down her cheeks. "That's how I got here— I got tricked with the box. Nisus told me how to make one. She said only kids can see it. But they almost never look." She shook her head, fingers tracing the sidewalk.

"Can I talk to her?"

She kicked a booted foot against the ground and shrugged. "Bad idea. Nisus just wants young kids. She doesn't even want *me* anymore."

The one thing that sounded worse than meeting Nisus was being stuck here forever, which was starting to sound like a real possibility. "Just take me to her. Please?"

She wiped her eyes and sniffed. "She's not gonna be happy."

We walked a few hundred feet down the trail to a densely wooded patch off to the right. From there, we made our way down a steep slope carpeted with dead pine needles. It leveled off beside a monstrous tree with feathery, reddish bark.

She pointed to a dark hole, like a small animal might live in, low on the trunk. "Put your hand in there."

"Do I have to?"

She shrugged. "You're the one who wants talk to her."

Did I really want to? I looked at the girl, so young and already so resigned, trapped in this dark version of our world.

"I'm going to try to get us both out of here," I said.

"That'll never happen, mister." She looked up at me, though, and I could have sworn I saw hope in her eyes. "Here, like this." She put her hand in the hole—and vanished.

I hesitated for a second before doing the same.

I found myself somewhere even darker than the eternal dusk outside.

Before me lay a downward-sloping tunnel with smooth, obsidian walls. Glowing blue strands dangled from the ceiling, lighting the way. Good thing I wasn't claustrophobic.

The girl was already heading down, and I hurried to catch up with her. Without a word, she passed several unusually tall doorways wreathed in the blue filaments, and then pressed her hand to a door on the right. It slid open, and we stepped inside.

My eyes were immediately drawn to an entire wall that was designed to look like a giant window. I knew it couldn't be real, given how far down we'd gone, but it was a convincingly lifelike image of a park. The grass rippled in an imaginary wind, and sunlight sparkled on the surface of a pond. I sighed, wondering if either of us would ever feel natural sunlight again.

"Pretty, right? She lets me come sit here sometimes." The girl pointed at a carved stone bench resting against the opposite wall. "Usually she wants me to go out on the trails and listen to people. She said the adults couldn't see me. Most kids don't, either."

An open doorway led to a hall that curved out of sight. "Is she down this way?" I asked.

The girl nodded. "Stay here. Nisus won't like this."

I nodded and sat on the bench as she headed down the hall, my eyes feasting on the image before me.

Minutes later, I heard footsteps approaching and stood up. A slim, unearthly creature with elongated limbs and pale gray-blue skin glided down the hallway toward me. She was draped in a filmy silver material that whispered against the floor as she swept into the room. I stood frozen in place, barely able to breathe, as the creature's inhuman black eyes met mine.

"Danielle," she hissed without looking away from me. "What have you brought here?"

"I'm sorry, Nisus," the girl said, cowering. "I made the box like you said. But *he* came through instead of a child."

"Danielle says you asked to speak with me," Nisus said. Her face was expressionless, unreadable.

I swallowed hard. "Please let us out of here. She said you don't want her anymore."

"I plan to release her," Nisus said, "as soon as she fulfills her obligation and brings me another child as a replacement."

"But it'll take another year," Danielle moaned.

"As it may, so it must," Nisus said.

"I can't just leave her here," I said, my hands clenched together so she wouldn't see how much I was shaking. "Please . . . let her go home."

The creature spoke dreamily, as if reciting. "I cannot. Without her, the summoning cannot take place. Through the oldest of our records, one child has always summoned the next."

"You can't just take children!" I moved into the center of the room and gestured to the image on the wall. "They need to grow up with their parents, not alone in the darkness."

"Unlike your world," she said, "no ill can befall them here. Our magic nurtures them, and the power of their youth keeps us ageless. My people cannot cross to your lands lest our powers be stripped away. I can let her go only when she summons another."

She paused, looking me over. "Fascinating as you are, your presence brings untold risks." She closed the distance between us and extended her arm toward me. "I'm afraid you must be destroyed."

Her hand touched my shoulder, and a shock like the one from the box surged through my body. I flew back against the image of the park, my vision going dark at the edges as I fought to stay conscious.

I gripped the wall to pull myself to my feet, and my shoulder screamed in agony. To my surprise the image rippled beneath my hand and gave way. My fingers slipped through, and I felt the sun's warmth on them.

I pulled away, and the film covering the hole resealed. I turned toward Nisus, expecting another blow, and was shocked to see her crumpled against the bench. She, too, must have been hit by the shock. As I watched, her arm reached out and clawed at the bench.

"Touch the glass, Danielle!" I shouted.

She hurried to press both her hands to the image, but the window stayed solid. "It doesn't work for me!"

Blue energy suddenly rippled around her, freezing her in place. Nisus had pulled herself up against the bench. "The child stays," she said, her voice weak with strain.

I pressed my hands against the image, crying out as warmth became searing heat. A hole opened around them.

Could I actually escape like this? A dozen horrible possibilities came to mind—getting sliced in half by the closing membrane, being trapped in an airless image—but I pushed them away. This would be my only chance.

I pressed my back to the image, screaming as a fiery sensation engulfed me. And then there was no question—I was slipping through.

I leaned once more into the room and grabbed Danielle's hand.

"She stays with me," I yelled, pulling her along to whatever lay beyond.

S unlight woke me, warm on my face. Beside me on the grass lay Danielle. I reached out to her, but she didn't move, and I felt as if the breath had been crushed out of me.

"Danielle!" I cried, shaking her limp form.

I turned her over onto her back and brushed a dirty lock of hair off her face. Her eyes opened.

"Are we . . . ?" Her voice trailed off as she looked around.

I nodded, smiling. "We're free, Danielle."

T he park we woke up in was several miles from my parents' house, and we caught a bus downtown to the police station. On the way, I thought of Nisus and the implications of helping Danielle escape. Had this ended the cycle of children being taken away to that realm? Had I doomed these otherwise eternal creatures? Did they deserve this?

And yet, could I have accepted the alternative? Of course not.

At the station, I explained I'd found Danielle wandering in the park. She told them she had no memory of what happened to her. To our surprise, they managed to contact her mother, Charlotte, who arrived that very afternoon.

"I never gave up hope," Charlotte kept saying, hugging us both.

Dad recovered from what his doctors assured him wasn't a heart attack. Though no one was sure exactly what it was, the shock of the experience appeared to be the wake-up call my parents needed. I spent Christmas with them, and they were both in high spirits. Better yet, they didn't fight once.

I ended up staying in Virginia, but not just for my parents. Charlotte called to say that Danielle kept asking to see me, and

I joined the two of them for dinner at her house. Danielle met me at the door and threw her arms around me.

As I stepped inside, I suddenly felt like I was just where I was meant to be.

Of course, that's my intuition talking. But this time, I'm listening.

....

Elisabeth Ashlin has a bachelor's degree in computer science from Bradley University, but she left software engineering to write and act. A member of SAG-AFTRA, she performed in several films and lots of live theater. Now a resident of Santa Clarita, she spends most of her time editing, writing, running, or cooking. Her stories appear in five editions of the Los Angeles NaNo Anthology, and she's been the lead editor for the last three years. Visit her online at elisabethashlin.com.

KATE WEIZE

....

ALL FUN AND GAMES

I t's hard to see what you've got till it's gone. Peripheral
vision, for example. If I'd had both eyes, I never would have
given myself that accidental undershave on the first day at
Academy. I never would have kissed Peony Kerner by mistake.
And I most definitely wouldn't have an Aolferian mercenary
holding me in a sticky tentacled grip with a machete against my
throat.

I get a lucky break—finally!—after two years of horrible
drudgery, and here I am ankle-deep in toxic moss that's hissing
against my boots, my commanding officer wounded and barely
standing, a blotchy purple canopy overhead rustling with
venomous creatures, plus the whole machete thing. I'd laugh if
it wasn't so very sharp and close.

Context: This was supposed to be a diplomatic mission.
A peaceful annexation of a small planet by an interstellar coop-
erative that could handle the Lozakkian's environmental woes.
The aggressive depletion of resources on their planet had led to
rapid biochemical evolution in certain wildlife. We're talking
huge reptiles suddenly producing acid spit—and let me tell you,

they like to spit. Not great when 37 percent of the population still lives in pre-industrial jungle settlements.

Lucky for Lozzakia, our xenobiologists loved it. They found the rapid widespread synchronous adaptation of the flora and fauna so fascinating that they were willing to pay to re-balance the planet's atmosphere. After they took samples, of course.

Only one problem. The Lozakks didn't *want* to be annexed and de-acidified. They wanted to *weaponize* the nasty buggers. Forget having a habitable planet, this was a profit opportunity. Big enough that whoever they'd sold their lizards to could afford to hire a respectably-sized cadre of Aolferian mercenaries.

End result: Our diplomat lies simmering in a soup of his own innards on the aeropad. Diving into the alkaline lake saved our skins but ruined our comms and blasters. Which is why something so Neolithic as a machete has stopped me in my tracks.

It's uncomfortably physical, the way the metal blade presses into my skin. The edge feels razor fine. I wonder if he gets it laser-honed or does it by hand. I glance at Peggy. Still there, fifteen feet away. My commanding officer, currently in command of bleeding way more than humans ought to. Still at it. Not good.

The Aolferian reeks like a damp crab carcass. His ethanol-laced breath tingles on the back of my neck. He snarls something at Peggy, and the translator on my belt whirrs to life, translating in not-quite-real-time.

[Drop your weapon and your friend gets to be a bad soldier another day.]

Hey, no need to get personal.

Peggy doesn't move. Not that the crude bow she's leaning on is much of a threat right now, since it's most of what's holding her up.

Odds are this Aolferian is lying. Mercenaries aren't known for their mercy, even ignoring the whole Human/Aolferian blood feud. I bet the Lozakkian Council wouldn't mind if we disappeared in an "unfortunate accident."

"You drop yours, or you'll end up like your friend here," Peggy snaps back.

Her hands drip black blood on the chalk-white moss. The other Aolferian twitches at her feet with an arrow through his neck. He went down fast, but not before ripping a grisly chunk out of Peggy's leg with a serrated whip.

His comrade doesn't so much as twitch a tentacle.

"Maybe we can talk this out," I suggest with as much chipper camaraderie as I can muster.

There's a pause as the translator shrieks, then the muscular tentacles squeeze tighter. The Aolferian makes a low guttural sound that the machine spits back as laughter.

[Even if we were not so well paid, I'd take the chance to humiliate Interstellar peons.]

"Really? I thought you Aolferians would rather sit on your hands—tentacles—like cosmic couch potatoes rather than do anything for free. There's no such thing as a free lunch, am I right?"

There's a trick to translator communication, which is a year one basic skill at the academy: short sentences. Avoid colloquialisms. Basically the opposite of what I'm doing.

The translator whirs and screeches through *that* slog of a sentence as I try to catch Peggy's eye. I can see by the little wrinkle between her eyes that she's thinking furiously—but that won't get us far. With me and the machete situation and Peggy bleeding like she is, we're easy prey.

Correction: I'm easy prey. Not Commander Pegasus Arbiter, the superior officer in more ways than one. She could take this chance and limp off, find cover, seal up that leg and regroup. Get the drop on this guy later. Try to hijack their craft. It has to be close. No way they bushwhacked out this far. I'd die, sure, but who doesn't? It might buy her time.

Rewind.

An hour ago. Deep in the Lozakk jungle, already lost. Magenta fronds and tangles of silvery vines blocked out most of the sunlight. We'd long lost track of the lake. We were both regretting goofing off during pathfinder training at summer camp so long ago.

It took about ten minutes of wading through dense foliage for us to realize two things: the flora and fauna had reached peak pH disparity, and either of them could kill us at any moment.

I nearly stepped on a spongy invertebrate methodically liquefying a small mammalian creature. Chalky spores drifted around us, tainting the filter on my air regulator with a hint of ammonia.

We found a Lozakkian skeleton slumped into a tree, bow and arrow still in its hands. The bow had survived intact, daubed in the same alkaline mud still coating our uniforms. The bones were slowly folding in on themselves like soft wax.

I laughed. "We're going to die."

Peggy pried the bow and arrow out of its bony fingers. "Not today."

When she got that look in her eye, things got done. Hysterical eleven-year-olds organized into a rescue team. Friends got dug out of deep space bureaucracy. People escaped acid-washed aero-pads and well-trained Aolferian deathmongers. We might even survive this killer jungle.

Maybe we did have a chance. This bow could be the sign of a lucky break. That'd be a new one, considering the rest of my not-so-illustrious career.

Rewind. Further back.

Interstellar academy. NeoAlexandria. Me, a bright-eyed, freshly minted cadet ready to shove all those space pirate gags down my uncle's throat at the next family reunion. I was having a nice clean evening of booze and bootlicking at my first alumni/graduate mixer. Rumor had it that if one of the admirals took a shine to you, your career was made—and I was right there with my pocket full of proverbial shoe polish.

When Admiral Armstrong expressed a desire for a Dusky Valentine, I dashed to the bar, elbowing away five other hopefuls to claim the tankard of smoky ambrosia. The fumes of the legendary cocktail made my head swim as I wove my way back through the throng of uniforms. The Dusky Valentine is a heady mix of alien substances first concocted on the Third Colony. It is potent, dangerous, and very, very staining.

Another thing about one functioning eye? Depth perception. I missed a step and stumbled. My elbow caught on the flared sleeve of a Somosian dignitary. The tankard flew high and splattered spectacularly onto an unsuspecting encroacher on my blind side. Gasps of horror came from all in a five-foot radius. I turned, and there he stood: Grand Admiral Matthew Vespa Houston the Third. *The* Grand Admiral Houston of the Battle of Aolferi 9. Impeccable, implacable, and in full snow-white dress uniform, now dripping with Dusky Valentine.

Safe to say, the scene got grisly.

Fast forward.

Delta Sector. My first assignment. Me, starring in one of the most ignominious careers to ever come out of old Interstellar Neo. They placed me under Grand Admiral Houston. Of course. If there was a sewage barge headed for a deep space dumping ground, a sloppy colonizer churning out toxic mud, an unpleasant dignitary that must be transported and plied with the appropriate level of groveling, I was assigned without fail. Two years this went on.

Then Peggy transferred in.

Pegasus Alegri Arbiter. Commander Arbiter now. My shining star. The only person who didn't scrape me off the bottom of her shoe after the drink debacle. My supposed ticket out of the hole I'd dug myself into. She vouched for me to Houston himself, and by the blessing of some infinite galactic being, he listened to this precocious young officer just barely out of Academy. He gave me a chance.

This was that chance. Our first assignment. A way out from under the backside of the wrathful girth of Interstellar United. A nice and easy diplomatic transfer of power. Like anything's *that* easy.

Of course, this wasn't the gruesome end I'd had in mind. No "faulty" airlock on the Grand Admiral Houston's ship or horrible acid creatures jellifying our bones. Just good old-fashioned tools of death, courtesy of an Aolferian thug.

Fast forward. Now.

The stench of dead crab intensifies as the Aolferian listens to the translator wheeze through my last communication. I can feel the old hardware heating up against my lower back, but that doesn't scare me like the twitching in the Aolferian's tentacles that say he's ready to snap my neck as soon as cut my throat. I'd better act fast.

I catch Peggy's eye, then wiggle my eyebrows and roll my eyes in the direction of the nearest bushes, mouthing *GO* too quietly for the translator to hear. I work a couple of fingers loose from the tentacles and jab them in the same direction for emphasis. She scowls.

The Aolferian slaps his translator with a free tentacle, and it abruptly stops squawking. He leans close over my shoulder and presses the machete into the soft skin of my throat. I get very, very still.

[I'm waiting, Human. Last chance.]

Peggy stands fifteen feet away, leaning on the crude longbow she took off the dead local. Blood streams from the ribbons of flesh below her knee. Her only arrow is still jammed in the throat of the dead Aolferian at her feet. That's it. No more ammo. Her best chance is to leave me.

Humans have this funny thing about pack loyalty, though. Peggy and I, we've been friends since the nursery fields. Friends through Academy and graduation. One glance at her fierce amber eyes and I know she's not going anywhere. Peggy doesn't run from fights. Besides, she still owes me. Big time.

That leaves us with one option. The thing I swore I'd never do again.

I look her dead in the eye. "Pegs, you'd better William Tell the *shit* out of this."

I can hear the Aolferian's translator box sputter and growl as it tries to work out a translation that makes sense. Good luck, software. That one's all about context.

Rewind. Way back.

Home Planet. Berljeing. Fifteenth colony. Summer camp. Fifth grade.

William Tell: Archer of Legend had just dropped at the 3Dplex, entrancing a whole gaggle of us neighborhood kids. Stunts, bravery, high stakes—and the novelty of using a physical projectile. It was magical. Every one of us dreamed of greatness bound up in fletching and recurves. We begged our parents until they sent us to the one and only camp on-planet that still had actual bows and arrows instead of holofields.

We had a grand old time sinking fiberglass rods into recyclofoam targets and terrorizing the instructor, but our eleven-year-old scrambled-egg brains craved more heroic feats. We took to sneaking off to the old orchard during free play to make challenges of our own. Apples on hay bales. Apples on trees. Apples chucked in the air as high as we could make them go.

Peggy outshone us all. She nailed it four times out of five—and that, we thought, was skilled enough for the ultimate challenge. William Tell's final feat. Granted, he did it upside down, chained to a pair of lions and looking through a mirror, but we figured we'd work out those details later.

I was selected as the one with the flattest head. I stood with my back against a gnarled old apple tree. Bark prickled through my T-shirt. I held perfectly still to keep the apple from rolling off.

We had that moment, you know, when you lock eyes as if to say: *Are we really doing this?*

Peggy set her skinny sun-browned legs in a wide stance, the bow stretched to her ear, eyes clear and focused. She let fly. The other kids whooped. My head smacked hard against the old tree, and the apple toppled from my head.

It took me a minute to figure out why everyone was screaming. A black line jutted out from somewhere close to my nose. My face felt warm and wet. I turned my head, and the black line moved. I screamed as loud as anyone after that.

We still can't agree whether she aimed a little low or I flinched at the last second. Either way, that was the end of our summer vacation, that camp's operation, and my peripheral vision. The big one she owes me? Yeah.

Fast forward. All the way to now.

I've just said the coolest thing I could possibly say while being threatened with a machete and held in fishy-smelling tentacles. The Aolferian hesitates, trying to work out what his translator is saying.

Peggy goes pale, and it's not the blood loss. We both know that this is our best shot.

Are we really doing this? her eyes ask. I grin, and she has her answer.

The bow swings up into her hand as she yanks the arrow from the dead Aolferian. She notches and draws in one fluid movement. The Archer of Legend would've been hella proud. The Aolferian holding me barely has time to flinch. I hear a *whoosh*, a *thunk*, feel a sting, and I'm thrown back on top of the Aolferian, still wrapped in its tentacles.

I stare up at the purple canopy. Strangely, not dead. A wild creature cries in the distance. There's a long wooden line sticking past my nose. I get an awful feeling of déjà vu. I turn my head and find the arrow sticking out of the Aolferian's skull, already blackening with ichor.

"You always go for the eye," I say as I wiggle loose from the clinging tentacles.

Peggy drops the bow and sits down hard. "What can I say? It's a good target."

I break open a bottle of Nuskin7 and pour it over her leg. She grimaces as the liquid bubbles into the wounds, disinfecting and sealing it in seconds. I'm about to put the bottle away when she catches me by the chin and tips my head up. I wince, remembering the sting and suddenly feeling the thin slice along my collarbone.

"He got you."

"Just a nick. He kept that thing sharp." I seal it with the last few drops of Nuskin.

"You were about two millimeters from death."

I shrug. "It's an art form. Like you and making reckless decisions." That's not exactly the thing to say to a superior officer who just saved your life. It's such a novel concept. I try again. "Thanks for not writing me off there."

She looks at me for a long minute. I don't have a word for the face she's making, but it's enough to make me suddenly very busy with wrapping her leg in the scraps of her pants to protect it from the toxic foliage.

"I didn't come halfway across the galaxy to have you die on our first assignment," she says at last.

I pat her leg lightly and stand up. "That would be pretty inefficient."

She looks up at me. "We're even now, right?"

I glance back at the Aolferian. An eye for an eye? Hmm. I help her up. "You're forgetting Houston the Horrible. Get me out of his jurisdiction, and we'll call it square."

"We have to get off-planet first. Let's find their craft and get out of here."

She shoulders the bow and flanks me, on my blind side this time. On our way past the Aolferian, I retrieve the machete. A little sticky on the handle, but the weight feels reassuring in my hand.

"You know something? I think we're going to make great interplanetary specialists."

Peggy brushes off a slug that fell from the tree onto on her shoulder; it leaves behind a smoking hole in her uniform. "Now you're the one forgetting Houston."

"The Horrible."

"He won't be happy that we lost his diplomat."

"Oh, I don't know." I give the machete an experimental twirl. It slices through a thick woody vine with a satisfying thump. "If we take out, say, a respectably sized cadre of Aolferian mercenaries, I'm sure he'll turn a blind eye."

The actual worst thing about lack of peripheral vision? I can't see her face as she takes in this little tidbit. I hear her stop, the bushes swishing around her legs. Then she laughs, and I have my answer.

....

Kate Weize decided to become a writer at twelve years old. She didn't plan on moving across the country, jumping off a waterfall, becoming a clown, or building a seven-foot-tall moon, but somehow all that happened too. Despite many distractions she's still at it, exploring genre fiction with a style nearly as colorful as her hair. She currently lives in Southern California with her husband and a fluffy rescue cat.

Made in the
USA
Lexington, KY